[Whiskey Tango Foxtrot]

Cat Connor

Book 4 in the Veronica Tracey Spy/PI Series.

Editor: Nicky Hurle
Formatting: 9mm Press
Publisher: 9mm Press, New Zealand
Publication date: June 2023
Country of first publication: New Zealand.

ISBN: paperback: 978-0-473-67067-2
ISBN: hardback: 978-0-473-67068-9
ISBN: ePub: 978-0-473-67069-6
ISBN: Kindle: 978-0-473-67070-2
ISBN: PDF: 978-0-473-67071-9
ISBN: Apple Books: 978-0-473-67072-6

A catalogue record for this book is available from the National Library of New Zealand.

Messages:

Strap in for an entertaining ride full of action and intrigue in [Whiskey Tango Foxtrot] where nothing is as it seems as Crockett, Ronnie, and Ben navigate the newest mission dumped in their lap. This mystery-thriller keeps you guessing until the very end!
- J.E. Taylor - author of Shades of Night and Season of the Dragon series.

"Cat Connor delivers another NZ spy thriller with plenty of twists to keep the most jaded reader entranced.
Worth reading all 4 of the series, so far, to realize the depth of espionage and intrigue in NZ – the novels feel too real to be fiction."
- Nick Spill author of the Jaded trilogy.

[Whiskey Tango Foxtrot]

Crockett, Ben, and Ronnie are asked to take a new off-book mission that none are thrilled about. They're asked to protect a young woman with hyperthymesia and get her safely to court to testify at a trial before sending her off to live a new life. Crockett has an extra task on his list; he's been asked to recruit the woman for an intelligence agency but he's not sure that is wise, or that the woman will be able to transition from 'social media influencer' to a career within the intelligence community.

Ronnie's cousin Donald suspects something dreadful has happened to their neighbours and manages to drag Nana and the *Cronies of Doom* into his conspiracy theory, despite Ronnie's many misgivings.

For Robyn and Duigald:

Good friends, good food, many laughs!

Chapter One:
[Crockett: Operation Hide and Seek]

I reached for my phone, then stopped. Instead of making the call I wandered into the kitchen and took a beer from the fridge, slid the cold bottle into a stubby holder, and popped the top with the bottle opener on my keyring. I settled on the couch, took a long drink, then placed my beer next to the-manila folder on the coffee table.

Wouldn't hurt to enjoy a beer and think about this for a little while. I flicked the cover of the folder open with my thumb. The first page was a photo of a young woman and some basic information. I already knew what the mission was - that was discussed in person. My part of this was to put a team together, pick up the woman, and keep her safe until she testified. Then there was the other part: try and recruit her as an asset for Australia. She was twenty, and I wasn't at all sure she'd be that much of an asset. Ageist of me, I guess. I flicked the page over and took another drink of my beer. At least Kiwis make good beer.

The preferred team for this undertaking? Ronnie and Ben. Of course, who else? Wasn't the kind of venture anyone'd particularly want my tradie team in on. They were a bit rough around the edges to have near a twenty-year-old. Under the team preferences was a short bio about Miss Alexandra Fowler. She had what some people call a photographic memory but hers was extra special: Hyperthymesia. Pretty sure there was a TV show a few years back where the female lead had H-SAM and was a New York cop. I thought about it. Why did I watch it? Because Poppy Montgomery was the cop. The show was *Unforgettable*. Those telly people know what they're doing.

I shook the bottle in my hand. That went down fast. Easing myself off the couch, I took the empty to the recycling, and grabbed another beer on my way back through the kitchen.

Glancing at the sheet of paper again, I read more about Alexandra. She liked to be called Alex. She used a pseudonym online in her interesting line of work as a social media influencer. Now there's a great use for a memory like hers. Nothing I read screamed 'ideal candidate for intelligence work' apart from her memory. Scream? It didn't even whisper. All I saw was a kid who somehow managed to land an impressive income from posting photos of herself wearing whatever, and going to events. A selfie queen, if ever I'd seen one. My head shook involuntarily, and I took a decent pull on my beer. I'd never seen a social media influencer in real life.

Halfway through my second beer, I rang Ronnie.

"Yo, it's me. I need your help on an assignment."

"Sorry, who is it?" I could hear the amusement in her voice.

"Very funny. You want in or not?"

"What's the pay like?"

I was quietly pleased she didn't ask about the guts of

the job before the pay. I'd gotten to know Ronnie quite well and I somehow couldn't see her thrilled with a babysitting stint.

"We won't need to do another job this year ..."

"It's early August. Can't be too bad, but not as good as if you'd said that in January."

"Aussies are paying."

"There you go; they can be a bit tight compared to the Yanks," she said, but couldn't disguise the smile in her voice.

"In, or out?"

"In. Anything is better than the wayward spouse cases on the books at the minute," she said. "Who else?"

"I'll let you know when I finish the calls. I'll pick you up at ..." I checked my watch. "Nine-thirty."

"Tonight?"

"Yeah."

"Okay, what's the happenings?"

"Babysitting."

"Not an actual baby though, right? I don't do nappies or puke or crying."

"Not an actual baby. She's twenty. We have her until Monday. Be armed."

"Okay, see you tonight. I'll be home."

I smiled as I said goodbye. Just before the call ended, I heard her cousin Donald squeal about something. He sounded in fine form. No wonder Ronnie said yes.

I finished my beer and made the next call. Ben picked up fast.

3

"Crockett, what's up?"

"New off-book mission. Babysitting. You in?"

"Who's paying?"

"Aussies."

"Sure, count me in. I mean, why not? Who else is coming?"

"Ronnie."

"And it's not an actual baby?"

"Seriously?"

"Have you met you? It's something that needs checking. Some of us don't do diapers, poop, puréed carrots, and screaming."

Didn't sound like Ronnie and Ben were keen on kids.

"If it was an actual baby, I'd be fine on my own. Jesus. I'll pick you up at nine. Sidearm."

"See you then. How long do we have the babysitting gig?"

"Until Mondayish."

"Yeah, that's not a day. Monday or longer?"

"It depends on how Monday goes."

"Great. Pick me up at nine. I'll be at home."

"Nine, then." I hung up.

He wasn't at Ronnie's for the weekend and that meant I'd be tooling around all over the show. Ben lived in Wellington, usually just referred to as the city, by Upper Huttians. Ronnie and I weren't too far from each other in Upper Hutt. The protectee was under wraps in Lower Hutt. She'd been snaffled up during the day and kept somewhere quiet.

4

I went over the details again. She was a witness to a murder nearly a year ago. Police knew about her, but no one else did until yesterday, when her name was given to the defence attorneys. Seemed like they didn't want to use her at all, keeping her name out of it for so long. I mulled over the details of the job. It came from my boss, which meant the Australian Office of Security, and that meant it was paid for by Australia. But surely this was a police matter, and they should be keeping Alexandra safe, not us. But then she had a memory that made her attractive to intelligence agencies. What'd they do? Hire us out as a security firm and promise the bloody moon to get Alexandra in our care?

I almost popped the top off another beer but thought better of it and made myself a coffee. Smarter move. After my coffee, I packed up the files. I still couldn't make sense of us having the business, but it was what it was. With a shrug, I shoved the folder into my overnight bag. I packed for four days, because it doesn't hurt to be prepared.

I rolled up the long mat in the hallway and opened the floor safe. I extracted two smallish black cases, a shoulder holster, a hip holster, and a box of 9mm ammunition. Wouldn't hurt to have a backup weapon. I put the cases, holsters, and the box in my bag then locked the safe and rolled the mat down. Nothing to see here.

It didn't take long for me to be ready and drop my bag by the back door. After a quick run-through of everything, I went back to my bedroom for my phone charger and tossed that into my bag. Everything was good. I rang Ronnie.

"Hey, rental cars ... who's good?"

"I'll do it. We used Omega last time and they're pretty chill."

"Thanks."

"They're in Wellington. Is that still okay?"

"Yeah, I'll ask Ben to pick the car up."

"Right, so it's you, me, and Ben." Ronnie laughed. "You could've said it was the Dream Team."

"Yeah, I could've. Hope Ben can grab the car."

"Be easier."

"Sure would."

We hung up. Plans were already changing. It didn't bode well for the weekend. Pick the kid up, gather the troops, head north to a safe house in Timberlea. Move again tomorrow. Move again on Sunday. End up at the Supreme Court building in time for her testimony on Monday morning. Hang around and hope it all ends there, but it won't. It never does. Maybe we'll get her jetting off to her new life by Tuesday night. Bye-bye Alexandra Fowler, hello new person that we've never heard of.

Why wasn't this a police thing, or maybe the question was, why did the police hand it to Australian intelligence? Or did they? This had to come from somewhere, we're not your average babysitters. A question kept coming into focus: What don't we know? I went back to the folder and looked over the last two pages again. The name of the police prosecutor trying the case was written down. It wasn't one I knew. But that didn't mean anything. I'd run it by Ronnie later, if I remembered. It felt like the unknown quantities would weigh heavily as the weekend progressed. We were overqualified for babysitting duty. Sure, the boss wants her turned into an asset, but does that warrant our presence all weekend? Doubtful.

Sneaky suspicions grew as I waited for Ronnie's call. She rang just as I made my second coffee. I wouldn't be going to bed, so it didn't matter if I'd be peeing all night.

"Did you get it?"

"Yes. Tell Ben the car is booked under *Wherefore Art Thou*. I'll invoice your boss for the car later."

"Fair enough. Thanks Ronnie."

"No problem. See you at nine-thirty."

I hung up and rang Ben. He was all good with picking up the car and meeting me in Lower Hutt. I gave him an address in Waiwhetū. We adjusted the times accordingly. He'd taxi to the car rental joint then drive out. Ben reckoned he'd be at the address by eight forty-five at the latest.

It was all coming together quite nicely. I drank my coffee. It wouldn't be that bad spending the weekend with Ronnie and Ben. How awful could a twenty-year-old be to take care of? They're pretty well human by twenty, surely?

I rang a cab, gave a false name and address for the pickup, and an address one street over from Alexandra's location for the drop-off, checked I had cash, and then wandered down the road to wait for the cab, with my bag dangling from my right hand.

Cold air made me wish I'd worn a beanie. I tugged the zip on my jacket higher and hunched my shoulders to protect myself from the wind. It was almost spring, but you wouldn't know it out here. Light spilled from houses only to vanish as people closed their curtains against the freezing night. Wood smoke in the air reminded me of nights by the fire in the Marlborough Sounds after a day fishing with mates. It'd be nice by a roaring fire instead of standing outside some random house in the cold, peering at cars on Fergusson Drive, trying to spot the taxi to give it a wave. The chill burrowed into my bones. Then I saw a car with a taxi light and gave it a wave. Moments later I was warm in the back of the taxi and heading south.

I warmed up quickly. Won't be that bad of a racket.

Chapter Two:

[Crockett: Alex the 'Influencer']

I sat deep in thought in the back of the taxi. I must be getting real old. I mean how on earth is being a social media influencer a real job. As far as I could tell it was right up there next to live streaming video games. Those thoughts were not helpful to the mission. I gave myself an internal pep talk: Reel it in, Crockett. That's not the attitude needed to ensure this operation runs smoothly.

The taxi pulled up to the curb of the fictitious address. I paid in cash, grabbed my bag, and climbed out of the car into the cold rain of Lower Hutt. I pretended to walk up a path to a house until I was sure the taxi was gone. I didn't have far to walk to get to the address of Alexandra Fowler. It wasn't exactly her dwelling place. It was a temporary residence. I'd would have said safe house, but if it was safe then there would have been no need for us to take her.

I approached the address with caution. I walked past it on the footpath for four houses. Nothing untoward happened or was happening. I walked back. There was no police car out front. Not even an unmarked vehicle. I walked up the driveway. There was a garage at the end. Not attached to the house in which lights were on. I walked up the five steps to the front door and knocked, thankful to be undercover on the small porch.

"Who is it?" A male voice asked through the closed door.

"Dave Crocker."

The door opened to reveal a tall bloke with short dark hair. He thrust his hand out and shook mine. "Andrew Chalmers," he said and stepped aside to let me enter. It was warm inside and it felt good to be out of the weather.

"Sorry, I'm going to leave puddles," I said, brushing water off my jacket and watching the droplets seep into the carpet. Not the best first impression.

"No worries. Not my house." Chalmers motioned for me to follow him. "She's in the kitchen."

"Hold up."

He turned and waited. "What can we expect?"

Chalmers shook his head. "Not a lot."

"How long have you had her?"

"Since this morning. There are two of us here and two more driving around the area."

I didn't see any sign of cops outside. Either they were very good, or they weren't there. "Where's your mate then?" I looked around. The front door opened into the lounge. Chalmers and I were the only people in there.

"Kitchen," Chalmers replied.

"We were eating."

"Sorry to interrupt your meal."

"No worries. Come on. I'd better introduce you."

I dropped my bag by the door and followed along. Through the lounge, down a short hallway, and left into the kitchen. The room was big with a table that seated six near the far wall. A girl looked up from a meal, frowned, and continued moving food around her plate. A woman pushed her chair back as she stood. She stepped toward me with her hand out.

"Cassie Clark," she said, pumping my hand enthusiastically a few times. "Grab a pew."

"Dave Crocker," I replied.

She smiled. "You're the guy they call Crockett."

"Guilty as charged."

Chalmers sat down. "Do you know him?"

Clark smiled. "I have heard of Crockett, never met until now."

"Must be nice having a fan club," Chalmers said with a grin.

I didn't respond. I was pretty sure that no one outside the circles I moved in knew about me. I doubted a dime-a-dozen cop would know my story even if they were handing someone over to me. I'd be a name and an ID. Not gossip. I took a chair, moved it away from the table, spun it around, and straddled it. No one asked for my ID and these two clowns didn't show me their accreditation. A small red flag popped up.

"ID," I said, letting a growl emerge from my voice.

They looked at each other, then me. I repeated the request.

Chalmers pulled a card from his wallet and passed it to me. Police ID. Looked legit. Clark followed suit. I handed them back. Still not convinced. I handed mine over and got it back with barely a glance. Putting my distrust on the back burner, I turned to the girl.

"You must be Alexandra," I said to her. She looked young.

"You can call me Alex," she replied, using her fork to push pasta spirals and vegetables in a tomato-based Italian sauce, around her plate. It looked like she'd eaten about half her meal so it couldn't have been that bad. Hard to screw up pasta and sauce.

"Not hungry?"

She wrinkled her nose and pushed the plate away. "No. I don't even know what this is, or what it's *supposed* to be."

Chalmers and Clark continued eating.

Great. I can see we're going to have a fun weekend. I studied Alex's face and tried not to be obvious about it. She didn't look much like the photo I had in the file. I could see she was that person but seeing her in real life made me pretty sure the photo was filtered.

"We'll be leaving soon." I glanced at my watch. "Our ride is about twenty minutes away."

"Can you cook?" Alex asked. "I hope you can because Clark can't." She picked up a glass of juice and drank some of the contents.

"It's been a long day," Clark said. "The longest twelve-hour shift ever."

"It hasn't been fun for me either," Alex snapped.

I grinned. "I can cook, Alex."

Chalmers and Clark finished eating. My phone buzzed.

Ben: Knocking on the door in three.
Me: Excellent.

"Our ride is here," I said to Alex. "Get your things together. Meet me by the front door."

Alex vanished from the room then returned wearing a long black leather coat with fur trim, a knitted beanie with a fur pompom, and carrying a black leather backpack.

I scooped the handles of my bag into my hand and swung the door open. Ben stood on the porch illuminated by the lounge light.

"Ready?"

"Yes." I ushered Alex out the door. "This is Ben, go with him."

Ben smiled at her. "Hi, the car's at the end of the driveway."

She didn't say anything, not even goodbye to Chalmers and Clark.

"Thanks," I said to them. "Catch ya."

"Good luck," Clark replied.

By the time I got to the car, Ben already had Alex settled in the back. He was driving. I sat in the front passenger seat.

"Let's get out of here," Ben said, firing up the engine. "Ronnie's waiting."

We were nearly at the Stokes Valley turn off when Alex said, "How are you going to keep me safe, Ben?"

Strange question. I let him field it.

"What are you talking about?" he said and shot me a glance.

I shrugged.

"Just because you play a cop on a television show doesn't mean you know what you're doing in real life."

"Lucky for you I have another job that's got nothing to do with my television character," he replied. "People can do more than one thing."

Alex blew out a puff of air that suggested she wasn't convinced. "They should've told me if an actor was going to be my bodyguard. I could've stayed with Chalmers and Clark."

"For some reason they'd had enough of babysitting duty," I half-whispered to Ben.

Ben grinned.

"I heard that," Alex said. "Why are you being mean?"

I left that alone. If she thought I was mean, she was in for a real treat if she kept this hostility up when she met Ronnie.

"No one is being mean," Ben said.

I looked ahead and saw we were in Silverstream already. Five minutes and we'd be pulling into Ronnie's driveway.

Alex sat quietly until the back passenger door opened and Ronnie clambered in. I twisted in my seat to acknowledge her presence.

"All good?"

"Yep," Ronnie replied. She plugged her seat belt in and turned to Alex. "Hi, I'm Ronnie."

Ben backed out of the driveway and turned the car to the north. "We are going north?"

"Yes. Timberlea."

"Seriously?" Ronnie muttered behind me.

"Who would look for her there?"

"Good point. No one, I guess."

Silence dropped like a blanket. Apart from the window wipers, and the sound of the tyres on the wet road, there wasn't much going on. Too wet and miserable for people to be out and about. Perfect really.

Just before the right turn into Moeraki Road, Alex spoke. "Ronnie, can you cook?"

She was quite preoccupied with food. Maybe there's an issue there.

"Yes," Ronnie replied, dead pan.

Ben and I laughed.

"Do not eat anything cooked by Ronnie," Ben said. "She's poisoned us all in the past."

"Oh my God, who are you people?"

"That is a gross exaggeration," Ronnie replied. "In my defence, that chicken was bought already cooked from the supermarket."

"Fine, amending my comment," Ben said. "For your own safety do not eat anything Ronnie buys."

"No one died. Nothing to get worked up about," Ronnie said. "It was one time."

"It was twice," I said. "Twice. Who is that unlucky?"

Ronnie laughed.

Alex huffed. "You people are weird."

"Ben, second street on the right, off Norana Road."

"How far up?"

"Gentian Street is a dead end; go all the way up, then turn and drive down about a quarter, I think. Looking for number fourteen."

Ben did as I asked. We found the house with no problem at all.

"This is us," I said to the occupants of the backseat.

"About time," Alex mumbled. She took her seatbelt off and opened her door. "Why is it so dark?"

"It's night-time," Ronnie replied.

Ronnie and Ben joined her on the driveway while I went to unlock the house. A dog barked somewhere down the street and another closer dog joined in, then another, maybe two houses down, barked. Good. An early warning system. Once inside I turned on the lights. There was security lighting, but it was off. I flicked that switch just in case someone wandered into the yard during the night.

Ronnie encouraged Alex to follow Ben inside. Ronnie came in last.

"Locked up?" I asked Ben.

"Yep." He dropped the car keys into a bowl on the table near the front door.

"Let's get settled then."

"Come on Alex," Ronnie said. "Let's find you a bedroom and check out the bathroom."

Alex grimaced. "Whatever."

Ben followed me into the kitchen. I opened a large pantry and found it well stocked. The jug on the bench looked workable.

"Coffee?"

"Sure," Ben replied.

I filled the jug and put it on while Ben went through the pantry and found coffee.

I made three coffees. I didn't make Alex one. I wanted her to get some sleep. Figured it might improve her mood.

Ronnie appeared without Alex.

"Where is she?"

"Lying down."

"Good. Made you a coffee." I passed a mug to her.

"Thanks."

We took our hot drinks into the lounge. It wasn't a bad set up. Separate kitchen, dining room, and lounge. It was tidy, clean, and warm. We couldn't ask for much more.

"Ronnie, have you ever come across a couple of cops called Andrew Chalmers and Cassie Clark?" I leaned into the back of the armchair and relaxed my shoulders.

"Names don't ring a bell," she said. "But I don't know many cops out the area."

"What's up?" Ben asked.

"Probably nothing."

"Spill it," Ronnie said.

"As I said, it's probably nothing. But, the woman, Cassie Clark had heard my name and knew I went by Crockett."

"Is that a secret?"

"Guess not," I said. "Not really anyway." I took a good-sized sip of my coffee.

"So, it's not a secret that you are Crockett, but it bothers you that she recognised your name ...?"

"Yeah."

"Interesting. Why?"

"Unlike pretty boy there, my face isn't all over the telly and there's not a lot of chatter outside of our sphere."

Ronnie drank her coffee. I could see thoughts crossing her face well before she voiced any.

"Okay, that is a little bit strange. I don't know what to make of it though."

"Nor do I. Guess I just wanted it out there. In case it turns into something."

Ronnie nodded.

Ben placed his cup on a nearby coffee table. "I'm starting to think an actual baby wouldn't have been that bad."

I didn't disagree.

"We should get some shut-eye," I said. "I'll take first watch. Ben, I'll wake you in three hours."

"Wake me next," Ronnie said.

"All right, if that's what you want." The watch order didn't make a difference to me.

Chapter Three:
[Ronnie: FML]

Morning arrived without much warning. Light streamed through a gap in the curtains right into my face. I heard cars moving on the street. One glance at my watch told me it was early. I sat up. Even quiet breathing from the bed occupied by Alexandra told me she was still asleep. It wouldn't hurt for her to stay that way for a bit longer. I got up, made the bed, and found the bathroom. Moments later I was standing under a stream of hot water in the shower.

Once showered and dressed, I heard wakeful noises coming from the kitchen, and light snoring from the lounge. I guessed Crockett was asleep and Ben was making coffee. I was correct.

"Morning," Ben said when he saw me in the doorway.

"What's the plan today?"

"Think Crockett said we're moving her this morning."

I nodded. "Breakfast?"

There are some commonsense rules that we live by when working and one of them is: when an opportunity presents, take it. Eat, shower, pee, whatever. There's no guarantee when another opportunity will come along.

There was a four-slice toaster on the bench. A quick look in the pantry turned up toast bread, jams, Marmite, crunchy peanut butter, and Vegemite. Ben handed me a butter blend and margarine from the fridge.

"I'll make a heap of toast." There was a table at the end of the kitchen. Perfect for breakfast. Ben added plates to the table, and knives. By the time we had a pile of toast, and the coffee was ready, Crockett ambled into the room.

"Looks good," he said. "Where is she?"

"Asleep," I replied. Running water caused a pause in our activity. "Okay, so not asleep. In the bathroom."

I slathered a piece of toast with butter and Vegemite. By the time I finished my second slice and first coffee, Alexandra appeared with damp hair and fresh makeup.

"Sleep well?" I asked, motioning her to sit at the table.

She scanned the table and didn't appear impressed. "What is this?"

"Breakfast," Ben replied. "Sit down and eat."

She screwed up her nose. "I'd like eggs bene with avocado and an oat milk latte." She sat at the table.

And so, it begins.

I smiled at her. "We have toast. There might be some cereal in the cupboard."

Crockett reached behind him and flipped a cupboard open. "Weetbix and some kind of muesli."

"Yuck," she said.

"No thank you," I said for her.

The cupboard closed. Crockett continued eating toast.

I added two slices to the plate in front of Alexandra. "Eat up. Might be a long day. There are spreads in front of you."

Ben filled a cup with coffee and handed it to her. "No

oat milk. Real milk is in the fridge."

She sighed. "I don't drink milk."

"Black it is then," Ben said with a smile.

I had a feeling our smiles were already waning and opted to continue with my breakfast and not worry about her.

Crockett made more toast.

We ate.

She glared at the barren toast in front of her and the black coffee.

"What's next?" I asked Crockett. "We have a plan for the day?"

He nodded. "We move closer to where we need to be."

"When do you want to move her?"

"I'm right here," she snapped.

"Yes you are. We're talking about you, not to you," Crockett replied. "Eat something." He motioned to me and Ben. We followed him into the lounge. "We drive south this morning."

"How far south?"

"I was thinking we head for Belmont. There's a place we can use in Belmont Regional Park."

"Can we drive right in?"

"Yes."

"Good, because I don't think madam in there is much of a tramper," I said, tipping my head toward the kitchen.

Ben smiled. "I like the idea of spending time in the bush, nice change of scenery from suburbs and cities."

I nodded. "Does sound good."

"Right, pack your stuff. Let's get going while the going is good."

Ben volunteered to do the dishes. Alexandra sat in front of her plate. She'd nibbled on the corner of a slice of toast.

"Pack," I said to her. "Times up."

"Where are we going?"

"Somewhere else," I replied.

"You can tell me. I'm entitled to know."

Entitled is right.

"We are moving you for your own protection. There, that's what you are entitled to know."

"I hate this." She scraped her chair across the Lino as she stood.

"Pack your bag."

I followed her out of the room leaving Ben doing the dishes. Crockett vanished into the bathroom.

"I can do this without you," Alexandra said, over her shoulder.

"I'm sure you can."

I zipped my bag up and dropped it by the bedroom door. When I turned back I saw a cell phone in Alexandra's hand.

"Hand it over," I said, reaching for the phone.

"No!"

"Now."

She tried to keep it out of my reach. I stepped forward and took it from her. She threw herself on the bed and screamed into the pillow. Such drama. I looked at the phone screen. She had a social media app open. I shut it and slid the phone into a side pocket of my bag.

"Get finished packing," I said. "This ..." I waved a hand at her as she pulled her face from the pillow. "Stops now."

She screamed again.

Crockett ran into the room. "Problem?"

"She had a cell phone," I replied. "Now I have it, and she's having a tantrum."

He leaned down to the screaming girl and with much menace said, "Knock it off."

She stopped and sat up.

So, it was an act then. Good to know.

"You people are going to ruin my life."

It's going to be a bloody long weekend.

I didn't say anything nor did Crockett. He left the room.

She finished packing and stomped out to the front door.

I did a sweep of the bathroom and bedrooms to make sure nothing was left behind.

Crockett put the whinger in the car, while Ben and I did a final check of the place.

I sat in the back with Alexandra, and Ben rode shotgun. Just before we pulled out of the driveway Crockett said, "River Road or Fergusson Drive?"

My phone chimed, so did Ben's. I read the Police alert. River Road was closed due to a truck versus motorbike crash.

"Fergusson," Ben and I replied together.

Chapter Four:

[Ronnie: This is New Zealand.]

"What's this all about?" Crockett said as we slowed to a crawl behind a line of traffic.

"Could be the traffic lights in Silverstream," Ben offered. It didn't sound like he believed it though.

"Not this far back," I said, and craned my neck to see past Crockett's head. "Accident maybe."

The crawl of vehicles came to a standstill.

"Both lanes?" Ben said.

"What are the odds of an accident blocking the north bound lane and the south bound lane in different places at the same time?" I said, more to the driver's side passenger window than to anyone in the car.

Pop, pop noises erupted from ahead of us in the traffic jam. That didn't sound good. Could've been a car backfiring. I scanned the road - still nose to tail traffic both north and south bound. Nothing was moving. Another pop. I leaned a bit so I could see out the windscreen from the middle of the car and saw a motorbike headlight coming toward us down the painted median strip. The rider looked like a gang member.

There were plenty of places we could go on foot, but the car was trapped.

The car was a trap.

Where exactly were we? Fergusson Drive. Heretaunga.

Lots of houses and a few side streets. What does Nana call it? The Golden Mile. Gunfire on the golden mile?

"Gunfire?" I asked. I reached under Crockett's seat with my right hand and grabbed the grip of a Glock I knew was there. I pulled my hand out exposing the gun.

Ben glanced at me. "You okay back there?"

I nodded, as I gently moved the slide and glimpsed a round in the chamber. I let it slip back into place.

"Definitely gunfire," Crockett said, and flung the driver's door open. I couldn't see the weapon in his hand, but I knew it was there. He ducked behind the open door and fired once using the door as cover. "Get her off the X."

I switched the Glock to my left hand, slung my backpack over my right shoulder, and grabbed our principal (protectee) by the wrist. She resisted. I tugged her arm.

"Follow me."

"Keep your head down," Ben said from the passenger side of the car. He opened the door. A bullet smashed into the windscreen. Cracks ran like a spider web away from the impact zone.

I heard another loud rumble from a motorbike, this time behind us. I flung my door open and saw the motorbike moving fast. A passenger leaned left and lifted a hand up bringing the barrel of a gun into my line of vision. I fired, hitting the rider. He swerved into a car. The motorbike, rider, and pillion, fell. Looked painful. I glimpsed a patch on the rider's jacket.

"We're gone," I whispered into the car as I led the reluctant protectee away. The plan was to stay as low as possible and weave through the cars to the nearest side street that ran toward the eastern hills.

"What's happening?" Alex whispered. She'd stopped struggling and let me lead.

"Did you not notice the motorbikes and the broken car windows?" I tugged her hand to keep her moving with me. "Stay low."

"Are we all right?"

"Of course." I didn't have free fingers to cross, so the lie flew free. "Stay close. We're moving." I peered around the boot of a stationary car. The first motorbike was in front of us about fifty metres and coming closer. There was a clear enough path and maybe thirty to forty metres to the nearest side street. Decent fences meant we could get a fair way down the street with cover. A bullet tinged as it hit a car. A quick glance told me it was too close for comfort. The motorbike was almost on us. I pointed at a doorway of a brick house. "Run," I said. "To there." I gave her a shove in the right direction.

She ran. I followed. Bullets chipped at the footpath and the bricks. Adrenaline coursed through my body as I skidded into the doorway behind her and spun around to face the danger.

Crockett waved one finger in my direction. I pushed Alex further into the doorway and knocked loudly.

Quit the espionage game, they said. Stay home in New Zealand where it's safe, they said. Be close to Nana in her twilight years, it'll be fun for her having you home, they said. A sigh escaped my lips.

A bullet hit the mortar in the brick wall of the porch. Dust puffed. I reached around Alex and knocked again.

The door opened a crack. "I hate to impose, but could we use your back door?"

I dropped my backpack down my arm, unzipped it, and carefully placed the Glock inside it. Probably not the best thing to be holding a weapon while knocking on doors in Upper Hutt.

The door opened wider. An elderly man with white hair, wearing a green V-neck jersey and tan-coloured cord pants, nodded.

"You better come in girls. There's a kerfuffle out there. Some fella with a gun."

"Thank you," I said, pushing Alex inside. "I'm ..."

"Veronica Tracey. My word. Look at you."

I was at a loss. "Sorry, I don't think I know you?"

"Veronica, I go to church with your Nana."

Of course, he did. Half of Upper Hutt went to church with Nana. I hadn't been to church with Nana for many years. I was a disappointment.

"I'm sorry, I can't recall your name."

"I'm Alan. Alan Christensen."

"And you recognised me, Mr Christensen?"

"You've changed a little bit, but yes." He smiled. "Come on through girls. I'll put the kettle on."

"I don't want to be rude, Mr Christensen, but we just need to nip out your back door."

"On another adventure I suppose. You were always off

27

on adventures, even as a child."

Alex looked perplexed. Welcome to my life. It doesn't get any easier even when you live it.

"This adventure has gotten a bit hairy. I'd rather not put you at risk. I just need to pop out the back and get this nice young lady home safe."

"Righto." He smiled and tapped the side of his nose. "Mum's the word. Down the hall and on the left."

"Mr Christensen, lock up after us," I said. "It was nice to see you."

"You too, Veronica. Maybe we'll see you at church sometime soon." He smiled. His old lips stretched taut, and laugh lines deepened on his weather-beaten face. "Be safe out there now."

"Yes, sir."

I found the back door where I expected it to be. The key was in the lock. I opened the door and checked outside. All clear.

Before I closed the door behind us, I called into the house. "Don't forget to lock up."

I took Alex by the hand and led her through the garden to the garage. The garage opened onto a side street. A plan formed. Down Bathurst Street, across Marion Street, and into an alleyway that I knew ran behind the houses which led to Heretaunga Railway Station. If we stayed on our trajectory, we'd cross the tracks and stick to the alleyway on the other side, which popped out in Weir Grove. Then it was up Maadi Place and along Sommes Road to the entrance of a driveway that led us to The

Messine Centre. To Alex's credit, she followed my lead without a complaint. We moved as quickly as possible but not so fast as to draw attention. At the front entrance of the Messine Centre, I wrestled my phone from my backpack and called Bill Bailey.

"Call me back. I'm outside." I hung up.

Alex frowned at me. "Where are we?"

"Somewhere we will be safe. Waiting for a call back from a friend who works here." He's more like the head of Army Intelligence, but she doesn't need that information. She also doesn't need to know the building is connected underground to joint command. "Didn't you see the sign before we walked up the driveway?"

She shook her head. "No."

She might have the world's best memory, but she wasn't overly observant of the world around her. In other words, her situational awareness sucked. My phone rang as a familiar male waved and walked toward me beyond the glass door. I answered the call.

"What do you need?" Bill said in my ear.

"Safety," I replied. "Cover up." I hung up. Through the glass I saw Bill stuff his ID inside his shirt and smile.

The doors opened.

"You'd better come in," Bill said. "This way."

He led the way to a small yet comfortable room not far from the main entrance.

He turned to Alex and offered his hand. I gave the most subtle shake of my head that I could.

Bill smiled. "Pleased to meet you. I'm Aaron, and you

are?"

"Alex," she replied, shaking his hand.

"Have a seat, Alex. I need a quiet word with your companion."

Alex plopped onto a leather couch. Bill motioned me to follow him out of the room.

"Nice to see you, Aaron," I said with a smile.

"You still Ronnie?"

"Yes."

"And the story here is?"

"A biker opened fire on us from a south bound motorbike on Fergusson Drive. And then for fun, another motorbike came at us from the north. I saw a patch, but I didn't recognise it."

"That was you. Why am I not surprised?"

"How do you know about it?"

"News travels fast. A motorbike crashed; the rider had a bullet in his shoulder. The pillion was injured in the crash. They are from a gang, but not a New Zealand one. If someone were to swab your hand for gunshot residue, what would they find?"

I shook my head lightly. "Probably don't do that."

"We have exercises with the Air Force at the moment. They've diverted two helicopters to help police look for the gunmen and the other motorbike."

"Good time to choose to be an idiot on Fergusson Drive." I smiled. "I'll let Crockett and Ben know we're here, and they can swing by and pick us up."

"The Armed Offenders Squad are on their way. Sounds

like armed police are going door-to-door looking for the missing gunmen. Cordons are in place from Barton Ave to Kiwi Street."

"Any word on what stopped the traffic in both directions?"

Bill nodded. "Four cars." He air quoted as he said, "Accidents."

That took some coordination and planning.

"Not going to make it easy for Crockett and Ben to get to us then."

Bill smiled. "We might have the dubious pleasure of your company for the rest of the day."

"Rude! I'm a delight and well you know it."

"What's her story?" Bill tipped his head toward the room.

"She's an unusual young woman." From our point of view, she was a living, breathing nightmare. "It's a protection gig."

Bill grinned. "Going well I see."

"Super well," I replied smiling. "I have a feeling this has just started to get interesting."

"And she can't know my name because?"

"She has hyperthymesia."

"Hang on, I've heard of that. Who's that famous actress with the amazing memory?"

"Marilu Henner."

"Yes. Her. It has another name hyperthymesia?"

"It does. H-SAM. Highly superior autobiographical memory."

"And Alex has that?"

"Clearly you do not." I smiled at him. "She will remember every detail from today, like she does every other day. But she'll remember details of everything that happens to her, or involves her, and not things that just happen around her."

"And you're badly protecting this person because?"

I rattled off the brief, "She's a special witness in a murder trial."

"Don't you have all the fun."

I shook my head but laughed. "Two days until she testifies. That's all. We just have to get her to court on Monday, alive, then safely on an airplane to her new life." I was super optimistic about her testimony only being a one and done kind of thing. Realistic me knew there would be a hold up somewhere and then a reason for them to call her back to the stand. Probably there'd be another reason to call her back for a third time while their experts tried to prove she wasn't accurately recalling information. We were stuck with Princess Alex until the prosecutor for the Crown, and the defence attorneys, were finished, and the alleged murderer was behind bars, or free.

"Where has she been until now?" Bill glanced out the glass door to the car park.

I followed his line of sight but saw nothing untoward.

"Under wraps. Or at least her involvement was kept under wraps. No one officially knew she existed until yesterday when the prosecution announced a special witness."

"Sneaky."

"Lawyers," I added with a shrug. "Par for the course."

I dragged my phone from my pocket and called Ben. He answered just before I hung up.

"We're good," he said.

"So are we," I replied. "Swing by and give us a lift, please."

"Crockett is giving a statement, then we'll get to you." There was a lot of background noise, but I could hear traffic moving. Police must've unblocked at least one lane. "Where are you?"

"Popped in on Bill."

Ben chuckled in my ear. "Bet he loved that."

"Of course, he did, I'm a delight. AOS?"

"AOS, two helicopters, about twenty armed police on the ground going door-to-door. It's busy over here."

"Sounds it. Any problems I need to know about?"

"No. I've given my statement. Police confirmed who we are via a call to Chandler, and the Police Commissioner."

"And being armed?"

"We're licensed to carry weapons while protecting the witness."

"No one saw either of you return fire? Or me, for that matter?"

"That's what we heard. They're looking for a male in connection to the shooting of one of the motorcycle riders."

"Are they bikies?"

33

"Yes. Not a Kiwi gang. Crockett probably knows more. Wasn't that his thing back in the day?"

"Yeah. Thanks for leading police to think a male shot the bikie." I guessed Crockett and Ben had something to do with throwing people off my scent. "Is the rider alive?"

"Yes. Receiving treatment in an ambulance inside the cordon. And not talking to police."

Par for the course. Bikies aren't known for being police-friendly. "We need to find out who hired them, or if someone hired them, and how they found out where we'd be."

"That might be difficult. He's under guard."

"How much are we getting for this suicide mission again?" I asked with a smile in my voice.

"Not enough. Be there soon. Hang tight."

I hung up and pushed my phone back into my pocket. Bill smiled and swung the door to the room open. "May as well wait in here," he said.

"Don't suppose you have coffee anywhere handy?"

He reached for a phone on the wall and made a call without looking at me or Alex. He asked for coffee for three to be delivered and said he was in a meeting. Whoever was bringing the coffee was to knock and leave the tray outside the door.

Good thinking.

I'm Veronica Tracey. Welcome to the chaos that follows me around like a lost puppy. Once upon a time I was an officer with the New Zealand Security Intelligence Service. Espionage was my game. I semi-retired a few years ago to be closer to my Nana and family. My best friends and I opened our own private detective company, *Wherefore Art Thou*. We mostly do theft as a servant and wayward spouse type cases but, more regularly than I'd like, I get roped into jobs for various agencies. It's not all bad. They pay well. I also get to work with my on-again, off-again boyfriend, Ben Reynolds. He happens to be a fairly famous actor and an officer working for the US government, stationed here in New Zealand. The other frequent flyer is a guy called Dave Crocker. He's with the Australians and also stationed here. Crockett is okay for an Aussie. The three of us have a good working relationship, most of the time.

Chapter Five:

[Ronnie: What on earth?]

"Where are we going?" I asked Crockett as he started the car. It wasn't the bullet riddled rental car he drove before. I imagined the rental was still on Fergusson Drive within the cordon with police and AOS. We'd made a right mess.

We were in Crockett's car. Good thing we always get a comprehensive insurance package with rentals. Even so, I'm certain Omega won't want us renting from them again. That's two rental companies on the 'don't bother even trying' list.

We'd switched places. I was now in the front passenger seat and Ben was in the back with our charge.

"I've got an idea, but I don't know if it's the best one," Crockett replied, driving out of the Messine Centre carpark and indicating to turn left. "We're already in Trentham. Your place or mine?"

"Yours," I said.

His place was down a longish driveway and a few streets north of mine. Crockett indicated right at the next intersection. He was taking the long way home. The long and evasive way. Nerves tweaked. Why did bikies come at us? I needed to discuss that, and any ramifications with Crockett and Ben, but not around Alex the memory queen.

My phone rang. My stomach leapt.

It was Cousin Donald, and the reason we weren't going to my place.

"How can I help?" I said as I answered the call.

"You not going to believe the across the road neighbours!"

"Are they back?"

"Oh, my darling cousin, no, they are not. And it's fascinating."

"So, they're not back, but other people are there?"

"Precisely."

"When did they arrive?"

"Yesterday evening. Where are you?"

"Working."

"Secret Squirrel bizzo?"

"Yes. Donald," I replied with a smile in my voice.
"Shouldn't you be at the salon?"

"Sweetie pie, it's my Saturday off. I'm home with my
hubby enjoying the spectacle across the road." Donald
sounded his usual happy self. No doubt Enzo was cater-
ing to his every whim. "And spectacle it is. First thing this
morning some crazed man screeched to a halt outside the
house, flew out of a car, and yelled at the upstairs windows."

"Who was he?"

"No idea. A fat white boy? Listen though. He used their
names, but I can't recall what they were. I think I heard
the name Summer. Anyway, he said, 'so-and-so has gone
to the police and told them everything. Told them what
we did.' And before he jumped back in the car, he yelled,

'Sort your shit out. We're all fucked.'"

"Exciting. Not at all like our street," I replied.

"Now I want to know what they all did, and who 'all' is, and where the real neighbours are. Because the couple that turned up last night are not the neighbours who are supposed to be there. All their stuff is still in the house, so they didn't move away, did they?"

"Most people don't leave without their belongings."

"And I saw them go. The real neighbours left weeks ago, with a backpack each."

"Intriguing."

"Ronnie, it's such fun. Don't suppose you could find out where the real neighbours are and what these Not-Neighbours have done?"

"Not right now. If you're that interested ask Steph or Jenn. They can do some digging. For funsies." His husband is in the espionage game. He could just ask him. Although, Enzo's skill set lies more in the interrogation camp when it comes to the gathering of intelligence, but he could still dig up a storm on someone if required.

"You don't mind if I ask Steph and Jenn?"

"Not at all. Word of warning though, Jenn is still not over that hair colour catastrophe you did on her." Sunset Fiesta, I think he called it. Donald is lucky to be alive.

Donald tutted in my ear. "It's been absolutely ages." He sighed dramatically. "I'll ask Steph."

"Good idea."

"When will you be home?"

"A couple of days, probably. Keep me posted though."

"You know I will. Toodle pip."

I hung up. Donald sounded more and more like our Nana every day. I couldn't decide if that was good or bad so I left it alone.

Ben tapped my shoulder. "Everything all right?"

I turned to see him. "Absolutely. Donald thinks something has happened to the across-the-road neighbours and is in full-on Nana mode over it all."

"Is it my imagination or is he getting more and more like your Nana?" Ben asked.

"I was thinking the same thing," Crockett interjected with a glance in my direction.

"You're both right. Must be hell on Enzo."

We chuckled to ourselves.

"Who is Donald?" Alex asked leaning forward.

"My cousin," I replied. "We share a house."

"Who is Enzo?"

"Donald's husband."

Alex sank back into the seat and asked no more questions.

Crockett eventually turned down his driveway. A garage door opened ahead of us. He drove in and shut the car engine off. We waited as the door closed behind us before I opened my door. The interior light lit the car. Alex looked up with a question in her expression.

"Come on," I said. "You're safe here."

"Are we staying here until court on Monday?"

We walked through the back gate and up the path to the house.

"I'm not sure yet," I replied truthfully. "We'll be here a little while at least while we come up with a new plan."

Crockett unlocked the door and flicked the lights on. We followed him inside. The drapes were shut making the lounge feel cosy.

"Someone knew we were on Fergusson Drive and what time, didn't they?" Alex asked.

"Yes." No sense sugar coating anything. "We have a problem. Make yourself comfortable while Ben and Crockett and I see what we can find out about today." I pointed to the couch in the living room and then a doorway. "The couch is comfy, and the kitchen is through there."

"Thanks." Alex wrapped her long, fur-trimmed, leather coat tighter around herself and plopped onto the couch. She then pulled out a cell phone and tapped hurriedly using the thumbs on both hands.

"You have another cell phone with you," I said, with a sigh. I held my hand out. "I'll take that."

She gripped it firmly and shook her head. "I need it."

"You really do not," I said, holding my hand out again. "Give it to me."

"Why?"

"Because someone knew where we would be in real time."

"You think I told them?"

"Not on purpose. Just hand the phone over." Bloody Zoomers with their device addictions and their 'me, me, me' attitudes. "It will not kill you to give me the phone, but it might if you don't."

"My followers need to hear from me. I can't just abandon them. I have obligations." She rolled her eyes. It was the loudest eye roll I'd ever seen. Her brown eyes righted themselves under long thick eyelashes. They weren't real, but I wasn't sure if they were magnetic or extensions. Either way they looked heavy. It wasn't a trend I'd be jumping into.

"What are you staring at?" Alex grumbled.

Saying 'Your weirdly heavy eyelashes' wouldn't help the situation. I behaved and slipped back into work mode.

"When I asked you for your phone yesterday - you gave me a phone. Where did that come from?" I pointed to the Samsung in her hand.

"It's a work phone. It was given to me to use for a campaign. I'm taking all my photos with it for the next month."

I snatched the phone from her death grip and looked at the screen. Instagram. Her followers numbered in the high hundred-thousands. She really was one of those god-awful influencers. I looked at what she'd posted recently.

Alex remained sullen and sulky on the couch, staring at the floor. "You can't just take the phone away. That's how I make my living!"

"Watch me," I said, and walked into the kitchen where Ben and Crockett were making sandwiches and coffee.

She shouted at me, "How am I supposed to work?"

I called back over my shoulder, "You are not supposed to be doing anything to draw attention to yourself."

When the guys turned to see what was going on, I waved a phone at them. "She had another phone and she's been posting photos."

"She's not super smart," Crockett muttered while cutting a sandwich diagonally and sliding the halves onto a side plate. "And she's not making it easy, is she?" He passed me the plate.

I put the phone on the bench.

"Is this for Alex?"

"Yes, can you ask her if she wants coffee, please?"

"Sure."

I took the plate out to the lounge and thrust it under Alex's nose. "Do you want coffee?"

"Is that gluten-free bread?" she asked, glaring at me. "I'd like a trim, soy milk, double shot cappuccino."

"You'll get an instant coffee with whatever milk is in Crockett's fridge. Are you a coeliac?" I knew she wasn't. We had a full brief regarding her health in case there was something that could impact her care.

"I don't eat gluten," she replied with a good deal of stroppiness. "I want a proper coffee."

"Eat the salad and corned beef, and leave the bread," I said, putting the plate on her knees. Before going back to the kitchen, I added, "We're not your servants. You'll take what you're given."

"I'm not eating this. I will not eat *dead* animals," she called after me. "And I won't drink instant coffee."

Buggery bollocks, she was a pain.

"Your decision," I replied. "Go hungry then."

Ben beckoned me closer. He had Alex's phone in his hand. "She posted a photo just before we left this morning. And there's one from inside the car. Hashtag, scary. Hashtag, OMG. Hashtag, so dangerous."

"What was the first photo?"

"The first one was her breakfast."

"Breakfast probably wasn't as scary as her lunch. The horror of meat! It's a dead animal! These people are barbarians."

Ben smiled. "She posted her breakfast with hashtags that implied toast wasn't what she was accustomed to eating."

"Oh, yay, she's one of them. A hashtag for everything and everything gets rated. No doubt we shall be rated poorly. Guess I took that second phone off her in time then, or she'd be posting the sammie she's refusing to eat as well. No doubt hashtagged, disgusting."

Crockett passed me a sandwich. "Wrap your laughing gear around this. I wouldn't be mad if you posted a photo with the hashtag delicious."

I grinned at him. "Of course. There is mustard on this corned beef?"

"You think I'd serve corned beef without mustard?"

"Well, I don't know what they do in Australia," I replied, lifting the corner of one sandwich to check.

"Holy smoke," Crockett said watching me.

I shrugged and took a bite of the sandwich.

Ben spoke again. "The second photo today has hundreds of responses from followers asking if she's okay." He scrolled. "She replied to several a few minutes ago."

Damn she's fast.

"So, while we were concerned about gunfire and getting her to safety, she took advantage and snapped a photo of the situation," I said, shaking my head. "And yet she acted like she had no idea what was going on when I took her out of the danger zone."

Crockett grumbled, "It's hard to help some people."

True.

"She posted two images last night: one of the river, and one of a tree behind the house," Ben said.

"And I bet someone scoured the metadata and knows where she was," I said, before taking another bite from my sandwich.

"Yes."

"How did they know to be on Fergusson Drive, and where we would be at that time?" I took another bite of my sandwich and wished I could post it with the hashtag delicious. "And bikers? Pretty unusual way of trying to get to a target. Great way to create absolute mayhem though." I thought about the patch I saw. A snarling wolf head with red fangs.

"And not a New Zealand gang." Ben put the phone on the bench. "Could the bikers be about something else?" He looked at Crockett.

"Me? You think the bikers are after me?"

"Well …" I said, "You were undercover in a gang back

44

in the day."

Crockett nodded. "I was. And I recognised the patch. Those idiots are in a gang that is affiliated with the one I infiltrated."

"Who are they?" I asked. The whole 'being inside a gang for years' thing was fascinating. "I saw a wolf head with red fangs; who wears a patch like that?"

"The Alpha Brotherhood."

"Should we have *you* in protective custody?" I ate another bite of sandwich.

"I don't think this is about me," Crockett replied. "But Alphas are associated with The Inferno Jesters, and one day the Jesters will catch up with me. It's kind of a given."

Alex's phone was chirping alert after alert and threatening my already dodgy mood. Ben glanced at the screen. "I think she's breaking the internet with her last picture. And I have a feeling that one or more of her followers could be tracking her."

"How do we find out?" Crockett asked, cutting the final sandwich in half, and sliding it onto a plate for himself.

"I think we'd need to go through the list and look for profiles that are newish."

"And she has hundreds of thousands of followers ..."

"Not ideal," I said. "This is a great sandwich, Crockett, thank you."

"You're welcome."

Our lunch was accompanied by the phone chirping and tweeting, and intermittent whining from the living room.

Just as I finished my sandwich, Donald rang. I walked into the hallway with my phone pressed to my ear.

"What's up?" I expected more nonsense from the neighbours.

"I really think we need a conversation about the behaviour across the road."

"Where's Enzo?"

"Out, he got one of those *phone* calls."

The sort he can't talk about. I knew them well.

"Talk to him when he gets back then."

Donald huffed into the phone. "Come and see me. I'm visiting Nana's."

"I'm in the middle of a thing ..." Yet, I relished the idea of getting away from the whinging and complaining for half an hour. "Don't do anything Donald-like, or worse, anything Nana-like. I'll be there when I get there."

I hung up before he could protest over my comment. Casually, I went back to the kitchen and the buzz of conversation, while shoving my phone in my pocket.

"Guys, I'm going to run home and take Romeo out for a walk." I didn't add that I intended to walk him to Nana's retirement village to meet Donald.

"Not a bad idea," Crockett said. "Make sure you run an SDR."

"Naturally."

Nothing suspicious about a woman walking her old greyhound.

Ben smiled at me. I knew he'd thought of something.

"Out walking in a familiar place, you might be able to spot any surveillance."

"That's what I was thinking. I know who's usually home or around the neighbourhood on a regular Saturday." One of the perks of keeping irregular hours is that I come and go a lot, so I see who is out and about.

"Get gone," Crockett said. "We'll keep an eye on the *influencer*."

"I'm going out the back. Won't hurt her to think I'm still here."

"She's so busy complaining and being bitchy, I doubt she'd notice if you walked right past her," Ben said. I got the impression he wasn't best pleased with our charge, and I suspected he wished *he'd* thought of sneaking out to walk Romeo.

You snooze, you lose.

"I'll be back in about an hour and a half. Text if something happens." Neither man batted an eyelid at the time I was planning on staying away.

It wasn't more than a twenty-minute leisurely stroll to Nana's, even with me doubling back and running a surveillance detection route and then taking a different path.

"Turn that phone off," I said as it chirped again from the bench. "Or at least turn airplane mode on."

Alex shouted from the lounge, "You're ruining my life!"

Crockett replied, "Put a sock in it, Alex."

I grinned at Ben. "Have fun with little Miss Drama."

I left via the back door in the washhouse with nothing but my phone and the house keys that I already had in my jeans pocket. The walk was peppered with gut tweaks and jumpiness. Every motorbike that sounded even remotely like a Harley had me looking the other way, no matter how far away the bike was, just in case I was recognised. Shooting a gang member wasn't a great way to ensure longevity.

Chapter Six:

[Ronnie: Donald and the neighbours.]

As I approached our house, I could hear a woman's voice yelling abuse at someone. I glanced at the house across the street as I checked our letterbox. I hadn't seen her before, but I was sure I'd heard her voice a few times. She was loud.

And there the lunatic was, standing on the front lawn and hurling things at the house while she shouted and ranted. I don't know who Timothy is, but if I was him, I'd be doing a vanishing act. The nonsense escalated quickly into a full-blown tantrum. Delightful.

I hurried inside. Romeo greeted me at the door, his long, thin tail wagging furiously. He leaned against me once the door was shut. I gave his bony head a rub. "Missed you too, Ro," I whispered as his tail slowed to a gentle wave. "I see the crazy neighbours are providing free entertainment."

I watched out the front windows for signs of anyone else I didn't recognise, while the woman over the road threw more objects at the house. She wasn't even remotely aware of her surroundings. I'd crossed the road right in front of their house and she hadn't noticed.

She took a shoe off and chucked it at a window. Then she hobbled over, picked it up, and did it again while screaming abuse. All of a sudden, she started wailing and pretending to cry. "Why are you like this?" she yelled at the house, while fake crying.

Enough of this nonsense.

Romeo leaned his long body against me again. A greyhound hug.

"Come on old boy, let's get your gear on, and go visit Nana."

Romeo danced sideways, happy feet in all directions. His tail whipped back and forth with pure joy. I took his harness from the hook by the front door and encouraged him to stand still so I could put it on him. That's tricky when a dog is so long, thin, and happy. Once I clipped his red lead to the D ring on the harness, he let out a long, excited whine.

One last check of the street, and the lunacy across the road, and off we went.

We walked right, the opposite direction to Nana's. Ro looked over his shoulder as if to tell me we were going the wrong way. He wasn't wrong. We were.

"Trust me Ro. We'll get there." He sighed, puffed his cheeks full of air, and glanced up at me. "I promise."

Walking north again on Fergusson Drive I saw something above a new building site, not more than power pole height. Very easy to miss. And I would've missed it if I hadn't looked up. It didn't move. We carried on until we were about thirty metres further up the road. I checked again. It had moved, rotated slightly, and travelled forward. It was a small drone. Not suspicious at all. Could've been there to take photos of the building site. I knew a few photography companies used drones to take aerial photos of properties. Two hundred metres ahead, I saw another drone, lurking at power line height.

Twenty-five minutes after leaving my place, and with no sign of any other surveillants watching me from the street, or bikies, Romeo and I walked into the retirement home reception. I made a note on my phone to keep a check for more drones. They might not be looking for us, but the odds weren't in our favour.

"Hi, Margot," I said, as a blonde head of hair popped around a door beyond the front counter.

"Hello, Ronnie," she replied, and stepped through the door to place a full box of blue surgical masks on the counter. "Lots of visitors today. This is box number two. Hopefully this will last the rest of the week."

I put one on, signed in, then squirted sanitiser on my hands and rubbed it in. Romeo waited. Bet, he wished he could sanitise against the oldie virus too.

Margot leaned over the counter. "Romeo. It's nice to see you," she said and smiled as his tail wagged. Margot lifted her eyes to meet mine.

"Your Nana and Donald are in the main lounge."

"Thank you." I steeled myself for the onslaught of old people smells. Masks did nothing to protect us from that joy. The old person aroma was strongest in the main lounge. I much preferred Nana's apartment where the elderly smell was drowned out by a reed diffuser that smelt like the beach or something equally nondescript, and I didn't need to wear a mask. Slowly we walked down the wide corridor avoiding the zombified, shuffling elderly and energetic, hunched walker users. The double lounge doors stood wide open. I was met with a bouquet of lavender, Chanel No.5, and creeping death. I whispered to the dog, "Breathe through your mouth."

I think he nodded.

Nana waved from her usual corner. I unclipped Romeo's lead. He made his way across the room to greet Nana. By the time I joined her, he was off to mooch biscuits from the gaggles of ancient folk playing pool at the other end of the large room.

I bent down and kissed Nana's papery cheek through my mask. There were some upsides to mask wearing.

"You're looking well, Nana." I smiled. "That deep red twinset suits you."

"Thank you, Veronica," Nana replied, smiling.

"You're welcome, Nana."

There were no masks on any of the relics, just those of us visiting. I'd always thought it was to protect us from the creeping death. Perhaps COVID-19 and Norovirus contained creeping death in their genetic code. Perhaps the COVID vaccine would protect us from ageing. Now that would be a worthwhile conspiracy theory and definitely cause an uptake in vaccine recipients.

"It's lovely to see you, and Donald, today," she said, stretching her old lips into another smile.

Donald beamed up at me from behind his mask. His brown eyes gleamed. He was ensconced between Nana's best friends, Frankie and Ester, otherwise known as the

Cronies of Doom. I said hello to them all.

"Donald asked to see me," I told the group, and chose a seat while hoping whatever virus caused old age wouldn't get me and again thankful for mask usage. I zoned into Donald. "What did you need?"

"I really think something dreadful has happened to our real across-the-road neighbours. Nana and the girls think so too."

My stomach churned. I knew how little it took for Nana and the *Cronies of Doom* to determine there was a mystery that they should investigate. They were like ancient Nancy Drews, and Donald seemed determined to pass himself off as a Hardy Boy.

Having witnessed a small amount of lunacy earlier at the neighbours', I did not want Nana involved.

"What do you mean, Donald?"

"They're gone. The man and woman left with a backpack each, and their tamariki, weeks ago."

"You told me that on the phone. They're probably on holiday," I ventured. "Could've gone to stay with rellies."

Donald huffed. "I don't think so, Ronnie. I think the Not-Neighbours did something."

"If you saw them leave why do you think that?"

"Because they haven't been back at all."

"Maybe they got sick of losers hanging around?"

Ever since they'd moved in across the road there had been loser wannabe gang members lurking around outside their house. Not just the idiot teenagers but also marginally older associated fools causing strife.

"They left all their belongings and furniture. And after that shouting from the fat white guy ... it can't be good for them, Ronnie."

"I'll give you that. People don't usually leave their worldly goods unattended, and the behaviour you witnessed does sound suspicious."

"Should we be doing something?" Donald asked. I didn't like the gleam in his eyes. It was all too much like the gleam in Nana's eyes. Trouble.

"What do you suggest?"

I could tell Nana and the cronies were itching to be involved. This was going to be bad.

"I've already spoken to Kāinga Ora. They told me that it's temporary housing while the tenants' house is re-fitted."

"Okay, so maybe, they did go to stay with rellies."

"Hang on, there's more." Donald consulted a small notebook. Good grief, now there's a notebook. "Kāinga Ora also said they haven't been able to contact the tenant in weeks. And whoever is there, shouldn't be."

"Ah, that's where the Not-Neighbours come from," I said. Clever.

Donald laughed. "It's what they are."

"Did you ask Steph or Jenn to look into this?"

"Not yet. I wanted to see how far I could get."

"And?" I checked my watch; as amusing as it was listening to Donald play detective, I had a job to do. Staying a little longer wouldn't hurt. I didn't relish being back with Alex the influencer.

"Ronnie, are you listening?" Donald reached over and tapped my leg.

"I am now. What were you saying?"

"I have determined the real neighbours have left and are unreachable. Meanwhile, the Not-Neighbours are having domestics and wreaking havoc at the house."

Ester spoke up, "Won't be doing house values any good." She shifted in her seat. "Have you called police on them?"

Donald nodded. "I called this morning when one of the women was outside screaming like she was being murdered. There was no one else in sight. I did hear a male voice yell from inside the house, but no one was near her while she was screaming and yelling saying that he was pushing her."

"Unhinged, poor woman," Ester said sympathetically. "Did police attend?"

"Yes, and they talked to her."

"There was a woman throwing things at the house when I picked up Romeo."

"Probably her then," Donald said. "Thin, long dark hair in a sad top-knot, big reddish-purple birthmark over one eye?"

"Yep. At first I thought it was a bruise."

"That's her."

Frankie leaned forward. "What could be triggering this behaviour? Is this a mental health situation or is she being pushed over the edge by an abusive partner?"

"My money is on the partner," I said, although it could

be both. "She was yelling at someone who I couldn't see, called him Timothy among other things that I won't repeat. Did you get a job number from Police?"

Donald nodded and handed me his notebook.

I wrestled my phone from my pocket and made a call to a friend. "Hey, It's Ronnie Tracey, is Detective Ryan available?"

The person at the other end said she'd put me through to his desk. There was a click and a single ring tone, then a deep voice, "DS Anthony Ryan."

"It's Ronnie."

"What's up?" His voice lifted.

"Got a query about a call out earlier today." I gave him the address and read the job number from Donald's notebook. "Have they kicked it to you yet?"

"I spoke to one of the attending officers about half an hour ago. They suspect family violence but can't prove it. No witnesses and the victim won't talk."

"Not unusual."

"That address is close to you. Tell me you've witnessed something."

"Only the alleged victim throwing stuff at the house and screaming abuse at someone I couldn't see. They don't live there. Do you know where they live?"

"She said she's staying with her cousin at the address."

"Interesting. Apparently, the real tenants are MIA. You wouldn't know anything about that would you?" There is always a chance that they saw something and are in protective custody.

"I'd need a name."

"I'll see if I can find out."

"Interesting situation. It was your cousin that made a complaint this morning. He said someone was yelling at the residents of that house about something they'd done and how police knew everything." DS Ryan chuckled. "We don't, but we'd very much like to, so if you see anything, let me know."

"Will do. Bye, Tony."

I hung up. All eyes were on me. Romeo returned and lay down.

"My advice is ... keep an eye on the situation. If you witness an assault, ring the police."

Donald huffed and puffed noisily. "If someone gets properly hurt and we see it, we can do something? Isn't that rather like the ambulance at the bottom of the cliff?"

"It's exactly like that," I replied. "She doesn't want real help yet, or she would've taken it."

Nana piped up, "The girls and I have a quiet weekend. Perhaps we could keep an eye on them."

No. No. No. No.

"No. Stay here," I said firmly to the group. Next thing we know they'll be in the thick of it and all hell will break loose.

"Donald can't keep watch alone," Nana said. "He might miss something when nature calls."

That was the instant I knew Nana and the *Cronies of Doom* were going regardless of my opinion.

My turn to sigh loudly. "I want to be on record saying

this is a bad idea."

Donald rolled his eyes. "They'll be inside our house, Ronnie."

"You know they're cunning. Do not let your guard down."

"Yes, Ronnie. Now don't you have to be somewhere?"

"I do."

Nana reached out and patted my hand. "Don't worry dear, we'll keep a good eye on that poor woman."

I narrowed my eyes at Donald. "Do you see the problem?"

He gulped. "I promise I'll keep them out of trouble."

"On your head then."

"Leave Romeo, Veronica. He can come with us. Donald's truck is plenty big enough."

I patted the dog. "Clearly, Romeo, you are the only sensible one here." I brought my face close to his. "You are in charge. Don't let me down, Ro."

I passed the red lead to Donald with a warning shot. "Don't let *them* out of the house!"

As tempting as it was to go straight to Crockett's I didn't. I went back the way I'd come. Drones, times two, were still lurking. They were definitely not taking photos for legitimate reasons, or it wouldn't have taken that long. I popped through the Lichgate at St. John's and walked quietly through the graveyard, then down the alleyway to Ngata Grove. From there I followed the streets to our house. The demented woman across the road was still going strong. Her stamina was impressive. If only she could harness that for good. I let myself into the house, ran upstairs, changed my mid-brown jacket to a black puffer, switched my shoes for a pair of grey hiking boots, and tucked my long brown hair inside a black baseball cap. From the kitchen I took a handful of Shapes crackers. I left the house while munching and scanned the skies for any signs of drone activity. Nothing. There was a car parked further down our road, facing me. It was not one I recognised as a resident's car. The driver alighted from the vehicle and walked up to the front door of a house. I slowed down to make sure they went inside. They did.

I ate another cracker and headed to Crockett's.

Chapter Seven:

[Crockett: The problem with Alex.]

Ben made the next round of coffee. Alex sulked on the couch. She'd picked at the sandwich and refused coffee and water. She did manage to force down a fruit tea and it felt like she expected a medal. She wasn't about to get one from me. I was in the throes of weighing the odds of her doing anything really useful with her incredible memory, against the strange occupation of social media influencer. Her memory would make her an extremely valuable asset in the intelligence community if I could get her to change her "career path" to a real career. Welcome to HUMINT recruiting one-oh-one. Sometimes it's an enjoyable pastime. Sometimes it's clandestine and the adrenaline adds to the payoff. And sometimes it's this type of bullshit. I'd successfully stopped myself dwelling on the biker situation by focusing on Alex.

Ronnie slunk in the back door wearing a black baseball cap. She'd gone with dark as her new colour scheme. Her long brown hair was out of sight. She'd changed her jacket to a black puffer. The black suited her. My eyes dropped to her feet. Dark grey hiking boots. I knew she wasn't wearing them before.

"Anything?" I asked, pouring her a coffee.

I motioned to the mug. She picked it up.

"Quiet as a church as far as traditional surveillance

goes here. I spotted a car near my place that could've been something, but I don't think it was." She sipped the coffee. "Then again, the across-the-road neighbours are drawing interest so it could be that, not us."

"You said traditional. What else did you see?" Glad she hadn't mentioned motorbikes or bikies.

She placed the cup on the bench and looked up at me. "A couple of drones. They were small, but not that small." Ronnie held her hands about thirty-five centimetres apart. "About the size of a kererū. The type of drone that takes photos."

"Where'd you see them?"

"The first one was on Fergusson Drive between here and the turn off to my place."

"Is that why the change of clothes and the cap?"

She nodded. "The second drone was further north past Ward Street near the Whakatiki intersection ... they were still there on my way back home."

"If it'd seen you on your walk to ...?" Ben queried.

"Whoever owns them would know I went down Ward Street. I was at Nana's retirement village," she said with a sigh.

"You visited June?" My turn, and I let my unimpressed tone do the heavy lifting.

"I walked the dog," she replied. "Never said where I was walking him."

"What else could they have seen?"

"Nothing. Me walking a greyhound and me returning without the greyhound."

"Where's Romeo?" I asked. "He's not small and I doubt you'd forget to bring him back."

"With Nana and Donald."

"Great," Ben said. "Donald too, huh? Family visit?"

Ronnie smiled. "It's all to do with the Not-Neighbours as Donald calls them. They're all bloody involved in that mystery. I was just checking they weren't ultra-involved."

"The drones," I said, bringing the family chatter to an end. "Is it surveillance or a couple of kids with new toys?"

"That is not something we can know." Ronnie picked her cup up again. "But they were up for a long time and if they're using drone surveillance, that might explain how they knew where we were this morning." She sipped her coffee. "They're easy to miss. I just happened to look up when I was crossing a road and saw it. At first glance I thought it was something attached to a power line, and I didn't take a lot of notice. When I looked again, it'd moved slightly. It wasn't very high, no higher than power lines really. And then when I was almost at Ward Street, I saw the second one, when I checked for traffic before crossing the road."

I chewed that over for a minute. I'd seen drones used to film rugby games at Trentham Memorial Park and occasionally teens messing with them near the river, but drones weren't commonplace. There was a photography company that used drones for aerial shots of houses for real estate agents.

"Let's say they're using drones. You can cover a lot of ground with a drone," Ben said.

"Or several drones," Ronnie added. "Whoever wants her must have cash to blow. They're not cheap, and one good wind gust could destroy them."

I hadn't considered that. We get decent wind here in the upper valley. Ronnie was right: drones are fair weather tools. They're probably shit in Wellington city where gusts can come from nowhere. Maybe we should relocate to the city and get lost in the crowd.

Expressions of unhappiness came from the lounge. This was a pretty damn annoying assignment. I knew better than to voice my thoughts, but I'd definitely had more fun. Alex was still sooking about everything and bemoaning her existence. It didn't bode well for the rest of the afternoon. I really think the powers that be missed the mark by even suggesting that I try and recruit that sheila. I've never met a more painful person, and I've met a few candidates for the title.

"What do we do here? Stay, or try for somewhere in the city to hole up until the court appearance?" I asked.

"Head into the city after dark?" Ronnie queried.

"Hmmm. I guess so."

Ben poked his head around the doorway then ducked back again. "She's still griping and carrying on. I doubt she would care where we took her. She just wants the phone back."

"That's not happening," I muttered. "I think they'll expect us to try for the city tonight." I looked at Ronnie who leaned a hip against the bench. "What do you think?"

"They won't expect us to go north."

"No, they won't."

Ben spoke up, "I know a place. Let them think we're going north, then we can head into Pinehaven."

I grinned at him. "Not Art's place, surely?"

"No. The other side of Pinehaven. A friend's."

"Trustworthy?" I asked. Someone had to; it was the first I'd heard of somewhere other than Art's place that we could go, and I didn't know Ben had friends.

"No. Not at all. I'm suggesting we dump her at some random house and let her take her chances," Ben replied, "She's a pain in the ass."

Ronnie laughed. "You've been in New Zealand too long, Ben. You're finally starting to sound like one of us."

I adjusted my stance and contemplated sitting in the living room, and then said, "I didn't know you had any friends."

"Cold," Ben replied. "But fair."

I chewed the inside of my mouth while I threshed out the logistics.

"We need decoys," Ronnie said, beating me to it.

"We need two blokes and two sheilas," I added.

"Can't use Donald," Ronnie said absently. "Enzo though, could pass as you, Crockett. In the dark with a hood pulled up."

"Maybe, if he wore five hoodies under a big jacket. He's not quite as big as me."

"Close enough if he's only seen inside a car."

"With masks on we can use almost anyone to play us, even Donald," Ben said.

64

Ronnie did not look convinced. "Not Donald. He is the last person ..." her thought process re-routed, I could tell by her expression. "Scratch that, Nana is the last person and Donald is bloody close to it. We need professionals for the post." She looked at Ben. "You know a lot of actors." It was a statement, not a question.

"I do, but I'm not sure actors are the best option here. Sure, they can pretend to be us convincingly, but we'd be putting them in harm's way. Actors are not agents or officers or even PIs."

Ronnie took her phone from her pocket. She glanced at the screen, then looked up at us. "We could use one of my surveillance teams to pose as me and the whinger in there." She nodded her head to the lounge. "Jo and Brie can pull it off without much effort, especially wearing masks."

She was right. I'd met them before, and we'd used them on a previous operation. They were good. That would work. I nodded.

"And we can use Enzo to double as Ben, and Art for me," I said. It made more sense that Enzo should be Ben. Wearing face masks was a great idea; hoods up, masks on. All they needed was to be wearing the same colour, and type of clothes as us, and to drive my car.

If they were using drones, then we needed to let the drones spot a couple of the ring-ins thinking it's us. Let's get the bozos chasing their own tails and doubting themselves at every turn.

"How nasty do you think the people trying to stop little

whingy from testifying are going to get?" Ronnie asked.

"Very." It hasn't exactly been a picnic so far. "It's not going to get any better."

"Right. I'll advise my team accordingly."

"Non-lethal weapons as first option, please," Ben said. "There's been enough gun play."

"And you think they'll opt for non-lethal?" Ronnie asked with a shake of her head.

"A taser will still drop them at fifteen feet," Ben said.

"Four and a half metres for the non-LEO taser cartridges. Eleven metres for the LEO ones. What do we have available?" Ronnie said quietly. She looked at me. "What do you have?"

I smiled at her. "LEO."

"So, we're using yours then."

"Yes," I replied, then added, "A 9mm from a Glock 17 will stop them dead at fifty metres."

"Ben would like us to play nice and shoot sparkly rainbows at them first. He just might be okay with riot guns shooting bean bags ..." Ronnie laughed. Ben's shoulders shook as he joined in the laughter.

"I'm just saying it'd be better if we didn't leave a trail of bodies all over the region and draw unwanted attention," Ben said, reining his amusement in.

A voice called out from the lounge, "What's so funny? This is not funny. Being here is not funny. This is a publicity disaster!" She paused, then yelled, "You are ruining my life!"

Ronnie poked her head into the lounge. "You'll get

over it."

"Pepper spray," Ben said.

"Sure. The gel spray goes the farthest," I said. "Five metres would be the extent of its reach, though. You're dependent on wind conditions and environment. You going to stop and put on a gas mask?"

Ben grinned. "Cancel that idea, then."

"You're a trier, I'll give you that, mate."

"Devil's advocate is what he is," Ronnie mumbled. "For the sheer hell of it."

Ben didn't refute her comment, which caused another chuckle to rise. True to form, a tirade of abuse sprayed from the lounge. It was tempting to leave her on my couch and let the bastards come get her. I needed to check my attitude before it got out of control.

A notion formulated, mostly because I honestly don't know how Ronnie's superpower really works. It wouldn't hurt to voice it.

"Ronnie, can you use your woo-woo and find out where any surveillance is?"

She sighed heavily. "That's not how it works." Under her breath I heard her mumble, "It's called dowsing, you moron. I'll woo-woo you."

Ronnie had her phone in her hand and started making calls. I did the same.

Chapter Eight:
[Donald: And the Socials]

I could hear Nana and the cronies talking quietly in the lounge as I settled myself in front of the computer. I doubted Ronnie would mind if I wrote a wee status update on the socials. I mean, it'd be like a report of sorts. I stretched my hands out and placed my fingers on the keyboard. Diamonds from my wedding ring sparkled under the light above the desk. That husband of mine has the best taste in sparklers. Makes it hard to focus with all the lights shining from my ring finger. I love a sparkler as much as the next man.

"Focus, Donald. This is important," I whispered to myself.

Nana's voice wafted from the lounge, "What was that, Donald?"

"Nothing, Nan, just talking to myself."

There is not a thing wrong with that old woman's hearing. Good grief. I took a breath and started to type.

* * *

Dear Readers, I've got to fill you in:

A few nights ago, a group of 'youths' arrived across the street. They weren't outside long. I don't know if they went inside, but I doubt it, because it was very quiet there.

When I took Romeo out the front (for a better look and a wee listen), and we walked across the road and around the corner, I noticed the living room light was on. That wasn't on the night before.

Someone was there.

It wasn't our *real* neighbours!

I'd forgotten about this wee morsel: I can't believe I forgot to tell Ronnie (that's probably why she doesn't believe there's a mystery in full swing!)

On Friday last week, a locksmith was there changing the front door lock. I didn't think much of it, except pretty much anyone can call a locksmith and have a lock changed, or a door opened - you just need to be slightly convincing.

And the one I call Big-Mouth, was there while the locksmith was. She and her partner (Mr Stupid) were in and out of the house and fiddling around with their car. They came and went several times that day.

I don't know who is there right now.

There is no car.

Someone was inside overnight the other weekend and being very quiet.

The whole thing is quite entertaining.

We are still left with a bit of a question: Where are the real neighbours and why can't anyone get hold of them?

Nana, Ester, and Frankie are staying for a few days. They're helping me keep an eye on the place across the road. We are sure something dreadful has happened to the real neighbours.

* * *

"Nana do you need tea?" I said, as I stood up from the computer after posting my update to every social account I had. I glanced at the screen as chimes sounded. My post was already getting likes. Who knew our wee saga would be so interesting?

I could see the tops of Nana and the cronies' heads in the lounge. They'd dragged the armchairs closer to the front window, and therefore had their backs to me.

"Yes, dear. Bring a tray through," Nana replied, no hint of frailty in her voice.

Funny how she does that and how she can move furniture one moment, but barely stand another. I think Ronnie may be right about Nana playing us all. Tricky old woman that she is. Who'd have thunk it?

I made tea; thankfully we had a teapot. I didn't think for one minute that I would get away with dumping teabags into cups. Not with this crowd. As the jug boiled, the kitchen door opened, and Enzo walked in with a smile on his lips.

"Hello, Lover," he said, sliding his arms around me from behind. "Tea would be nice."

"Your wish is my command," I replied, leaning against him for a moment. With Enzo anything was possible, and nothing was difficult. He had a calming effect on everyone. I'm a lucky man to have such a spectacularly beautiful and good husband.

"We have guests?" Enzo's words tickled the side of my face as he looked over my shoulder at the tea tray on the bench.

"You know how the neighbours have disappeared? Well, it's gotten a lot more interesting. Nana and the girls are helping me surveil the house."

Enzo stepped sideways. I looked at him just as he tried to hide a smile. Caught.

"What's the smile about?"

"Nothing at all, Lover," Enzo said, and planted a kiss on my cheek. "I'll get some biscuits out, shall I?"

"Yes, please."

Enzo took a large square Sistema box from the pantry, unclipped the lid, and inspected the packeted biscuits it contained. I poured the boiling water into the tea pot and arranged the cups to make room for an extra one. I chewed my bottom lip, while I watched Enzo open a packet of Mint Treats and arrange the chocolate covered deliciousness on a pretty plate. He added serviettes to my tray before putting the box back in the pantry. I'm such a lucky man.

I wished Ronnie wasn't so caught up in whatever she was caught up in. I'm sure she'd be able to get to the bottom of the neighbour situation if she was here.

"I'll take the tray," Enzo said.

"Thank you. I'll take the bikkies."

"What a team." Enzo's hand lightly brushed mine as he reached for the laden tray.

"I'll go first, might need to move the coffee table. I think the girls have done some rearranging."

Enzo chuckled. "I'm sure they have."

I carried the plate into the lounge. The coffee table was behind the chairs now that they'd moved them closer to the window. So, they must've gone around the table. Frail old ladies be damned!

"Ladies, can I trouble you for a moment? Just need to get this coffee table in the right place for the tea tray."

Nana's head spun toward me. "Donald, I don't know that we'd be much help at our age." The generalised feebleness was back.

Ester and Frankie tutted quietly before Frankie said, "You're a big strong lad, I'm sure you can move the table."

Wow. This must be what Ronnie was talking about: frailty being an act to get us all doing her bidding. Now I'd seen it with my own eyes. She plays a good game, does Nana.

"The chairs need to move back to make a space," I said, keeping a smile in my voice.

"One moment, Donald," Nana said, with a good deal of annoyance. "We don't want to miss anything with all this moving of chairs and carry on."

Enzo strode across the lounge, no tray in sight.

"Let me, Nana. If you ladies could stand up for a moment, I'll move the chairs back a fraction, and bring the table around," he said, smiling kindly.

I knew what was beneath that smile and it made me

smile. Enzo really did like Nana, but he tolerated none of her nonsense.

"Very well, Enzo, if you insist."

Nana called for her cane. I found it all the way down-stairs by the front door. Hmm. She didn't need it earlier, obviously. There was much huffing and puffing from the trio as they stood and shuffled about, while Enzo and I moved chairs and together lifted the table into a suitable position, without the biscuit plate shifting at all, and more importantly, without clouting any old women with a table leg. I dragged Romeo's bed closer to us. He didn't like to feel left out.

"There we go, Nana," Enzo said. "Sit yourself down. Tea's brewed. I'll duck out and bring the tray through."

With the cronies seated and tea poured, the next fif-teen minutes were most delightful.

Enzo and I pulled the couch around and cosied up to-gether. Good thing we have massive front windows and plenty of room for nosiness.

"Now, we noticed that there are some young people in the house," Frankie said.

Ester lifted a notebook off her knee. "I've been making notes and writing descriptions."

"Do you mind if I read your notes?" Enzo asked, stretching his hand out for the notebook.

"Of course not." Ester passed the book to Frankie who passed it to Enzo.

Enzo leaned back into the soft cushions next to me and flipped through pages, reading the spidery writing quickly. I don't know how. I could barely make out words.

"This is thorough and well done."

"I used to be a policewoman in my younger days," Ester replied. "I should think it would be thorough and well done."

"Frankie, the young man you spoke to ..." Enzo's voice drifted. "He was bringing the rubbish bin in?"

Frankie sipped her tea for a moment. "Yes, that's right. He came over. I was out the front with Romeo." Her lips stretched taut over aged teeth. "The young man said the neighbours were away and there isn't supposed to be anyone at the house." She took another sip of tea. "He asked that we call police if we see anyone inside the house."

"Did he give you his name?" Enzo flicked back through some pages and then looked at Frankie.

"I think he said his name was Caleb. I'm not certain though."

Enzo pulled a pen from his inside jacket pocket and wrote on a page in the notebook.

"This is a good description," he said. "I think we'll know him if he's seen again."

Ester cleared her throat. "We called Kāinga Ora."

That was the first I'd heard of it. I leaned closer and watched the old faces perk up with the joy of telling what they knew to dear Enzo.

"When did you get that phone call in?" I tapped Nana on the arm.

"This is why I said we should be here to help, Donald.

You can't be watchful all the time. You have things to be getting on with."

"Where was I?"

"I don't know dear. On the phone in the other room, I think."

"So, I was on the phone while Frankie was talking to a young man, and while Ester was speaking to Kāinga Ora ... right, there was a semi-crisis at the salon. This is why I don't like opening in the weekends!"

Enzo smiled reassuringly at me. "It's all okay, Lover. We've got the girls here to keep an eye out."

Didn't we though.

I was beginning to see what Ronnie was on about. Nana is by far too eager to be involved and so are the cronies.

***

Dear Readers, I quite have my hands full with Nana and co. Now, to continue my update about the other weekend because I feel that's going to become relevant as this weekend continues.

Last Saturday went like this ... one police unit and a K9 unit arrived after three phone calls to police while they tried to get to the bottom of the nonsense across the road.

Two young idiots were there earlier that morning, so I called police because our neighbours are not there. And when I called Kāinga Ora on the previous Friday, the housing manager asked me to call the police if anyone showed up there, and the person Frankie spoke to also asked that we call police if anyone shows up. So, duty done. They can thank me later.

It was highly entertaining having police and a K9 officer present. Romeo was glued to the window because of the dog. It was a beautiful dog and had been standing in the carport in full view of our lounge. And you know how the old boy loves police dogs.

Now, later that day I popped over next door and saw our lovely neighbour Annie - she told me there were three males and one female in the house across the road.

The house that no one is supposed to be in.

I saw two males inside when Enzo and I got home from walking Romeo: one in the kitchen and one in the lounge. The old boy is a bit slow now, so we were walking slowly, when we heard a lot of crashing about going on in there. It didn't sound good.

Police sent another a unit as soon as they could.

I very much hoped it would be another K9 unit that attended and one of the morons would try to run. I would pay good money to watch that unfold. No such luck though. Police said one of the youths had permission from the tenant to be there and showed the cop a message on FB Messenger, supposedly from his aunt, the tenant. Because if it's on Facebook, it must be true?

Currently, Nana and *the Cronies of Doom* are happily ensconced on our gorgeous lounge suite watching the craziness across the road. I'll write more when I can!

Chapter Nine:
[Ronnie: Best laid plans]

Crockett's phone rang. He looked over at me as he answered it, "Enzo. What's up?"

Enzo spoke. We couldn't hear the words, just a muffled sound of speech. A few seconds later Crockett said goodbye and hung up.

"We're switching it up again," Crockett said. "Enzo is going to be me. Art is Ben."

I didn't have time to ask why before my phone rang. Jo's name and photo were on the screen.

"Hi, Jo," I said as I answered.

"Brie can't make it. It's just me."

"Bugger. It's okay. You're similar in height and build to our charge. So that's great."

"Okay. But you still need someone else?"

I weighed my options; it took a split second. Yes, we did, and I knew just the person. "Yep, but I'll take care of it."

I hung up.

"Crockett, how are we going to get our doubles into your place without a drone potentially spotting them?" Ben asked. His fingers spun a lighter on the stainless-steel bench.

"Carefully," Crockett replied.

"Might be best if we left in your car, like we arrived in

your car," I said, thinking while I spoke. "We need to switch cars and people, but not anywhere we can be seen from the sky."

"Staying off Fergusson Drive is going to help. That's where you saw the drones, right?" Ben asked.

"Yes."

"What do you suppose the range is on those little things?" Ben's voice remained low. None of us were speaking at our usual volume. No one wanted to explain anything to the 'influencer' at this stage. It'd generate more complaints, and I for one, was running out of patience.

"Something around the five hundred metre mark, would be my guess," Crockett replied. "When we leave, I'll take the Harley. You game to be my pillion?" Crockett nudged me.

"Sure."

"And how is the Harley going to help?" Ben asked.

"We're not all in the one car," Crockett said. "And now Enzo is being me, I can switch bikes with him."

"And pillions," I said.

"Exactly."

"Okay." Ben didn't sound convinced. "So, I take her." He flicked his thumb toward the lounge. "To where?"

I was trying to find a place that meant we didn't cross, or use, Fergusson Drive and kept us at least five hundred metres away from where I saw the drones. What about Upper Hutt College? Easy for us to get to. It was the weekend, so apart from sports on the fields, the school itself wouldn't be open. They had a covered section of the quad between the hall and A block. We could just park right up the reception side of A Block, under cover.

"I think I have it. Upper Hutt College."

I watched their faces as they considered my idea.

"That might work," Crockett said.

"I want you wearing armour," Ben said to me. "It's your back on the line."

I nodded. "I know. Kevlar will be worn."

"And silk," he said, giving me a look that said no argument would be allowed.

"What do you think I'm wearing under this jacket?" I asked Ben, and grinned.

"Clothing?"

"A silk shirt. A deep red silk shirt. So, silk is covered."

Ben laughed. "You know that's not what I meant."

"And you know, it's what you're going to get."

"She can wear a bomb disposal suit if you want," Crockett said with a mile-wide grin. "Might be a bit tricky sitting on the bike, but I'm sure we could make it work."

Ben laughed. "Just tell me she'll be wearing fucking good armour, and I'll be happy."

"She will." Crockett's attention shifted at a noise in the lounge. He took two long strides and landed in the doorway. "What are you doing?"

I moved to him. Both of us saw Alex the influencer standing in front of a window, looking out.

"Curtains were closed when we arrived," I said.

"Yep," Crockett replied. He walked across the room

79

and grabbed Alex by the arm. With one fluid motion she was again sitting on the couch.

"Don't touch the curtains." He pulled the curtain to cover the exposed windows.

"You can't keep me on this couch!"

"Stay!" Crockett said, pointing a finger at her. "Right there."

He lifted his Glock from the holster in the back of his jeans.

"Ben," I said quietly. He moved up beside me. He, too, had a gun in his hand. He gave me a nod and stepped back. I knew he'd go to the back door. Crockett was about to open the front door. I slipped my Glock from my holster and seated it comfortably in my right hand. I angled myself in the doorway and leaned my back against the door jamb. I could see both doors and both men.

Alex squawked indignantly. I held my fingers to my lips and shushed her.

She rolled her eyes.

Fine, be a dick and die then.

Wow. She really brought out my worst. Quite a talent. I took a breath and let calmness wash over me while I listened for sounds that meant trouble.

In, one, two, three, four.

Out, one, two, three, four.

Ben slipped silently out the back door.

Crockett glanced at me before letting himself out the front.

"You, Alex. Come to me. Now," I ordered. I could see

Crockett as he walked down the steps. Then he was gone.

Alex stomped across the room.

"This is lame."

So are you.

"Sit over there," I said, pointing to a chair at the dining room table. Alex muttered under her breath. The dining room was at the end of the kitchen. She was no longer in my line of sight but behind me. I remained where I was so I could see both doors.

I heard Alex drag a chair out and sit heavily in it, she was still complaining about everything. I wasn't sure how she could make much more noise.

A few minutes passed and I saw Ben come up the front steps as the back door opened. Crockett stepped into the house from the back door. Ben closed and locked the front door behind him.

"Anything?"

"No," Ben said. "No sign of anyone out there or any electronic devices."

"Good to know," I replied, then turned to Alex. "You can go sit back down in the lounge. Keep away from the windows."

"I want my phone!"

"No," I replied and pointed to the lounge. "Off you go."

"It's right there!" She yelled pointing at the phone on the bench.

"It is. You're not having it."

"But I need to check my accounts."

"No. It's too dangerous."

She huffed and puffed and stomped past me. "It's not dangerous. You're ridiculous."

"Do you remember the shooting earlier?" I asked, holstering my Glock. "Thought you remembered everything you saw."

She glared at me. "Of course, I do. Hardly my fault you three can't keep me safe!"

"It was entirely your fault," I replied, quietly. "You could've gotten us all killed."

She tossed her head back and laughed like a maniac.

Crockett appeared next to me and spoke to Alex. "Do you have a death wish?"

She continued her borderline hysterical laughing.

"Maybe. Or possibly a mental illness," I whispered to Crockett.

His deep laugh flowed and stopped Alex in her tracks. So, it was an act. Good to know.

"We need to get moving before she causes any more chaos." I kept my voice to a whisper. "I wish we could fast forward to Monday and get rid of her."

"Keen of you to think we'll be able to send her away on Monday."

"She testifies Monday, right?"

"I doubt she'll be called once. I expect her to be called back for cross-examination."

"Don't say that."

Crockett laughed again. "Just think how good we'll feel when it's over and how happy our accountants will be."

True.

Steph will be glowing when she sees how much this enterprise brings in. I'd like to be alive to enjoy spending some of it.

And that reminded me I needed to ring Emily. She and I were close in height and build. Even our hair colour wasn't far off. Hers was a slightly lighter shade of brown.

I made the phone call.

"Emily, it's Ronnie. I need you for a job."

"Hello, Ronnie." She paused. "I have a job."

"Yes, I know. You work in the bookshop."

"Yes."

"This is a different job and only for a few hours today."

I knew the bookshop wasn't open today.

"What do I need to do?"

"Go for a ride with Enzo on his Harley."

"Okay," she said and hung up.

I smiled at Crockett's dumbfounded expression.

"Really? You're bringing Emily into this?"

"I am."

Chapter Ten:

[Ronnie: This isn't good!]

I leant on the stainless-steel kitchen bench and gazed out the window while I pondered about Alex. I really didn't know what to make of Miss Fowler. I tried to imagine what her world as an 'influencer' was like, but it was a million miles from my world, and I couldn't get my head round it. Perhaps I don't have that much imagination. So far, I'd managed to fail at saying the word 'influencer' without making speech marks with my fingers. She gets shirty when I do that. Guess I'll be doing it forever then. Come on, Ronnie, that's not very professional. Behave yourself and do your best. Keep her safe. Get her to court. See her off on her new life. Sometimes I needed to give myself a pep talk. This was one of those times.

In my view, the last part of the assignment was going to cause the most trouble. I couldn't see her leaving her life and her eight-hundred thousand, or whatever silly number it was, followers behind.

Ben waved his hand in front of my face.

"Earth to Ronnie," he said with a smile. "You looked a hundred miles away. What are you thinking about?"

"Not much," I replied.

Crockett came into the kitchen with a black leather jacket over his arm. It matched the one he wore. His other hand held a bulletproof vest. He handed me the vest. I dropped it over my head and fastened the left shoulder then the side. It wasn't the most comfortable thing to wear, but better than a bullet in the back. Marginally.

Crockett lay the jacket on the table and took a photo of it.

"I'm pretty sure Enzo has a spare jacket like this, I know he has one the same as mine. Would you mind? A full-length photo please." He handed Ben his phone. Ben took a photo of Crockett and handed the phone back.

Crockett sent a text.

"Just making sure Enzo has exactly the same jackets as we do, and he's wearing what I am, right down to my boots," he said, and looked at me for a second. "Black jeans," he said and typed another text. "Does Emily have black jeans? I've never seen her wear them."

"She does. They're in her wardrobe in a box." I glanced at my feet. Boots. "She has these grey boots as well."

"Will she know where?"

"Same box."

His eyebrows rose. "What else is in that box?"

"A black balaclava, black leather gloves, a black hoodie, a few long sleeved black tee shirts." Her life before the accident. Clothes she wore when we were doing night surveillance work or some of our other covert night-time activities. I still miss that version of Emily.

I handed Crockett my phone. "Full length photo, please."

He walked back a few paces and snapped the picture, then returned my phone. I sent the photo to Emily along with a text asking her to wear the same clothes as me and where she could find those clothes in case she'd forgotten.

There was one problem. The motorbike jacket. Neither of us had those. I was borrowing one from Crockett. I thought for a second. No, two problems. Crockett said Enzo had a jacket Emily could wear. She needed a bulletproof vest under the jacket.

"Emily needs ..." I started.

"I know. Enzo will take her the jacket and a vest. I got this," Crockett said.

"Good," I replied. I should've known Crockett would be onto it when it came to Emily. "Then as soon as everyone is dressed, we can make a move." I inclined my head to the lounge. "How about her clothes. Jo needs to wear what she's wearing."

Ben smiled. "Alex has on a long, black leather coat with fur trim and a knitted pompom hat. I couldn't tell you what was under the coat or what colour the hat was. I doubt anyone saw her shoes or anything much of her."

"Yeah, but we should behave as if they did."

Crockett walked into the lounge with his phone in hand. I heard the protesting from Alex, the whiner. He strolled back in, wearing a tight-lipped smile. Crockett showed me the photo he'd just taken. Sneakers; she was wearing branded sneakers. Mid-blue straight legged jeans. The pompom hat was deep red and lying on the couch next to her. The black coat she'd wrapped around herself covered everything else but the bottom of her jeans and her sneakers.

I poked my head around the doorway into the lounge. "Hey, Alex, what size shoes do you wear?"

"Why?"

"Just answer the question."

"Why should I? It's a weird question. You people are not normal."

I took a deep cleansing breath and walked into the lounge. "What size shoes do you wear?"

"Do you have a shoe fetish?" she snapped back.

"No. Tell me what size they are, or I'll take them off you and look myself."

She glared up at me from under her heavy eyelashes. "Why are you like this? Why does it even matter?"

"Answer the question," I said and took two steps towards her.

"Fine. You're a bully. I wear a US eight," she grumbled. "Leave me alone."

I spun on my heels and walked back into the kitchen.

Crockett had a grin plastered across his face. "Nothing is easy with that one." He tipped his head toward the lounge.

"Her choice to make everything hard," I said. "She wears the same size as Jo. I'll tell her to wear sneakers, mid-blue jeans, and a warm jacket but not worry about a hat. They can swap coats and shoes. Jo can put the hat on."

"Sounds good."

I made another phone call to Jo and told her what we

were planning. She was happy to play along. I knew she would be.

Ten minutes later our phones alerted. I picked mine up and saw the alert on the screen.

"A new police alert," I muttered, opening the message. Armed man seen in Wallaceville. Great. People in Ward Street and Martin Street were told to stay inside, lock their doors, and keep away from windows, as AOS and police searched for the gunman. There was a police road-block from the Fergusson Drive entrance to the retirement home, and another at Whakatiki Street roundabout. "Maybe Nana and the *Cronies of Doom* staying with Donald this weekend, was a good idea."

"I think so," Ben replied, making eye contact with me. "Armed man in Wallaceville. Related do you think?"

"Be odd if it wasn't. Just this morning we had armed men shooting in Heretaunga. What are the odds that this isn't related?"

"Slim to none," Crockett said. "Perhaps they think we're in Wallaceville. I hope they do. Because we're not."

No one mentioned bikies. Police didn't mention a bikie connection in the alert either.

"Will this affect our escape plan?" Ben asked.

I turned my face toward him slowly. "You're the one who came up with the place we're going, so, will it affect our escape plan?"

He chuckled. "No. And I better make a call and check that my friends are ready for visitors."

"Oh, right, we have a plan, but the people involved

don't know?" Crockett said. "You Yanks do things arse-about-face."

"It'll be fine. The call is merely a courtesy. I'm always welcome."

Ben chose a number from his phone and put the call on speaker.

A woman answered, "Hel-laire."

"Ginny, it's Ben."

"How are you, darling? Been a while."

"I'm great. Keep meaning to call in. But you know ..."

"I do. Gets a bit like that here too."

"I need a favour, Ginny, and it involves me bringing some colleagues over."

"Tom and I are home this afternoon. It'll be lovely to see you." She paused. "What's wrong?"

"You'll see when I get there."

"Are you staying for dinner?"

"Yes, please. Tell Tom it's an extra four for dinner."

"Are we having a party?"

Ben laughed. "I'll grab some bread rolls and a few groceries on my way over."

"Just yourself is fine."

"See you soon."

He hung up and looked at me. "Definitely getting groceries. These are really good people, and that in there." He pointed toward the lounge. "Is not."

"Harsh," Crockett said half-under his breath. "She might be a really nice person in different circumstances."

We all chuckled quietly.

Yeah. Maybe. But I had a feeling that she was the same no matter what. Overly concerned with appearances and praise from internet weirdos. Shallow as spit.

Her voice rang out from the lounge. "Are we staying here forever?"

No one responded.

She tried again. "Well, are we? If so, can someone get me some real coffee? I don't know how anyone can drink this grossness."

Ben rolled his eyes and looked at us one at a time. Neither Crockett nor I took the bait. Ben shook his head and walked over to the entrance to the lounge. He cleared his throat and said, "We will be moving again soon. Logistic organisation is underway. Be patient." He turned abruptly and walked back to us.

"Well done," I said with a smile.

Crockett's phone buzzed in his pocket. He dragged it from his jeans and read the message. With a glance at the screen again, then a quick smile at me, he said, "Time to get geared up. Enzo is riding over to pick up Emily. Then it's go-time."

I heard something in Crockett's voice. Worry? Concern?

"Are you all right?" I asked him.

He nodded, then shook his head. "Emily on the bike. She doesn't know when her artificial foot is on the peg."

"She's been on the bike with you?" I knew she had, and she'd loved it.

"Yeah. I know she can't tell so I check. And I get her to

put a bit of weight on it. What if Enzo forgets?"

"Just text him and remind him about her artificial leg. He'll make sure she's safe." I watched Crockett for a spilt second. "That's all that's bothering you?"

"Using Emily at all ..."

"She's the perfect person to be me, as long as no one glimpses the bionics under her jeans."

"See? It's risky involving Emily."

Wow. He had it bad for Emily. I grinned at him but before I could toss a smart remark my phone buzzed. Jo. She was ready and Art had arrived at her place. We kept everyone involved in this little problem away from our office. If the bikie gunmen from earlier knew who we were, then they'd be watching the office. It'd be better if Steph and Jenn carried on as usual and none of the rest of us showed up there. People can only watch so many places at once. Unless they have an army. I pushed that notion away. As far as we knew there were four bikies, two drones, and at least two people in cars that caused the accidents. One man was wounded and one arrested. Down to two men and two drones. It was safe to conclude they had support from somewhere, so there were more people that we didn't know about yet. It could be a reasonably fair fight if it came down to it. Out of country bikies: how many friends could they have?

Ben touched my arm. "What are you thinking about?"

I smiled. "Wondering how many people we are up against."

"Ah."

"Not that it matters," I added. "We'll be fine."

"Course we will," Crockett said. He sounded a lot surer than I was.

"Has that gang got friends here?"

"Probably. Be stupid to think they didn't. And a lot would've changed since I was involved."

"Let's get Alex the pain-in-the-butt ready," Ben said as another phone buzzed.

It was Crockett's phone. "Enzo and Emily are on the move."

I checked for an update from Jo. Nothing. So, I fired off a text to her. Seconds later she replied saying they were leaving.

"We are closest," I said.

Crockett grinned. "The Harley could do with a run. We'll head north and then take back streets to our rendezvous." He handed me a black helmet. "Come on."

I jammed the helmet on my head, fastened the jacket over the bullet proof vest and then tightened the helmet strap under my chin. What were the odds of us coming across trouble? A voice inside my head said, 'Don't even think about it.'

"I'll give you ten minutes then I'll leave with her," Ben said, tipping his thumb toward the pain-in-the-bum young woman in the lounge. "We'll go back streets south, then swing back and meet you."

"Cool," I replied, and followed Crockett out the back door and around to the garage. "We can't go up Fergie because of the cordon."

"I know," Crockett replied as the garage door rose.

Chapter Eleven:

[Crockett: Can't be good all the time]

It'd been a little while since I'd taken the Harley for a run. As usual, it started first time. It was a hell of a bike and always reliable. I got Ronnie to climb on behind me out in the driveway. She settled fast. I was going to have to remind myself we were two-up because I could hardly feel her weight.

I roared out of the driveway and turned left. There wasn't much traffic, so I got across Fergusson Drive easily and down Liverpool Street. Before long we were travelling north on Ararino Street. From Ararino, I took Miro, crossed Ward, and veered right all the way to Lane Street.

Within five minutes, we were through town, and riding south down McLeod Street. There was no sign of any other bikes.

I didn't see any police cars, which was probably a good thing, as I wasn't exactly sticking to the speed limit at times. Can't be good all the time. A little bit of fun never hurt anyone.

We cruised down Moonshine to the main gates of the school. Ronnie tapped my right shoulder and pointed to a covered area between the hall and reception. Slowly, I took us in and under the sails that shielded the area from rain, sun, and hopefully, nosy drones. We parked up and climbed off the bike. Fun. Ronnie seemed to have enjoyed herself. I set my helmet on the seat. We wouldn't be staying long. Ronnie followed suit. In the distance I heard the rumble of another Harley, and I hoped it was Enzo.

It didn't take long before the rumble closed in and eased around the corner to pull up next to us. Emily hopped off, steadied herself then removed her helmet and smiled widely. Enzo killed the engine, kicked the stand down, and removed his helmet.

"Hi, Emily!" Ronnie said.

"Hello, Ronnie," she replied, still smiling. Her eyes moved from Ronnie to me. "Hello, Crockett."

"Hey, Milo. Did you enjoy the ride?"

"Yes. I did enjoy the ride." She smiled. "Enzo has a motorbike like yours."

I nodded. "They are Harleys. His is a soft-tail and mine is a wide-glide."

I heard a car drive slowly in through the driveway that connected to Hikurangi Street. Car doors opened and closed. Another car cruised through. We waited in silence. Art and Jo sauntered around the corner chatting. Their conversation stalled when they saw us. Ronnie waved. Jo waved back. All we needed was Ben and Alex the annoying 'influencer' and we could execute Part Two of the plan.

Footfalls rang out among the buildings. I peered toward the noise. It was Ben and Alex. They'd come in from between the buildings, not up the driveway. Good thinking.

Sounds of people cheering filled the air. Someone

must've scored a try. The happy yelling made me think it was Upper Hutt College who got the try. When the noise died down a bit, I could hear Ronnie and Jo discussing what would happen next. Jo and Alex were to switch coats and shoes, and Jo would wear Alex's hat. Art already matched Ben. Enzo and I exchanged helmets. Ronnie and Emily did the same. Then the bike swap.

It wasn't easy handing the key to my Harley to Enzo. I imagined he felt the same.

We did it.

Nothing bad happened.

I watched Emily and Enzo ride off on my bike. They'd take Fergusson Drive as far south as Silverstream, use the underpass and head back to my place via the back way, through Heretaunga, over the railway line at Trentham, back onto Fergusson Drive, and then down Tararua, around Ruahine, to Rimutaka, and up Merton. Emily had a key to my back door. It was no problem for them to park the Harley up in the garage and go inside. Enzo was aware that I had a gun safe in the floor and where to find it, just in case.

Ben and, the now changed, and still bitching and sooking, Alex, switched cars with Art and Jo. Art and Jo left next; they'd go north up Fergusson Drive, then follow the detours in place to Upper Hutt itself. They would make like they were going to a supermarket, then, when they were sure they'd been in the open long enough to be spotted, head further north. Art was keen to make it look like they were going back to the starting point of this disaster, but then veer off to Jo's place. That was a pretty good move.

All that was left was us. Ben and Alex headed for Jo's car. Ronnie and I took Enzo's Harley. If all went well, we'd rendezvous in Pinehaven, free of bullet holes.

Ben had given me directions. I was to approach the house from Blue Mountains Road and then go down Forest Road to Elmslie. They were going up Pinehaven Road to Elmslie.

Ronnie settled herself behind me on the Harley. She tapped my shoulder to let me know she was good.

I gave myself a few minutes on the road to get used to how the bike felt. Cruising. Nothing silly. Just cruising. I chose Brentwood Street to cross Fergusson Drive. As soon as we turned onto Ararino from Islington, I turned my head a bit so Ronnie could hear me.

"Ready for some fun?"

"Yeah," she replied.

"Hang on."

She moved her arms up a little, so they were around my waist and the fun began. Good luck to any drone trying to keep up with us. There were no holdups at all when we got to the railway lines. And it was smooth riding from the crossing to Gloucester Street and up to Chatsworth Road. I misbehaved a little bit until we started the descent down Chatsworth to Whitemans Road. I figured if I'd been clocked by a cop by that point, I'd scramble to keep all my points. It'd be worth it, though. I behaved a little better going down the hill, knowing there was a tight

left turn at the end. Once we rounded that into Whitemans Road, I was ready for more fun. It was big bends
the rest of the way and good fun. Down Forest Road I
slowed to the speed limit in time to turn into Elmslie.
Then we cruised; I didn't want to risk taking out kids. I
knew we were looking for a house quite a way up the
street and then down a longish driveway.

Ronnie tapped my left shoulder and pointed to a driveway coming up. I nodded.

The driveway turned right just before the bottom. It
was a shared driveway until the right turn. Ben waited
and motioned to a large carport. I saw the car he'd driven
in there and eased the Harley in beside it. Ronnie hopped
off and had removed her helmet before I'd killed the engine. The smile on her face said it all.

"Everything all right?" Ben asked her.

"Yes. That was a little bit of fun."

Ben smiled, then frowned. "Drawing attention to yourself, were you, Crockett?"

I placed my helmet carefully on the seat and took
Ronnie's from her. I put it next to mine then grinned at
Ben. "Little bit of fun never hurt anyone."

"Come on, I'll introduce you to Ginny and Tom." Ben
moved closer to me. "I hope you're wearing clean socks.
Leave your boots by the back door."

"Funny man," I said, with a slight nudge of his shoulder with mine. "How's the brat?"

"No change there."

The back door opened. I unzipped my steel cap boots

and pulled them off, then placed them neatly beside Ben's shoes. Ronnie unlaced her hiking boots and took them off. A blonde-haired woman smiled at me from the top of the back steps.

"Hel-laire ... and you must be Crockett," she said. "I'm Ginny." She looked past me to Ronnie. "And you must be the infamous Ronnie. Bring your shoes inside, Ronnie."

She welcomed us into her light, warm, and inviting home.

"Come on through," Ginny said. "Ronnie, your shoes will be fine next to Alex's just inside the laundry there." She led the way through the kitchen to the dining and living room.

Alex was on the couch with cats all around her. Big, fluffy, cream-coloured cats. I counted five.

"Hope you're not allergic to cats," Ginny said in a tone that suggested it was too bad if I was.

"No allergies here," I said. "We appreciate your hospitality."

"It's not a bother. Ben and I were overdue a catch up, and I've wanted to meet Ronnie for ages. Have a seat, Crockett, make yourself at home."

Ronnie had a small smile stuck to her face. I guessed she didn't know she was a topic of conversation on the regular.

I sat down near Alex. Two cats looked at me. A big cream one with gingery ears came to investigate.

"That's Pierre," Ginny said to me. "Ronnie, come and sit with me. Can I get you a drink of anything?" Ginny picked up a mostly full, tall glass from the kitchen island. "Cocktail? Tea, coffee, something cold?"

Ronnie's smile grew. "As much as I would love to say yes to a vodka cocktail, it better be a coffee, please."

"As long as you're sure," Ginny said, wiggling her glass at Ronnie. The many bracelets and bangles on her wrist clinked and jingled.

"Tempting. I'll stick to coffee, thanks," Ronnie replied with a smile.

Ginny wore bracelets up both wrists. The expansive collection of gold and silver ended about ten centimetres from her elbows. I imagined they were semi-permanent due to the effort it would take to get them off and back on. It was impressive that she could lift her arms to get the drink to her mouth.

"You all right, Crockett?" Ginny's voice pulled me away from the jewellery she wore.

"Sorry. Zoned out for a minute."

Her arm rattled as she put her glass down. She smiled.

"When we have time for a proper visit, I'll tell you the story behind each bracelet," she said.

"I'll look forward to it."

Chapter Twelve:
[Donald: The Not-Neighbours]

"Nana, where are you?" I strolled around our house looking high and low. Who knew where that woman could be? I found myself back in my bedroom and was about to try the kitchen one more time. How could she vanish like that? Ester hurried down the hallway.

"Goodness Donald, there's a set-to out front. I could hear the commotion from the dining room. Do you know where June and Frankie are?"

"No, but I have a horrible feeling."

I spun around and hurried down the hall to the living room, followed by Ester. Dread filled me as I flung the ranch slider open and stepped out onto the balcony.

"I found them," I said to Ester, as I patted my pockets and realised I didn't have my phone. "You better call police."

Down below, on the footpath directly outside our house, were Nana and Frankie. Frankie appeared to be taking photos, or perhaps filming, what was going on across the street. Ronnie would kill me if she saw that situation.

The big-mouthed crazy bitch was out front of the Not-Neighbours, in their carport. She was hurling abuse at a tiny wee girl who was sitting on the grass. Poor wee poppet.

I saw Nana ready herself to move, and I shouted from the balcony, "Stay where you are, old woman!"

She looked up at me, gave a small smile, and tottered across the street leaning heavily on her walking stick. Frankie was close on her heels.

I couldn't hear what she was saying but I know she said something to Big-Mouth. The nasty thing turned on her. She yelled, "It's none of your business, lady!"

Nana spoke again. Frankie had her phone in her hand as if she was filming.

"You better not be filming me, you old bat!" Big-Mouth hollered, making a grab for Frankie's phone.

Frankie is surprisingly nimble for an oldie. Big-Mouth missed.

Nana spoke again. I couldn't believe Big-Mouth could even hear her.

Big-Mouth let loose, "You old c ... nothing to do with you. She's my fucking c ... kid. Fuck off c ..."

I was appalled that Nana was hearing that language. I was appalled that the wee girl was hearing that language.

A motorbike roared up the street from the direction of Trentham Memorial Park. It didn't sound like Enzo, but I crossed my fingers and prayed it was. I saw the Harley as it closed in on us. It was Crockett's Harley and a pillion. Cold sweat crawled up my spine. If that was Ronnie, we were all in big trouble. Even Crockett wouldn't have a show at saving us. I heard the garage door start to rise before he got to the driveway. That was strange. Crockett didn't have our garage door fob unless Enzo gave it to him. I had just enough time to pray that it wasn't Ronnie on the back of the Harley before Crockett stormed across the road still wearing his helmet. It was definitely his helmet, but Crockett walked differently. That man was not Crockett. I'd know that backside anywhere. That was my husband, Enzo. Relief flowed over me like a wave then rolled back when I thought about Ronnie. But why was Enzo pretending to be Crockett? Ronnie wouldn't tell me she never does. Secret squirrel and all that.

The door to the garage stairs opened. I prayed while my head turned toward the kitchen door and then back to the scene outside, rinse and repeat. The swivelling made me dizzy.

"Hello, Donald." The owner of the voice was not Ronnie. She pulled her helmet off.

A thankful whoosh of air left me. "Emily!" I grabbed her and hugged her hard. "I'm so glad to see you."

She smiled as I let her go. "I am happy to see you as well, Donald."

I dragged her over to the ranch slider. "That's Enzo?" I pointed to the man in black wearing Crockett's helmet.

"Yes."

"Thank God."

"Do you not want to see Crockett? He is your friend."

"It's complicated, Emily."

"What is Nana doing?" Emily pointed to the old woman who had her boney hand around that of the small child.

"Hopefully not getting into trouble," I said very quietly. I watched Enzo's body language. He was unhappy. That did not bode well for the potty-mouthed witch screaming at Nana.

"What is happening. Why is that lady yelling awful things at Nana?"

I sighed. "Because Nana can't help herself and went over there to interfere with the parenting of that wee girl."

"Who is that woman?" She pointed at Big-Mouth.

"I don't know, I call her Big-Mouth."

"She has a bog-mouth," Emily said.

"Yes." I chuckled. "That can be her new name. Bog-Mouth."

"That might make her mad," Emily replied.

"Don't think she can get much worse."

Ester spoke from the couch. I'd forgotten she was there. "Police are on the way."

Enzo had Nana by the elbow and turned her back toward us. Frankie followed along. Nana tried to grab the child on her way. Bog-Mouth pulled the kid from her.

"Stay here Emily," I said, and raced across the lounge and through the kitchen to the stairway door. I swung the door open and witnessed Nana and Frankie ascend with Enzo behind them. He still wore his helmet.

"Nana! I am mortified at your lack of sense," I said, and flapped a hand at her and Frankie. "Get in the lounge and take a seat."

Nana smiled her old lips stretched taut. "I've still got it," she said to Frankie. "Old be damned."

Frankie shook her head slightly as a small smile crept across her aged face.

"The pair of you need to take stock. If Enzo hadn't come home when he did ..." I couldn't even finish my sentence. It was too terrifying. "Get in there and stay put!" I dismissed them both with another flap of my hand. Enzo closed the door and pulled his helmet off.

"Give me a minute, Lover," he said and planted a kiss on the side of my head. "We'll talk about this." He indicated to the helmet in his hand.

"I'll put the jug on," I said, and headed for the bench. I saw Enzo put the helmet on the dining room table as I turned to flick the jug on. He went into the lounge.

Ester called out, "Donald, police are here. There are four cars."

Right then and there, I knew I had to tell Ronnie and get in front of the situation. She had too many friends on the force; someone was bound to mention the ordeal. I knew she was working, and she'd be furious with me and Nana. I decided I'd talk with Enzo first. He'd know if telling her right away was the best thing. I made coffee for all. The cronies were not getting a choice this time.

Ester called out again, "Donald, two officers are coming over here."

Of course, they are. Nana tried to kidnap Bog-Mouth's kid. What did they think would happen next?

Enzo came in. "I'll go take this jacket off."

"Hurry, police are about to knock."

He ran down the hall and got back, just as the police

knocked. "I've got this. You carry on making the coffee."

I blew him a kiss. "Thank you."

More proof that I'd married well.

I could hear the voices downstairs but not the content. I didn't imagine for one second it would end easily or prettily. As I loaded coffee mugs and a plate of biscuits on to a tray, I heard footsteps coming up. I took a deep cleansing breath, and I carried the laden tray into the lounge.

The coffee table was in a convenient place, not where the Cronies had left it. No doubt they got Emily to move it when they heard the jug boil.

"Coffee, not that you deserve it," I said to Nana. "The police will be wanting to speak to you. If you're lucky they won't arrest you."

"When did you become such a drama queen?" Nana asked, then giggled. "I believe it was at birth, wasn't it Donald my dear boy?"

I tossed my fringe out of my eyes and plonked into my favourite chair. "Not me going to jail, old woman. Who do you think will do your hair in there?" I snapped my fingers at her. "Good luck. No doubt Bog-Mouth's rellies would love to meet you." With another finger snap I said, "And by meet you, Nana, I mean rearrange your face."

"Don't be so melodramatic, Donald." A wicked smile settled. "I'm sure you'd be allowed to do my hair in prison."

"I don't think so, old one."

"I don't think anyone is going to throw three old

women in jail," Nana said, with a double injection of feeble ringing her words.

"Who's Bog-Mouth, Donald?" Frankie asked.

I wiggled my fingers toward the road. "That filthy beast over there. The unfortunate looking one."

"And you think her relatives are in jail?" Ester reached for a mug while suppressing a smile. "You're probably correct."

I looked toward the kitchen. Enzo and two police officers approached us. Enzo made eye contact; a small reassuring smile settled on his lips. He nodded at me. It would be all right.

"Officers," I said, standing. "Can I get you refreshments?"

They shook their heads. Enzo ushered them closer to the ranch slider and the *Cronies of Doom*.

"June Tracey?" a plain clothes officer wearing a kevlar vest, asked.

Nana waved a finger at him. "That's me, dear."

"I'm Detective Liam Sanders," the officer said. "Could you tell me what happened this afternoon." Liam had his notebook and a pen in his hand.

"The woman across the road was wailing, screaming, and screeching the most foul things at whoever was in the house, and that was disgusting enough." Nana took a breath and injected as much frailty into her voice as possible as she started to speak again, "She launched a vile attack on that poor wee girl. She can't be more than eighteen months old."

I piped up before I could stop myself, "She lives in Hikurangi Street, as far as I can tell. Pretty sure I saw her at her house when I walked Romeo one day the other week. Or maybe she lurks at other people's houses and lives under the bridge like the troll she is?"

Enzo squeezed my hand. "Let Nana answer."

"Sorry," I said.

Detective Liam wrote then looked at me. "So that's not her house?"

I shook my head. "She does not live there."

He nodded and turned back to Nana. "And did you call police?"

Ester spoke, "I did," she said. "I am Ester Mulholland, former constable, now retired from the New Zealand Police." Ester flipped back some pages in her own notebook. "I've made notes." She handed the notebook to Lovely Liam.

"Thank you." He read the notes and added notes to his notebook. "Ester, you mention in your notes that you feared for the safety of the child."

Ester nodded.

"Did you see the woman physically hurt the child."

I waited, hardly daring to breathe.

"Yes. She hit the child with an open hand," Frankie said.

"And what happened next?"

Nana spoke, "We went out there of course. The child was not in a safe situation, young man. And police were a long way off."

"We've had a busy day in Upper Hutt," Liam said. "It happens."

"We're not saying anything is your fault," Nana said. "We felt we had to do something for the sake of the wee one. We would not be good Christian women if we stood by and allowed a small child to be treated horribly."

"I see," Liam said. "Do you understand that it was dangerous and reckless on your part?"

I nodded in agreement. It was.

"I thought," Nana said. "That if we were there, then she might settle down."

"And how did that work out for you?" Liam asked, passing Ester her notebook.

"It got a bit heated," Nana said, quietly.

"You were lucky that Enzo came home in time to prevent a violent escalation," the second police officer said.

"I don't think we've been introduced." Nana said, sweetly.

"Constable Doug Edmunds, ma'am."

"Nice to meet you, Constable." Nana applied some well-considered contrition to her manner and voice. "I certainly didn't intend to act so rashly. It was the wee girl. I couldn't stand by and watch her maltreatment."

"I understand that ma'am, but I don't imagine your granddaughter is going to be very pleased."

My heart sunk. He was one of Ronnie's friends. I thought it was going too well.

"I don't think there's any need to involve Veronica, do you?" Nana said. "She's working. It would cause her distress. That could be dangerous."

Enzo stepped up beside Nana and said, "She will be told just as soon as I can do so."

"There's no need, Enzo. Everyone's fine."

Liam intervened, "Everyone is not fine, Mrs Tracey. You tried to take a child from its mother."

"But the mother is unfit."

"That's for police to decide, or Oranga Tamariki, and often the courts make that decision, but not you," Liam said. He was doing well to maintain his calm. "Do you understand?"

Nana nodded demurely.

I wasn't fooled.

"What will happen now?" Frankie asked.

"You will turn over any notes, photos, and video taken of the situation across the road. I will put a special authority on your address."

"What for?" Nana asked. Not what it was, but what for. Strange.

"And what is it?" I asked. "Nana doesn't live here, nor do the *Cronies*."

Liam smiled. "We know. As for why, because there could be retaliation from the woman and her associates."

That sounded bad.

"Associates," I mumbled. No wonder Ronnie wanted Nana kept out of this.

"And as for what it does," Liam said, "If you call emergency services from this address you will get a swift response."

"Swift?" I queried.

"As swift as possible. Police will attend with K9's, and police officers will be armed."

"Nana! Ronnie is going to explode!" I said, moving as far from Nana as I could while still being part of the conversation. "Get away from the windows, for goodness' sake!"

Enzo appeared next to me. He slung his arm around my shoulders and whispered in my ear, "It's okay, Lover. I'm here."

"Is Nana going to jail?" I whispered back.

"Not today," he said.

The police continued talking to Nana and the *Cronies of Doom*. They told them to stay inside and not to get involved for the safety of everyone. Liam said the woman wasn't pressing charges, but that was an attempt at self-preservation because she didn't want Oranga Tamariki involved.

Clearly, she didn't realise it was too late to bargain. As if Nana was going to let this lie!

Enzo and I walked the police to the front door.

"Good to see you Enzo," Liam said, shaking his hand. He nodded his head toward the interior of the house. "You have your hands full with those three." He paused and looked at me. "Have you ever noticed how much your Nana resembles our late Queen Elizabeth?"

"I knew she reminded me of someone."

"Do I ever have my hands full," Enzo said. "Her Royal Highness is going to give us heart failure." His deep laugh vibrated. "Let's catch up properly soon, yeah?"

"Definitely." Liam turned to me, and we shook hands. "Good to meet you, Donald. Try to keep your Nana out of trouble."

I nodded. There was no way in hell to keep that old woman out of anything.

Liam opened the door.

Constable Dave shook our hands. I stepped into the doorway to say goodbye and wave them off. Then I saw a drone hovering in the air in the middle of the street. I'd not seen one in our street before. Maybe the police used them.

"Is that yours?" I asked Dave.

"No," he replied. "Probably a kid playing with a new toy."

Enzo moved behind me. I glanced at him as he stepped into the shadows of the entrance way.

"Catch you later," Enzo said. "Flick me a text when you have time for a beer. Both of you."

Liam and Dave waved and headed back across the road. Enzo reached around me and shut the door.

"That was close," he said. "Must've picked me up when I rode home."

"What was close, the Nana thing? Yes, too close."

We climbed the stairs, side by side. "No, the drone. But yes, the Nana thing was very close too."

"You're losing me. What's going on?" I spun over the events I'd witnessed. Enzo coming home wearing Crockett's helmet, and on his Harley. Emily as a pillion. And it made sense. "Ronnie is in trouble."

Enzo shook his head. "She's fine. They're all fine. Emily and I were helping them remain that way. It would be best if that drone never sees me or Emily. And whoever controls it believes that Ronnie and Crockett are here."

"You can't go near the windows," I said spinning in circles. "We'll shut the curtains. What else can I do? There must be something. Lock the doors!"

"Just close the sheers, you don't need to shut out the light or batten down the hatches." Enzo kissed the side of my head. "It's all going to be fine."

Chapter Thirteen:
[Ronnie: WTF]

There was no way on God's little green earth that Alex was going to be anything more than famous for being famous. Whatever influencers did was still beyond my comprehension. I could not see a point at all. Is that where we are now? Life so shallow, people are literally famous for nothing, and everyone clamours for attention. I guess approval from random strangers is what drives them. Daddy issues?

Some days I think the internet has a lot to answer for.

My phone rang. I jumped. One glance at the screen told me I needed to answer it. It was Bill.

"Sorry, I need to take this," I said to Ginny, as I stood and made my escape from the dining room to the back door. I let myself out with Bill ringing in my hand.

"Bill," I said as I swiped my finger across the screen.

"We have trouble."

"We do?"

"Yes."

"How bad is this trouble?"

"Someone recognised your charge while you were here."

"We put her in a quiet room. No one came in but you and me."

"Yes. As I said we have trouble."

"How was she seen?"

"CCTV at the front door."

That made sense. "Okay, and?"

"I was sent a photo of you and Alex with red crosses over your faces."

"Charming. But if it was from your CCTV, then that sounds like a *you* problem."

"This is a head's up, Ronnie. Someone either hacked into our feed or it was someone who has access."

"How would anyone know where we went?"

"That's what I don't get. You weren't followed, right?"

"Correct." A bad feeling grew into words. "Surveillance Drone."

"Really?"

"I saw two earlier. I didn't see any when we escaped the gunmen slash bikies, but that doesn't mean they weren't up watching." It means I wasn't looking. That was a me problem.

"Say that a drone saw you running my way and then couldn't find you. Assumption made that you sought shelter at Messine. What happens next, means you are up against some sophisticated criminals."

I didn't for one second think it would be easy to hack into the CCTV at Joint Command.

"Could also mean there is someone inside Defence that they called on to get images, or the drone took the images."

If it was a drone, then there were more than the four people we saw, after us. Were they even after Alex or was that a Crockett situation?

"Either way is not ideal." I heard something in his voice.

"It's someone inside, isn't it?" I looked at the photo on my phone again. It was front on as it would be from a security camera. We might have been seen by a drone and followed, or they guessed where we'd go and reached out to a contact for confirmation.

"There were no attacks on the system. So, that's unlikely. If there is, or was, someone feeding them information, but they then sent that info to me, I have a feeling a body will turn up soon."

"I hope this woman is worth all the mayhem." I thought about his body remark. "Let me know if you get a body dump."

"Try not to be the body they dump," Bill said.

"I'll do my best."

"Who is she testifying against?"

"You know I can't tell you that."

"Worth a shot."

I laughed. "Get in line. Pretty sure every agency that's heard about her will want a shot." So far, I only knew about the Aussies wanting her, or at least wanting to sound her out. I was about willing to let them have her with the blessing of New Zealand.

"I don't doubt that. How likely is it that she'll accept an offer?"

Currently the only people with direct access to her are me, Crockett, and Ben. So, her offer choices are limited.

"She's an *influencer*. She thinks the photos she posts on Instagram, and every other possible platform, are where it's all at."

"You've spent the most time with her; is she malleable?"

"She's a tantrum in designer clothes. And you're on the hunt for a way in to grab her for Defence."

It was Bill's turn to laugh. "You can't blame a man for trying."

"Stay safe."

I hung up and went back inside. Now I knew Defence wanted her, too. She could pick her price and work for any agency, and all she wanted to do was gather millions of likes on social media. What a waste of a natural born talent.

I checked on her when I rejoined Ginny at the table. Alex appeared more relaxed than I'd seen her. She was petting cats and playing with the kitten. The break from her whining and complaining was welcome.

"Is everything honky dory, Ronnie?" Ginny asked.

I nodded. "Was a friend who had information for me." I tipped my head toward Alex. "She's causing quite a stir in our world."

"She strikes me as someone who likes attention. I'm sure she'd love to know how much of a stir she's causing."

"She likes people fawning all over her images on social media."

Ginny considered my comment for several seconds before forming her response, "She's hard work for you, isn't she? You don't like her much."

"There isn't a lot to like so far, and I don't see the point of her chosen career."

"It's not yours to see. Her path is her path. Yours is yours."

She wasn't wrong.

"That's a very good point." I smiled. Being here was a great idea. "I need to reframe how I think about her."

"It can't be the first time you've had to deal with someone you didn't see eye-to-eye with."

I nodded. "Definitely not the first time but this one pushes all my buttons."

"She's twenty," Ginny said. "She's still a kid."

"Yes, she is." I sat with that for a second or two. "I needed to hear that, Ginny. Thank you."

"You're welcome."

I felt tension leave my body. I wasn't sure if it was the huge number of crystals in the house or the accepting, caring atmosphere of Ginny's home. But I felt better than I had since meeting Alex.

"You're smiling," Ginny said.

"Ben's idea to come here was a smart one," I replied. "Where is he, anyway?"

"He's out in the garage with Tom. They'll be talking about screws and screw drivers or drop saws and hammers." She laughed. "Those two can rabbit on for hours."

Crockett strolled into the dining room and pulled out a chair. "All quiet on the cat front," he said.

"Tell me about Crockett," Ginny said, turning her attention to him. "You're not a Kiwi; there's a hint of Australian in your voice, but also American."

Crockett grinned. "That's about right. I'm Australian but worked in the States for a long time before landing here and joining up with this crew."

"You're in the same line of business?"

"More or less," he said. "I usually work for the Australian Government."

"And today?"

"Feels like we're working for everyone today."

I didn't disagree and his answer was noncommittal.

"Ronnie? You used to work for the New Zealand Government?" Ginny asked.

"Yes, I did. Now I work for myself."

"Ben is still working for the Americans?"

Crockett and I shrugged. Not our story to tell. "You'll have to ask Ben who pays his bills," I said with a smile and a wink.

"You all seem to get on very well," Ginny said, then she changed her approach. "Oh, Ronnie, didn't your cousin get married recently? I heard it was fabulous."

"Did Ben show you photos?" Of course, he did. He spent the day chuckling to himself.

"Just a few."

"The *Spy Who Shagged Me* was not my ideal theme for a wedding, but I must say it suited Donald and Enzo down to the ground."

"I don't know anyone who could carry off that best woman dress. You have my respect for getting though the wedding without killing your cousin, or his new husband."

"They were lucky there were so many witnesses." And Nana was there. She's the one who kept them alive by intercepting me every time I got near them. "Tangerine and purple should be removed from all colour pallets," I said.

"I think that was more aubergine."

We laughed. "It was an atrocious, aubergine abomination!"

Ben barrelled in the back door with Tom right behind him.

Crockett jumped to his feet. "What's wrong?"

"Drone." Ben peered out the kitchen window.

"Might not be them; how would they find us here?" I said.

"I don't know." Ben was still looking out the window. "But there is definitely a drone going up the street and pausing at driveways."

"Did it see you? And maybe stop leaning over the sink and peering out the window?"

"I hope not. We heard something. Then Tom's neighbour came over and said he'd seen a drone hovering above the street." Ben turned around to face the room and stepped away from the bay window and the aloe plants growing there in ceramic pots. "He watched it pause at the end of driveways and that behaviour seemed suspicious."

"Is the car visible?"

"No, it's under the carport and we put the Harley in

the garage a while ago," Tom said. He leaned on the marble kitchen bench to look out the window above the sink. "Could be a kid with a toy."

Could be. Not everything in our lives is sinister.

"Could be burglars casing houses, trying to see who's home or away, and if it's worth breaking in," Crockett offered and sat back in his chair. Emergency over.

That was a good point. How long before crooks used drones to case houses?

Ben handed me his phone with messages open. "Read."

It was a message from Enzo. He'd spotted a drone outside our house. He didn't know how long it'd been there or if he'd been seen from the doorway. The drone moved up and down the street for fifteen minutes, then left. He'd let us know if it returned.

Fingers crossed they still thought he was Crockett, and that Emily was me. That should confuse the watchers for a little while.

I passed the phone back to Ben.

"They're not giving up," I said. "Even more reason that we need to stay out of sight and keep Alex safe."

"Wonder how much the contract is worth," Ben said as if he was thinking out loud.

"I hope there isn't a contract and I especially hope there isn't an open contract. We have enough problems with the lunatics from this morning," Crockett said.

Ben and Crockett had good points. If this was an open contract situation, then we could be up against many assailants. As it was, there was nothing solid to link the four bikies slash gunmen to the surveillance drones.

"We have to change this up," I said. "Think of the gunmen and the drones as separate situations." They had to be separate if a drone followed us or saw me and Alex leaving the scene of the shooting. No way was either pillion or rider operating a drone during that attack.

Ginny's jaw dropped open. "It was you in the middle of the Golden Mile shooting."

"Yes. We've had better days," Ben replied. "And the AOS call out in Wallaceville later was probably about us as well."

"This is the most exciting thing that's happened in our house ever," Ginny said with a wide smile as she stood up. "I need another cocktail."

Alex piped up from the lounge, "Did someone say cocktail?"

Oh, dear Lord.

"Coffee, Alex?" I suggested.

"Tom makes fancy coffee with his top of the range espresso machine," Ben added.

"I do," Tom added. "Name your poison, Alex, I can make any coffee you'd like."

"Vodka cocktail."

"That's not coffee ... anyone for a coffee?" Tom sounded keen to use his machine.

"I'd like a cappuccino, please," I said. "If you're offering."

"Coming right up," Tom replied.

"It'll be a while," Ginny said. "Takes time to make good coffee."

"Last chance for a decent coffee, Alex," I said.

"I'd like a vodka cocktail," she insisted.

Crockett met my eyes. He shrugged.

"One," I said. "Make it weak."

Maybe it'd relax her a bit and ease the whinging.

Chapter Fourteen:
[Ronnie: How does this work?]

"Hey, Crockett? Where are you?"

He strode up the hallway to meet me. "You summoned me?"

"Yes, I did. We need to find out who is after her and how we can avoid them. We can't stay here forever." I kept my voice soft.

"Can't we?" He too used a quiet voice. Crockett smiled and looked back to the lounge. "She's not whining and it's not too shabby here."

I sensed his reluctance to leave and set off the whinging again.

"True, all true, but sooner or later we will need to move on. Probably time we decided where our next port is."

"Moving closer to Wellington city to make Monday easier makes sense, but."

A smile grew on my lips. "But? I haven't heard you say 'but' at the end of a sentence in ages. Sometimes I even forget you're an Aussie."

"At least I can say six."

"Now who's dreaming?"

He laughed.

"Lie low until after dark and then move," I said. I was thinking we needed a destination – somewhere the drones wouldn't find us.

"A hotel with underground parking would be ideal but that would mean travelling into the city tonight, because I don't know of any in the valley. Do you?"

I shook my head. "Can't think of any."

"The problem with going into the city, no matter what time of day, is the Hutt motorway. But we have to negotiate that at some stage."

He was right. It was unavoidable. There was no cover from Petone to Wellington city. But on Monday morning it'd be full of commuters. Safety in numbers might be a thing that'd work in our favour. Time to ditch the car and the bike and take one of my fleet vehicles.

"What's on your mind?"

"Making our run to the city during rush hour on Monday morning."

"That could end just like this morning with gridlocked traffic and bikies but worse, there is nowhere to run."

"Hmmm. You're not wrong."

"You could just say I'm right you know?"

Not happening. "How about this then ... ditch the Harley, ditch the car, go to Naenae, and grab an SUV from my garage."

He nodded. "Good plan. I have a modification. You and I take Enzo's bike down, then leave it in the garage and come back in one of your fleet cars."

"Or two cars," I said.

"Wait until dark," he said. "We need to find a motel and book a couple of rooms."

"Let's make sure Enzo and Emily move at the same time we do. Get them out riding around in Upper Hutt."

"And Art," Crockett said. "He and Jo should stick close to Enzo. Make it look as though we're moving Alex to a location in the north."

"Back to where we came from this morning," I said. "Let's set them up and see what we catch."

"Where's Cary Grant?" Crockett asked.

"Dead," I replied.

Crockett laughed. "You know who I mean."

"Not sure where he is." I puzzled over the Cary Grant reference for a moment and then the penny dropped. Cary Grant was an actor and also a spy during World War Two. "Cary Grant. Very funny."

"Suits him."

Apart from Ben having dark blond hair, not black.

"I suppose it does."

I could tell Crockett was thinking, so I let him think and went to find Ben. On my way through the lounge, I noted Alex was still enjoying the cats, her vodka, and Ginny's company.

Noises that sounded like the preface to cooking drifted from the kitchen. I found Ben. He was in the kitchen wielding a potato peeler like it was an everyday occurrence.

"I didn't know you knew how to peel potatoes," I said, leaning on the marble island bench from the dining room side.

Ben looked up with a smile on his lips. "I could say the

same about you."

Tom passed Ben a large pot, then turned his attention to tenderising steak with a vicious looking mallet. Water ran into the sink. Ben flicked a switch on the wall by the taps and peelings disappeared down the gobbler. The domestic scene conflicted with the version of Ben that I knew.

"Crockett and I were talking about sending the teams out again, and us all moving south, later tonight," I said.

"Okay," Ben replied, cutting a potato into quarters, and letting it splash into a pot full of water.

"And setting a trap at our location last night."

Another quartered potato splashed into the pot.

"That's risky."

"Yes," I agreed. Another potato hit the water. "Might be the only way we can find out who is after Alex."

"How?"

That was the part I wasn't super sure of. I decided to speak and see what happened. "If we send the teams out together, as if we're all moving to a new location, but have them circle around then head back to last night's safe house."

"Dangerous."

"Not if we send in someone to rig the house first. Wire it for sound and get some video surveillance in place."

Being two thirds of the way up a hill gave whoever got there first the advantage.

"If they leap ahead of Enzo and Art, then what?"

"Then Enzo and Art are heading right into a trap."

That wasn't the best.

"We don't know if they found where we were last night, but there is a chance they did. Or at least they know now. All they had to do, was have people watch Alex's Instagram and grab the geotags from her photos."

"Good point."

"They might already have the place staked out."

"So, we need counter-surveillance prior to making the call for the teams to head to that address. We need to know who they are, who exactly we are up against."

"Yes." Ben's eyes rose to meet mine. "How sure are you that the bikers were after Alex?"

"Bit of a coincidence if they weren't."

He picked up another potato and put it on the chopping board. "Just a thought."

If they were after Crockett and not Alex, then that would add a whole new dimension to the weekend.

"Steph and Jenn," I said. "I'll call them."

Another chopped potato landed in the water. I walked behind Tom and Ben and down the hallway. Crockett was gone. Good. I wanted a bit of privacy as I made the group FaceTime call.

Four rings and Steph and Jenn answered on separate phones but from the same room.

"How's it going?" Jenn asked.

"Not sure," I said.

Steph frowned from the screen. "What do you need?"

"Counter-surveillance. I'll message you the address. Check it out on iMaps before you head up there. Take two cars. Run SDR's. I can't call in anyone else at the moment. Enzo, Jo, Art, and Emily are tied up. Brie is on another case."

"Okay," Jenn replied. "We got this."

I checked the time. "And I need you to deep dive into Crockett's past and an American bikie gang called The Alpha Brotherhood. They have ties to the Inferno Jesters; they're in Australia and the USA. Find out who they're affiliated with here."

"Bikies?"

I nodded. "I need to rule something out. If they're here for Crockett then he's a liability. If they've been hired by a third party to get to our protectee, I'd like to know who. It'd be very helpful if you could find out how they got to New Zealand with gang patches, and which gang here is helping them."

Jenn nodded. "I'll dig in and get back to you ASAP."

"Great. And for the surveillance of the property … plan to be there for the rest of the evening. Ideally, I need you in place at least half an hour before I send the teams out. If you see anything, including any drones, get back to me ASAP."

"What are you up to?" Steph asked.

"Hopefully laying a trap. If it's all clear of surveillance, I'll keep you two positioned while we send in a tech to rig the place with cameras and mics."

"Do we need to know anything else?" Jenn asked. "I'll take a laptop with me if I haven't finished the dive into gangs."

"The bikers that might already have the house under surveillance opened fire on us on the Golden Mile this morning. But I think there is more than one lot of surveillance at play here. I think we have a messy situation with way too many hands in the mix."

"Ssshhiiit," Jenn hissed half-under her breath. "I'll tap a mate at AOS. Might pay to have back-up."

I nodded. That was good thinking. "He cannot know about Alex; she's got to remain zipped up tight."

Jenn's blue eyes stared out from my screen. "You know we'll keep this buttoned up."

"I do."

"The drones in the tech room, are they fully charged?" Jenn asked.

"Should be. And yes, deploy them during your surveillance." I thought for a split second. "Deploy them from the bottom of the hill and probe for surveillance before you drive up there."

"Will do."

"Check out the map, stay safe."

"You'll hear from us later this evening," Steph said. "Hi to the boys."

Jenn and Steph waved. The call ended.

Bugger, I should've asked if they'd heard from Donald.

Chapter Fifteen:
[Donald: Whingy-Chick]

"What's going on out there, Donald?" Nana asked, waving her stick toward the front window.

"Sounds like more silliness," I replied. "How about we make dinner?"

"You and Enzo can handle that, Donald dear. The girls and I must keep an eye on the proceedings." She leant her cane next to her chair, then her arthritic gnarled index finger stretched toward the ranch slider.

"The ranch slider stays closed, Nana." I used my firmest voice. "Do you hear me?"

"Yes, Donald. Off you go and start on dinner."

Dismissed, again, in my own home. The audacity!

I latched eyes onto Ester. "Please keep those doors closed."

She bobbed her old head.

Frankie piped up, "Not to worry, Donald. I'm here to keep an eye on things."

That was comforting. Not. They gave her the slip last time. Whatever smarts she had as a school principal back in the day, were rusty as.

A women's screeching, loud voice rose from outside. "You're hurting me! Leave me alone! Go away!"

"Who's she talking to?" Ester said, leaning forward to ogle out the closed ranch slider.

As much as I didn't want to leave, I knew dinner needed prepping and I wasn't sure if Enzo was going to be around all evening. He'd mentioned he was helping Ronnie out with something. Secret Squirrel bizzo. I hurried into the kitchen to find my beloved already getting the veggies organised.

"All right, Lover?"

"They're carrying on outside again," I said, sliding up beside him and giving him a peck on the cheek. "Thank you for this."

"I need to eat too," he said off-handedly while he chopped a carrot and then slid the carrot circles into a saucepan.

"Are you here all night?"

"Don't bank on it. I'm sure Ronnie will need us again."

"Us ... Emily, where is she?" I glanced around in case she was standing behind me or lurking near the pantry.

"She asked if she could take Romeo to the park." He slipped another sliced carrot into the pot on the stove. "I think she needed to get away from the oldies and get some fresh air."

The me-crow-wah-vai dinged.

"What's in the me-crow-wah-vai?" I just love Nigella Lawson and her gloriousness. She makes everything sound so fancy.

"Defrosting some mince. Shepherd's pie tonight."

"I love your shepherd's pie. I'm sure Nana and the Cronies will too."

"Chop the onions for me, Lover." Enzo placed two big

brown onions on the chopping board in front of me. "I'll get the mince browned."

By the time I'd cut both onions, Emily and Romeo came up the stairs. Her hair was stuffed inside a black baseball cap on her head and dark glasses hid her eyes. She looked every bit like Ronnie.

Emily wore a frown and Romeo a thirst. He stopped at his water bowl and lapped noisily.

"What's wrong Emily?"

"There is a person yelling outside. Across the road."

"Same one as before?"

Emily's evaluation process played out on her face. I tipped the onions into the pan Enzo had going to brown the meat.

"A different woman," she said. "She has dyed hair. Red, like a ..." she searched for the word. "Not like a fire engine. Like ..." her eyes scoured the bench. "An apple," she said, pointing to the pinkest red on a pink lady apple. "That part."

"She's the one I call Whingy-Chick," Enzo said. "I've seen and heard her on and off over the last few weeks. I don't know if she lives there or is related to someone who lives there."

None of us know the relationships in that house. I'd need a big board and lots of coloured string to even begin to work it out. Pretty sure someone fornicated with a first cousin to create the disasters we keep hearing. A mess of cousin/brother/uncle and sister/auntie/mum, combined with drugs. How is it, people like that can breed?

"Then, Whingy-Chick is shouting that someone is hurting her, and they should leave her alone."

"Did you hear or see anyone else?"

"A man yelled; he was very loud. I do not know where he was."

"What did he say?" Enzo asked, stirring the meat and onions.

"He said, go away. He said it twice."

"Did Whingy-Chick go away?" I asked.

Emily shook her head slowly. "She did not. She fell on the ground and screamed that he pushed her."

Crying wolf is going to bite them on their skanky, in-bred arses one day.

"Did she say anything to you?"

"Yes. She asked if I saw him push her."

"Did you?"

"No, there was no one else there." Emily took a deep breath. "Why are those people like that?"

"Maybe it's their hobby," I replied. Enzo motioned towards the jug full of beef stock, and I passed it to him as Emily spoke.

"That is not a hobby, Donald. A hobby is something you do that is not work and is fun for you."

"Well, they don't work. And I really think they enjoy the drama."

Nana's voice rose. I listened, in case it was trouble. Enzo flashed me a smile and said, "Go and see what they're up to."

"Come on Emily, let's go see Nana."

She walked beside me into the lounge. The ranch slider was wide open. I hurried over and slid it closed. Nana, Frankie, and Ester groaned their disapproval in unison.

"What did I say?" I addressed them like naughty children and waggled my finger. "Keep the door closed!"

"We needed to make sure there was no one out there hitting that poor girl," Ester said. She'd tried for authoritative, and it fell short.

"I said, keep it closed. If you can't behave, I'll have to lock it."

Nana ignored my protests and launched into a question, "Did you see the car in their carport?"

"Yes. What of it?"

"That other woman, what'd Emily call her?"

"Bog-Mouth," I said with delight. "Suits her way more than Big-Mouth."

"Her, she is in that car. And the other one, she got in it too. They shut the doors, turned the music up, and the car filled with smoke. I didn't know what to think."

I know what to think. Hot-box.

"I see."

"When Emily came home, just a few minutes ago, she said Whingy-Chick, the one with the funny reddish-pink hair, was yelling at someone who she said was hurting her."

"Oh, yes," Nana said. "That was going on and on. In between shouting at the house, they were jumping in the car and fogging it up with smoke."

"Did you see any males?"

"None. We did hear one yell from within the house though," Ester said. She flipped her notebook back a page. "I've been taking notes."

"If I can trust you to keep this door closed, and the net curtains shut, then I can go back and help Enzo make our dinner."

"You can," Frankie said. "I'm here to prevent non-sense."

"Frankie, you failed me last time," I said. I turned on my heels and hurried back to the kitchen.

"Everything all right?" Enzo asked as soon as I stepped foot on the linoleum.

"They had the door open."

"Where's Emily?"

"Not near the door."

"Good, she needs to keep up the charade that she's Ronnie, so, we don't want Emily spotted by any drones."

"What on earth is this case that Ronnie has you both on?"

Enzo smiled. "You know I can't talk about it."

I screwed up my nose and huffed a sigh. "I know ..."

Enzo's arms circled me. The warm spice in his after-shave was delicious. "What's happening outside?"

"The freak Not-Neighbours are sitting in their car in the carport playing absolute shit music, so loud that the bass is probably vibrating right through their poor neighbours' place, and hot-boxing."

"That's not new. They do it on and off all day long and quite often into the night. They're the most inconsiderate arseholes."

"The other day, that Whingy-Chick had a massive tantrum in the car and chucked bread all over the lawn. I think they'd just got back from the supermarket. I could tell because the women were wearing their tatty jammies and scruffy old slippers."

Enzo chuckled. "I think I came home after the worst of the tantrum. She was doing her usual screaming and yelling while picking up some of the bread. He sort of helped. He's a skinny little white dude with an attitude."

"Haven't heard his name though. She screams at him but never uses a name."

"Maybe she doesn't know it," Enzo said, giving me one last squeeze before turning his attention back to cooking dinner. He stabbed a potato in a pot that was boiling. "These are ready to mash."

All of a sudden, the music from outside got louder.

"The door," I muttered and hurried into the lounge.

Sure enough, the cronies were out on the balcony watching. Emily wasn't. She'd found a book and was settled in a chair a long way from the open door.

I felt a change in the room; a glance over my shoulder told me that Enzo had appeared from the kitchen. He shook his head and went back to finish assembling the shepherd's pie.

"Nana!" I shouted from the middle of the lounge. My voice mingled with the music outside. I tried again, "Nana!"

Her old head turned my way. I beckoned to her. A

small smile graced her lips before she refocused on the scene across the road. I couldn't see much from where I stood, so I stomped right up to the door.

"Nana, Frankie, Ester ... get back inside, immediately."

Ester nudged Frankie. They both looked at me then at Nana. She was busy pretending to be deaf.

"Inside!" I repeated.

The nudging happened but no movement followed.

Ronnie would murder me if I didn't get those old crones under control. They were testing the limits of my patience.

Chapter Sixteen:

[Ronnie: Who are they?]

My phone rang. Steph. I looked at the time.

"Hey, okay?" I asked.

"All good to send the techs in."

"Excellent." I could hear Jenn in the background but not what she was saying. "What's Jenn on about?"

"Nothing. She's chatting to her mate, the AOS guy."

"Okay. Which of our techs are available?"

I heard a page turn. Steph had her notebook with her. "Keith and Brian. Also, Paul and Bevan."

"Can you get Keith and Brian in ASAP to install video and sound? Keep surveillance in place for another hour after they've gone."

"No problem. They're rostered on so it's not overtime."

You can't take the accountant out of the woman even on surveillance, apparently.

"Keep me posted. Get one of them to send me the code for the app once they're done."

"Will do. Bye."

The screen dimmed. Steph was gone. And my phone rang again. This time it was Jenn.

"Forget something?" I asked.

"Yes. I dug into the potential problem. Looks like Inferno Jesters are affiliated or associated with a smallish gang here in New Zealand."

"How small are we talking?"

"Fourteen patched members. The club is called The Storm Mavericks. They originated in Wainuiomata, and it was formed in nineteen eighty-five. Membership hasn't changed since."

"How bad are they? Considering I've never heard of them or seen them."

"I hadn't either until I started drilling down into the Inferno Jesters and affiliates. Not a lot is known about them. They have a club house in Wainui, been raided a few times over the last few decades. They had, and probably still have, a grow operation up in the bush and were/are supplying cannabis locally. My AOS mate, Kev, says they're mostly quiet. Keep to themselves and smoke a lot of weed."

"Sounds like their name is cooler than they are."

Jenn snickered.

I hung up, pushed my phone back into my pocket, then walked down the hallway past large glass and wood cabinets filled with crystals and precious stones. I stopped at one cabinet. Some of the stones fluoresced green. They were pretty cool to look at. I wasn't one hundred percent focused on the stones, though; I was thinking about how The Alpha Brotherhood were affiliated or associated with the Inferno Jesters, and how they were affiliated with Storm Mavericks. So, by proxy, The Alpha Brotherhood had help in New Zealand to do whatever they were here to do; either take out Crockett or take out Alex. Maybe it was a twofer. Either way, it wasn't going to be fun with bikies roaming all over the place, looking to catch sight of us.

Ginny's voice behind me said, "Aren't they stunning?"

I shook myself from my thoughts. "Yes. They are."

"I had Tom put black lights in the case so we can see the fluorescence. Before we had the lights, I had to get each piece out and use my black light torch to see the colours."

"This is very cool," I said. "Amazing."

"Nature is beautiful," Ginny said.

We walked into the lounge together. Crockett was playing with the kitten. He had a feather on the end of a wobbly stick and the kitten was having a lot of fun trying to catch it.

"You've got a new friend there," Ginny said. "Laila will play for hours. I bet you get tired before she does."

"Probably," said Crockett, moving his arm so the kitten chased the feather.

My phone rang. I extracted it from my pocket and saw Jo's name on the screen. A second later Crockett's phone rang. He passed the stick to Ginny and pulled out his phone. He showed me the screen. Art. I showed him my ringing phone.

We answered our respective phones in unison, "What's up?"

I walked toward the kitchen, Crockett stayed where he was.

"We've picked up surveillance," Jo said.

"Where are you?"

"At home with Art."

"Talk me through it."

"We did our tour of duty, as it were, and because we knew we were going to go out again once you all wanted to move, we decided we'd stay together. Keep up appearances."

"Good thinking, and?"

"We ran an SDR before going to the supermarket, half an hour ago. We ran another before coming back here. Both times, we spotted surveillance. Two cars. One followed us for a few minutes then handed off to another."

"Same again on the way back?"

"Yes. And now there's a car, about five doors up, parked in a driveway, and another at the other end of the street."

I pictured Art's street in my head. There was no way out without going past those cars. There were no side streets or alleyways off his road.

"They haven't made a move?"

"No. They're just watching, for now."

I wondered how long they'd keep that up before moving in to grab 'Alex'. Our splitting up must've worked. Except something felt off. Someone deployed drones in Pinehaven. Why? How many factions were looking for her?

"When you first left Upper Hutt College, did you pick up surveillance?"

"Nope."

"Interesting."

"Yeah, they know where we are, and we had only moved once in a couple of hours."

That didn't bode well. I wondered if there was a tracker somewhere, probably in something that Alex wore, and now Jo had. The coat.

"Check her coat," I said. "Might be a tracker in it."

"I'll text you back."

I hung up. Crockett moved towards me as he hung up. "Has to be a tracker," he said.

"That's what I think."

I settled down on the leather couch next to a cat and waited.

The text arrived two minutes later.

Jo: Tracker in the bottom seam of the coat.

Me: Don't destroy it.

Jo: Okay

Me: When I get the okay from Steph, I want you and Art to head north to an address we'll provide.

Jo: And then ... I leave the coat and we bugger off.

Me: Yep.

Crockett picked up the cat next to me and sat down. He ruffled its fur and scratched under its chin and received a rewarding purr.

"And?" he asked.

"Tracker in her coat."

"Someone has always known where she was, but until the Fergusson Drive incident no one made a move. It's interesting," Crocker said.

"Would've been easier to get her last night," I said, then changed my mind. "Or nab her this morning before we left Timberlea."

"Last night they probably didn't know how many of us there were."

"Good point."

"And we had the advantage of being up the hill," Crockett reminded me. "As for grabbing her on our way out of Timberlea, they could've easily blocked Norana Road."

"What's mystifying me is that the bikies knew where we were," I said. "If they weren't connected to the Alex thing they wouldn't know, would they?"

"Does look like the bikers are connected to Alex, and not me." Crockett looked a little relieved. "That also means that they knew we were at Upper Hutt College. I'm picking that wasn't a feasible place to grab her due to the rugby games and spectators."

"Do you feel like there's something underpinning this nonsense that we don't know, or aren't supposed to know, about?"

Crockett ran his fingers through his hair. "We better use that tracker to our advantage ..."

"Of course. My question is, where did it come from?" I leaned back into the couch and sighed. "Now we know how the bikies found us in the traffic." I turned my head to see Crockett. He didn't react that time. "And there probably was someone outside your place in your backyard."

"The drones in Pinehaven; what were they for?"

"I don't know. Throw us off. Make us think they didn't know where Alex was. Or it wasn't related at all. Just a kid being nosy with a new toy."

"Second question." Crockett patted the cat on his knee. "Where did she get the coat?"

"Third and fourth questions ... who is it tracking her, and how many people are privy to the info coming from the tracker?"

Crockett lifted his voice a little, "Hey, Alex the Influencer, come over here."

She looked over from her seat at the table with Ginny. Surprisingly, she stood and followed Crockett's instruction.

"What witchery is this?" I whispered, nudging Crockett.

"Cat witchery," he replied. "She's looking at the cat, not me."

Alex perched on the edge of the couch near Crockett. Her fingers ran through the cat's fur. "Her name is Meg," she said. "Isn't she beautiful?"

Crockett nodded. "I have a question about that really cool coat of yours."

Good start.

"That's real fur on the collar, down the front and on the cuffs, you know," she said. "I hope the lady who is wearing it looks after it."

"Real fur," I said. "I didn't think Zoomers liked fur.

Aren't you all vegan?"

Crockett elbowed me.

"It's like those Furmoo bags, you know the ones they make in Christchurch. They use the hides left over from the diary and meat industry. I mean it's already dead, why not use the fur?"

I bit my tongue. I saw her coat. That wasn't goat, or cow; it was something much smaller and cuter. The coat itself was probably cow leather.

"Good point," Crockett said. "Where'd you get it? Do they do jackets or long leather coats like that for blokes?"

"It was a gift. I am using it to do some promo work for the company that makes them."

"When did you get it?"

"Recently, maybe two weeks ago." She tickled the cat under the chin and was rewarded with a purr. "I think they do men's coats. You could ask."

"Who would I ask?"

"The company is called *Alexandrite*."

"I see why they wanted to hire you," I said. "Clever."

She almost smiled. "I was working with a public relations person they hired to run their PR campaign and I was part of that campaign, so I don't know who you'd talk to at *Alexandrite*."

"What was her name?" I asked.

"Andie Jones."

"And she's not part of the fur company?" Didn't hurt to double check.

"She told me that she worked for *Forest, Jones, and*

Richards in Lower Hutt."

"Is she the Jones in the name?"

"I think so, I didn't ask, though." She shrugged.

"Thanks," I said, and made a mental note to do a search on that company after we'd looked into *Alexandrite*.

Crockett eased his phone from his pocket, almost dislodging the cat in the process. Lucky she has claws. He opened a browser window.

Alex stood up. "I'm going back in the dining room," she said.

At least she gave us a contact name at the PR firm.

Crockett held his phone so we could both see the screen and typed in the company name. There was a showroom in Wellington.

"Something about that address feels familiar," he said, opening the website link and scrolling through products. "Nice jackets."

"Any names?"

"Not yet." He scrolled more and pointed out a few long coats he liked. As much as I hated to admit it, he'd look good in one. Crockett abandoned the product pages for the *About Us* page. "They source their leather from the dairy and meat industry, like Alex said."

"I didn't know sable were food," I replied.

"Nor did I. Maybe it's rabbit."

I shook my head. "If you need to think it's rabbit, then it's rabbit. A gorgeous meaty rabbit with silvery tips on its fur that became a scrumptious pie."

He chuckled and moved on to the contact page. "There is a contact for orders and the CEO is listed as Josef Baranov." Crockett rubbed his face. "I wonder how common that name is in New Zealand."

"What's going on? You clearly know something about this Baranov guy."

"Once upon a time, I worked with someone called Josef Baranov."

"Last time you said that ..." I didn't particularly want to vocalise what he told me last time he said the words once upon a time, but I did, quietly. "I was under the impression that everyone was killed in a drone strike."

"Depends which version of the story you've heard."

I felt a frown form. "There are different versions?"

"So, I heard."

"And in the other version everyone survived?"

"That's the gossip," he said with a smile. "Can't say I believe it. I mean, I was there."

"It can't be the same Baranov."

"You'd think not."

Ginny waved at us. "You honky dory over there?"

"Yes, thanks," I replied. "Crockett is looking at leather coats. Fancies himself in one."

"Black leather, not brown," Ginny replied. "He'd look magic in black leather."

She wasn't wrong, but I wasn't about to agree.

"Alex goes to meet this public relations person and is given a four-thousand-dollar coat to wear and take photos of herself wearing for social media ... and a bloody tracker is sewn into the bottom seam," Crockett said, his voice low. He typed into a new browser screen and brought up the New Zealand Companies Register. Into the search bar he typed the name of the company. I watched the screen. It was a registered company and Josef Baranov was the Chief Executive Officer. He pointed at a phone number and address for the company. "It still feels familiar."

"The number or the address?"

"Address."

"Sit with it for a minute, see what pops up," I suggested while I typed the name and phone number into my contacts. New contact: Josef Baranov from Alexandrite.

The tracker being in the coat for two weeks, before we got involved, prickled. If it was malicious someone could've grabbed or killed her at any point, and no one would've twigged until it was too late. Why wait until we have her?

I hauled myself off the couch and went down the hall to the bathroom.

The big mirror on the wall reflected tiredness back at me. As soon as this situation was over, I was going to sleep for a week. No Nana, no Donald, no drama, just sleep.

I walked back into the lounge and said, "Alex met with the public relations person at *Alexandrite* and was given a very expensive coat to wear. What's the tracker all about?"

Crockett's right eyebrow lifted. "She could've seen

something she shouldn't have. Maybe the Russians want to talk to her too."

"The Russian coat makers want to talk to Alex? Mhmm." Sounds plausible I thought, shaking my head slowly.

"Okay, then she saw something."

"But what?" That didn't feel right. "I think the tracker was there ahead of time, so it was ready to go. It might have nothing to do with this."

Did I really believe that?

Maybe.

Chapter Seventeen:
[Crockett: Who does that?]

"What did you find?" Ronnie asked me, pointing to Alex's phone in my hand.

"A code."

"How did you find it?"

"I was snooping. Looking at her photos to see if there was anything of interest to our current predicament."

"Okay and you're sure it's a code?"

"Uh huh. I know a cypher when I see one. It's not sophisticated," I showed her the photograph. "Reminds me of the type of codes kids use to communicate when they're playing spy games."

"Fun childhood you had there, Crockett." Ronnie chuckled. "But that definitely is a code or a cypher, and you're right, it isn't sophisticated."

"It might be a way she and her mates communicate," I said. "She's famous for being famous. Maybe they have a way of talking privately."

"That's just great," Ronnie said. "Do you think she's clever enough to chat with her friends in code?"

"With her memory it'd be fairly easy," I replied. "She doesn't have to be Einstein to remember a code."

"Did someone send it to her, or did she take the photo herself of a code she saw somewhere?"

"Easy enough to check." I opened the photo and

scrolled to the properties. "It was sent by a different phone. Another android, but not a Samsung."

"Does she know what this is?" Ronnie asked.

"I don't know, but I assume so. Otherwise, why would anyone send it to her?" It made sense for her to know and be able to read it.

Ronnie held her hand out for the phone. I gave it to her. She looked at the time stamp attached to the image. "Right before we left this morning, before the shooting, this was sent to her." Ronnie dropped the phone into my outstretched hand.

"She had her phone discoverable and Bluetooth on. She does nothing to help herself." I looked at the photo again. "Groups of five numbers. Each set of two numbers probably corresponds to a letter."

Ronnie grabbed a pen and a piece of paper. She drew up a grid. "How far do you think it goes. Highest single digit number?"

I read the numbers out loud, and she wrote them all down. "Four, four, three, one, three and then seven, one, three, two, seven. Next set is, two, seven, three, one, three. Then six, two, one, two, two, break; one, four, one, five, one, break; six, three, four, three, one, break; two, six, four, four, three, break; one, three, seven, three, five, break; six, two six, one, one, three, break; six, one, six."

"The last group is only three. An anomaly," Ronnie said. "Sounds like the code goes from one to seven. So, one to seven across the top, and one to four down. And the alphabet fits in the middle."

"Reasonable."

She wrote for a few minutes then handed me the paper. "Wasn't difficult at all. Not like decoding flowers in a rug."

I smiled. "Yeah, Zillah went all out to protect that information." I read the writing on the paper in my hand. "'You cannot hide from your fate.' That could be a threat, or maybe it's prophesy."

Ronnie smiled. "Yeah, a prophecy. I like that. Like a coded fortune cookie sent via an image, and minus the cookie part."

"Never did like those cookies." Not much to like, and not really something you get in New Zealand or Australia.

Ronnie's eyebrows rose. "Do you think she knows what it says straight up without having to work it out, and that the picture was there?" She pulled the hair tie from her ponytail and re-tied it. "More importantly, do you think she will lie about the code and picture?"

"Let's go and find out."

Alex was sitting at the table with Ginny because we were still in Pinehaven. As much as I didn't think it was a good idea to hang around and risk dragging them any further into the disaster, it was still the safest place we had.

"A word, Alex," I said, sitting in the chair next to her. "Where did this come from?"

I tried to show her the photo, but she refused to look at the phone screen. "You need to look at it." Ginny made a move to leave the table. "It's okay, you can stay."

"Crockett, I wouldn't leave if I didn't want to. I need a drink."

That sounded like a beaut idea, but we'd have to wait until Alex the influencer was off on her new life, or working for whoever snaffled her because of her fascinating brain.

"Look at the photo, Alex," I said, and thrust the phone in her face again. "Do you know what it says?"

She nodded, then shook her head. "No."

"Try again."

She shrugged. "It's a cypher. Someone sent it to me."

"How?"

"Bluetooth, you know anyway," she said looking away.

"You had your phone open and discoverable," I let disapproval slide into my voice.

She frowned. "Yeah, so?"

"Security, Zoomer. Ever heard of it?"

"Of course. This is work."

"And work means broadcasting your location to the world and letting anyone send you images directly to your phone. Talk about 'let the freaks in'. I bet the dick pics alone are worth it."

She shrugged one shoulder. Her face flushed. "My followers need me to be accessible."

"And your parents are okay with this kind of accessibility?"

"They're old, they don't get it."

Probably in their forties. Ancient. No doubt she thinks we're all old. I felt old. The more time I spent with Alex the older I got.

Ronnie sat across the table from us. Her hands rested on the surface. She looked at Alex and waited for the girl to make eye contact.

"The photo, Alex, it's a little bit weird don't you think? Grown-ups sending coded messages, all very James Bond. I think this came from someone you know." Alex's head moved in the tiniest of increments suggesting Ronnie was correct. "What bothers me, is that you knew what it said, and you didn't share it with us. We found it. As amusing as it sounds, it could be a threat."

"Found it going through my phone and invading my privacy," Alex snapped.

"In this situation, there is no privacy," Ronnie continued. "To know what that said when you saw it, means you've seen the cypher itself and hence, you knew how to read it. Where did you see it?"

"It was on someone's desk."

Hang on. What the hell?

"Someone?" I asked. "Does someone have an actual name?"

She shook her head. "It was on someone's desk. I thought it was a strange thing to have written on a notepad. A cypher. That's old school. Probably even older than you two. It amused me."

"Give me some context around this discovery," I said.

"I was waiting for a sponsor. I'd been invited to wait in the office while the personal assistant went to get me a coffee." Her eyes flashed up to mine. "That's how normal people behave. They go out and get coffee. They don't drink instant rubbish."

Nice.

"Who were you waiting for? Who were you supposed to be meeting?"

"The marketing person for a shoe company. His name is Nigel Scott."

"That wasn't so hard, was it?" Ronnie said. She was watching Alex pretty closely. "So, someone did have a name after all. If you'd told us what we needed to know in the beginning, this would be much easier on you."

"This company does what?" I asked.

"They make sneakers, you know, shoes. They're targeting late teens and early twenties."

I suppose it made sense to get Alex involved, then. That was her crowd, for sure.

"Did you meet him?" Ronnie asked. "Because if Nigel Scott had the cypher on his desk, there's a good chance he sent the photo to you."

"I did, but only briefly."

"Describe the man to me," I said.

"Not as tall as you. Older looking. More lines around his eyes and mouth than you have. He had white hair, faded blue eyes, no scars that I could see."

"Anything stand out at all about him?"

"The white hair. I don't think he was old enough for it to be age white. You know?"

"Good," I said.

"What was his voice like?"

"He had a New Zealand accent."

"Describe his office to me."

I grabbed a pen from the table, and my notebook. While she recalled images, I wrote what she'd told me so far.

"Okay. It was a big office with lots of windows, so there was a lot of light. His desk was large: a combination of wood and chrome. Very modern. His chair was an executive leather chair with arms. In front of his desk were two leather chairs; they had arms and they were deep blue. One entire wall was windows. That's why it was so light. On the back wall he had a large wall hanging of the countryside. Underneath it was a bronze plaque that said the wall hanging was silk and created by Ashley Chu. The name of the wall-hanging was 'A study in North Canterbury'." She stopped talking and looked at me. "On the other side of the room were high windows out to the rest of the office space. Other offices. Under the windows against the wood panelled wall were boxes. They were shoe boxes. Probably around twenty shoe boxes."

"What else?"

"There were two frames hanging behind his desk. Both contained affirmations. One said, 'I am not pushed by my problems, I am led by my dreams' and the other one said, 'Happiness is a choice and today I choose to be happy'."

"And these were hanging in an old bloke's office?"

She nodded.

"Anything else to add?"

"He took a shoe box off the top of the pile of boxes and

handed it to me."

"He knew your shoe size ahead of time?"

She nodded. "Yes. That information is sent to clients in advance by my manager."

"I didn't realise you had a manager," I said.

She scoffed. "Of course, I do! Everyone in this industry does. It's huge. How else would I get gigs and keep everything straight?"

"And your manager's name is?"

"Trisha Perkins."

I wrote it down.

"How long has she been your manager?"

"How does that matter? I thought you wanted to know about the shoe guy?"

"Humour me. How long has Trisha Perkins been your manager?"

"Six months."

"Does she manage other clients?"

"Of course, she does."

"Who?"

She shrugged. "I don't know. We don't talk about her other clients, and usually if influencers get together, we've got other things to chat about. Managers only get talked about if they're not doing their jobs."

"Thank you."

Ronnie spoke, "And you witnessed the murder when you left his office?"

"No, it wasn't that day. It was a few days later. Nigel's office was in an office building on Vivian Street in

Wellington. That's not where the murder happened."

"So, a delivery guy wasn't stabbed to death outside that building?"

"Maybe, but I never saw it." Her face paled.

"Did you witness a murder?"

"Yes. But not there." A flash of something lit her eyes, then vanished, and was replaced by the usual stroppy expression. "What is going on? Why so many questions?"

"Not sure what's going on," I said. "The way we find out is by asking questions."

"But you don't know?"

"Not yet, but we'll find out."

Ronnie made eye contact with me. I knew by the look that she'd come to the same assumption as I had. We'd been lied to, and it was not just by Alex.

"Hang here for a minute, I want to have a chat with Ronnie." I pushed the chair back with my legs as I stood.

Why the hell wouldn't they live video stream her testimony from a secure location instead of having her in the court room? I motioned to Ronnie to follow me.

We convened in the hallway. "Why would they risk her life by bringing her to the courthouse?" I asked. "And why were we told the murder took place on Vivian Street?"

"I've been wondering all this time why they didn't just live stream her testimony. Much easier to secure her somewhere and live stream," Ronnie replied. "But now we know we were fed lies. Maybe someone doesn't want her to testify. Have we considered that?"

"We are now," I said, and nodded. "We are now."

"She's supposedly a witness for the prosecution. or crown, or however you want it phrased." Ronnie words landed like a punch. "It's not making a lot of sense."

"Why would they want her silenced?" I could think of many ways to do just that, which were easier than trying to get to her while she was actively protected.

"Because she knows more than we're aware of. She probably knows more than she's aware of, and under cross-examination it might all come out." Ronnie shoved her hands in her jeans pockets. "We were thinking there was an open contract, but we didn't think wide enough. It might not be connected to the murder, but a convenient way of getting rid of someone who knows too much."

"You don't think this is connected to the murder?" I was trying to wrap my head around what Ronnie was telling me. If it wasn't the murder that sparked the attempts on Alex's life, then we could be digging in all the wrong places trying to find answers.

"Easy to say she's at risk because she witnessed a murder, and no denying that she did, but was it a drug-fuelled blitz attack on a delivery person? I don't think that's right. How much danger would she really be in from associates of that lunatic?"

"Wasn't he connected to a couple of gangs?" I scrambled through my memory, hauling that info to the fore. "And we have a few bikies in the mix."

Ronnie smiled and nodded. "That's what they said. Isn't that why the security, and her name being kept out of the court proceedings until a day or so ago?"

"You don't think it's true?"

She shook her head. "Do you?"

Up until Alex said it didn't happen where we were told it did, there wasn't much point in formulating any theories regarding the job. The operation was multifaceted: try and recruit her for Australia and keep her alive to testify. Ronnie had a good point.

"All right, let's lay this out." I leaned on the wall behind me. "The blitz attacker was supposedly a gang associate. We know he was a meth addict and a loose unit. How many gangs want someone like that bringing the wrong kind of attention to them?"

"Don't imagine many would," Ronnie replied. "What gangs was he supposed to be an enforcer for?"

"The report I read said he was vocal about ties to the Head Hunters and Mongrel Mob."

"Okay, so this loser goes off his tree at an innocent delivery person and threatens the person's family, and then posts addresses on social media sites."

"Doesn't sound very likely, does it?"

"You were undercover gang-guy. Does it sound likely?"

"He threatened women and children, there's a code. Families are off limits. They'd be scrambling to get distance from him. No one wants loose units bringing the police to their door. Good chance they'd put out a hit and get rid of him. People like that are liabilities."

"Code amongst crooks," Ronnie mumbled. "Good to know they don't just bash everyone."

"Where does that leave us?" I knew where it left us. Up the creek.

"It leaves us with Alex and the possibility that the threat/prophecy thingy is not related to the murder, but someone is making it look that way. It also leaves us with lies. The whole thing is based on a lie. There was no blitz attack on a delivery guy outside that building on Vivian Street."

"We need to act accordingly and protect ourselves, and Alex. If we're right, then someone is going to try and take her out at the courthouse, and she'll never testify."

"Yep," Ronnie said. "Do you know who the judge is?"

"No, but we'll find out." I still had the phone in my hand. "Let's go through this thing properly before we go back in there." I'd flick the phone into Airplane mode as soon as I turned it on, then enable WiFi. Those steps should enable me to go through the phone without drawing unwanted attention from any electronic surveillance. "That she disabled the lock feature on the phone is disturbing."

"Does she have TikTok on that thing?" Ronnie asked, stepping across the hall to lean on the wall beside me.

I held the phone so we could both see it. "Let's start at the home screen and find out exactly what little Miss No-Security has been up to with her so called work phone."

"Her other phone was locked, yes?"

"Yep. But it makes no difference locking one if she's going to carrying an unlocked one around with her that's pinning little flags in a map and telling the world her location."

Ronnie sighed. She pointed to an app icon. "She does have it."

"Do none of these Zoomers understand how dangerous that app is?" I grumbled as I scrolled through another two screens. "She has all the crap you could imagine on here when it comes to social media."

"Check her email."

I opened the email icon. Lots of emails. Mostly from fans or people suck holing. I opened the draft folder because I saw there was an unsent email. A double tap on the email revealed something that surprised me.

"She's talking to someone," I said. "The old convo in draft folder is the kind of thing people like us do."

We read in silence.

"Why would they talk in code?" Ronnie said, but I knew she didn't want an answer. We both knew why it was a coded draft inbox conversation. Also, if you don't send it there is no electronic trail. But for it to be a conversation the other person has to have access.

"I'm surprised whoever the other person is, didn't jump in here when she stopped communicating and delete this."

"Maybe she does talk to her friends using a code?" Ronnie said with a shrug. "They might think it's cool."

"No doubt. She's too cool for school."

"We need to decode it. I have a horrible feeling she isn't what she's cracked up to be. I don't doubt she's an *influencer* but there's something else going on here."

Ronnie pushed off the wall. "I'm getting a pen and paper. Go ask Tom if we can use his office."

"You don't want to go ask Alex to tell us what this means?"

"Nope. I don't want her knowing we know. Screenshot it with your phone just in case it disappears."

I did as she asked. Ronnie's a smart cookie. Then I went to find Tom and Ben. Alex the influencer had secrets.

I heard their voices coming from the workshop, or shed, or garage, whatever. I opened the door to find them deep in conversation about a ratchet screwdriver. I get it. They're pretty cool.

"Sorry to interrupt, Tom, could Ronnie and I camp in your office? We just need an hour or so in a quiet place to work something out."

"Go ahead," Tom said. "We'll be in soon. Just showing Ben some new tools."

"So, I saw." I turned to leave, pulling the door closed behind me. "Cheers for the use of your office."

Ronnie was in the hallway waiting for me.

"What's happening in the dining room?"

"Ginny is talking to Alex. Sounds like a bit of straight talk. Reminding her she's being protected, and she could be nicer." Ronnie grinned. "What I heard anyway."

"Good luck to her getting through to Alex." I led the way to Tom's office. Once inside we moved two chairs nearer to his desk and closed the door.

I opened the email again and saw a new message.

Using my phone, I took another photo.

"It's the same cypher," Ronnie said, then frowned. "But not quite. Looks like it goes to eight on the x axis but only three on the y. So, there might be no z and no y in this alphabet. Or I'm wrong."

"I'd pay money to see that," I said, with a grin.

"The bit I don't get, is the photo. If it's the same person, why send a semi-threatening image or whatever photo? Why not just use the email draft?" Ronnie said, as she wrote sequences of numbers on the paper under a drawing of the cypher. "It makes zero sense."

"And two unconnected people wouldn't use such a similar code," I said. Unless they had absolutely no imagination and used the easiest thing their pea brains came up with. Even then it was a long shot.

"She said she saw the code on Nigel Scott's desk. If she saw a code similar to one she was using to communicate with someone, wouldn't that set off red flags?"

Ronnie and I looked at each other.

"They're connected."

"It's too much of a coincidence."

"Don't suppose there's a name in all that?" I asked, as Ronnie turned numbers into words.

"Not so far. I'm not even sure which part of the conversation is Alex and which part is someone else. Would've been nice if they'd attributed sentences to each other. All I have is red and blue text colours. I'm going with Alex first, because this is in her draft folder. But the other person has access, so they could've set it up."

"Read it to me," I said, leaning back in my chair and resting my eyes for a moment.

Person One: I do not see why I have to do this.

Person Two: It is all part of the big picture.

Person One: The big picture. What is that?

Person Two: It is need to know. You do not need to know yet.

Person One: What if I tell the world and take away your hold on me.

Person Two: You work for us.

Person One: I quit.

Person Two: That is not how this works.

Person Two: You are painting a target on your own back.

Person Two: We will find you.

Person Two: People do not quit us.

"Person One has to be Alex."

"Seems she's pissed someone off," I said. "But who, and who is she, or was she, working for?"

"And what was she doing?"

"That I can guess," I said. "Someone got to her before any of us could. My guess is she isn't working for anyone involved in Five-Eyes, or an allied country."

"Espionage for unfriendlies. Why did we get the task to supposedly protect her?" Ronnie twisted in her chair to watch my face as she spoke. "You have a tell, so go ahead and make my day."

"I do not have a tell. You know why we got the job. We have skills."

"Are you both supposed to be flipping her?"

"Probably," I said. No sense in lying about it. "We want her, and if we want her, you can bet the Yanks want in."

"So, Australia is trying to steal something else from New Zealand. How unusual."

"It's not us stealing anything from you," I replied with a grin. I knew where this was going.

"You've already got Pharlap's heart, and we graciously gave you Russell Crowe." Ronnie grinned. "No backsies on that one by the way."

"Are you going to mention pavlova?" I stifled a laugh. She was on a roll.

"You know that's ours. So are ANZAC biscuits, so don't do anything shady there." Ronnie wrinkled her nose. "Why don't you Aussies lay claim to feijoas or bloody zucchini. No one wants them."

"Are you done?"

She nodded and took a deep breath.

"Back to work."

"If you go ahead with your directive, then you're creating a monster, not a double agent but an honest to God monster. She's already being used, and we both know it's not the 'good' guys. Don't forget Baranov and her leather coat. What the hell is going on there?"

Ronnie wasn't wrong. "We need to find out who she's working for and what that really means."

"Right, let's reply to the email. We've got the sad arsed

code so we may as well use it," Ronnie said.

"Not a bad idea."

Ronnie rolled her eyes. We crafted a response. Added a certain amount of contrition for not responding sooner but offered no explanation as to why. And we waited.

Twenty minutes ticked by. Two cats came in to check what we were doing. The big one with ginger ears was very nosy and friendly. He jumped on my knee without any encouragement. Guess he liked men.

Ronnie spent the entire twenty minutes waking up the phone and checking the draft message. Nothing.

"I could murder a coffee," she said, tapping the screen yet again. "Hold up. We have a response." She grabbed the pen and wrote the number sets on the paper. Less than a minute later we could read the response.

"'Stay in touch. You have missed too many check-ins'," I read out loud, then thought for a second. "Do we have a time stamp for any of the other messages, something we can work with in regard to the check-ins spoken of?"

"Nope. It's just the messages, one after the other. The top of the screen gives the time of the most current version of the email. Don't think we can backtrack it to earlier versions and times."

"Just another thing to think about. Don't suppose you have anything capable of doing that for us?"

"I'd have to go to the office to access the computer and see if there is anything on Justin Case's drive."

"Is it worthwhile?"

Ronnie shrugged. "Probably not. She hasn't responded

since we grabbed the second phone at your place."

She had a point. The timing wouldn't tell us much beyond her chit-chatting with the unknown subject earlier today, and by the look of the conversation, yesterday. It wouldn't tell us who it was.

"Let's go talk to Alex," I said. "I think we need to know what exactly we're up against."

Chapter Eighteen:

[Ronnie: Here we go]

Crockett and I entered the dining room and found that Alex was still at the table talking to Ginny. Ginny smiled up at me. I smiled back. I quite liked her. Truth be told, I really liked her.

"Could I have a quick word, Ronnie?" Ginny asked.

"Sure," I replied.

Crockett sat across from Alex. Ginny and I went into the kitchen. Ginny reached up to a cupboard near the back door and retrieved a pack of cigarettes and a lighter. She took one smoke from the pack and put the pack back. She then opened the back door. We stepped outside, but I stayed on the porch. It was the safest option if a drone happened to be flying around. You can't be too careful with those pesky things lurking.

Ginny lit her cigarette. "I don't think Alex is telling the whole truth," she said, exhaling smoke.

"Nor do I," I replied. I was curious, though. "What makes *you* think that?"

"She's been asking a lot of questions about you and Ben."

"And Crockett?"

She shook her head. "I don't imagine she would because I just met him today. But she knows Ben has talked to me in the past about you. She listens to what's going on around her. When we all think she's sulking, or whatever expression that face of hers portrays most, she's actually listening." Ginny waved her cigarette hand in front of her face. "You know when she gets that look on her face, like a tantrum is about to let loose."

"I know that look. Interesting that you've picked up on her listening, because I imagined she was dreaming up her next screaming fit." I was tricked by her tantrums into thinking she didn't know what was going on around her. Do better, Ronnie. Do better!

"She's playing you all," Ginny said.

"It now seems that way. What questions?"

"Who do you usually work for? Has Ben told me about someone called MacKinnon? Had I heard the word Genesis?"

Buggery bollocks, they're not innocent questions that have come from nowhere.

"Quite the chatty little miss. Fascinating question choices," I said. "She's nosy, I'll give her that. You must look friendly."

Ginny exhaled more smoke and laughed. "She thinks she can weasel info out of me because I'm drinking."

I doubted that would happen. Ginny didn't strike me as the sort of woman who would reveal a confidence no matter what state she was in. We wouldn't be here if that was the case. Loose lips don't just sink ships, they kill spies. Why were we here in this place with these people, right now?

"Thank you for telling me," I said. "Let me know if she

tries for more information. We're pretty sure she isn't who she'd like us to think she is."

"How did you get this assignment?" Ginny asked then back tracked. "Am I allowed to ask that? You don't have to answer. I'm as bad as Miss Nosy Pants in there."

"It's just another assignment. We often get unusual ones via my business. Nothing different here."

I lied. It wasn't even me that got this job for us. Sometimes lying isn't that easy. Ginny struck me as perceptive.

She smiled at me. "I get that you can't tell me. Could whoever hired you, be someone nasty, or in cahoots with someone unpleasant?"

Yep. They could be. Cold from the concrete seeped into my backside when I sat on the top step. Ginny sat next to me. Smoke wafted past me from her cigarette. I watched it disappear into the garden.

"Between you and me, yes, it's possible." And this time it's highly likely. With everyone's eyes on the prize, which in this case is Alex, it was not the easiest of jobs. The more we uncovered, the tougher it became. The more I knew, the more I saw a messy future as we tried to unravel the knots and make sense of everything. Nigel Scott, the manager - Trisha Perkins, the lies from the brief about where the attack took place. I don't doubt there were lies about who was attacked. The shroud of secrecy was wearing thin.

"Is she really testifying at a trial on Monday?"

"As far as we know," I said. "We're given a certain amount of information, not a lot, because it's not necessary."

"I don't suppose you need many details or anything to do your jobs," Ginny said, blowing smoke away from me.

"Nope. All we need to know is if she's allergic to anything, has any medical conditions that could impede our care of her, and where and what time to drop her off." And part of it was to deliver her to Courtroom Six on Monday morning at ten.

All of it muddled in my head as I tried to knit the pieces together. I knew the job was coming but I didn't know I'd be quite so involved. My contact, Garry, was an old friend in the espionage community. He'd heard there was a person with H-SAM who needed protection and the Australians had skin in the game. Gossip indicated the person was a *special* witness. I set that aside.

What I didn't know was why she wasn't put into a safe house for the duration, or why she was removed from a safe house. If police were truly involved like Crockett's information suggested, then a safe house would've been the sensible thing with a police guard. Why didn't they just do a video link instead of insist on her being present?

That it was an Australian job, meant Crockett had an agenda. Ben probably had one as well. Crockett was told to use me and Ben. He had to know the Yanks would want dear Alex as soon as they heard about her memory. Me, I didn't care. I'm not technically in the espionage game anymore, no agenda here apart from keeping the kid alive. The three amigos together again. We work well together, most of the time.

I knew Defence were interested in getting their grubby little mitts on Alex, but they may not have known about her before I introduced her to Bill.

And Alex was working for someone who was potentially in the espionage field, and not us, or a friendly handler, because that would've been included in the brief. I wonder who knew about that and who she really worked for. The G word pressed into my mind and wouldn't let go, probably because Ginny mentioned it. *Genesis*. Surely not. The *Genesis* program had caused upheaval and chaos since its conception. Our last tango with a *Genesis* related piece of nonsense, cost the lives of the creators. Why would Alex ask about MacKinnon?

William MacKinnon and his son James created and ran *Genesis,* an off-book program. William ran an American team here for years, then switched to the Aussies, and was Crockett's boss. Ben and I knew more about *Genesis* than Crockett. We were both once intelligence officers; I retired, Ben didn't. But retirement isn't always the end. And I had access to something no one else did: the *Genesis* files. MacKinnon gave them to me before his death and my access was never revoked. That means, I have access to everything. There's a link hidden in the files that takes me to the *Genesis* servers. To my knowledge, the person who took over *Genesis* is not known to the espionage community. There was no chatter suggesting who it could be. I don't share *Genesis* information, not even with Ben or Crockett. And I knew damn well Crockett was not part of the program. MacKinnon wanted him in before his untimely death. MacKinnon may have wanted Crockett on the inside, but it didn't happen. No doubt the new head of the program will invite him if he or she deems it a good idea.

My mind's eye scanned the most recent reports sent by the analysts. Nothing stood out. I needed to get in front of my computer and check for anything that could've cropped up in the last few days, or any chatter that was missed during my cursory scans. Our analysts are the best in the world, so I doubted they missed anything, but I could've.

Ginny touched my arm. "Rapt in dreamland, Ronnie. What do you need?"

I felt the lines of concentration on my forehead smooth as a smile took over at her question. So simple. So straightforward.

"The first thing I need is to go home for an hour."

"Will that help you?"

"Absolutely."

"Then go."

"You make it sound so easy."

Ginny laughed. "Sometimes things are."

"Yeah. Sometimes."

"I'll go back in and leave you to organise whatever you need to do." Ginny stubbed out her cigarette and picked up the butt before she went back inside.

I rang Enzo. He answered on the third ring.

"Hey, Ronnie." I heard a lot of commotion in the background.

"Everything good over there?"

"Yes, of course. Donald is playing a game with the ladies."

Sounded legit, but I'd lay money on that not being true. I had enough going on without questioning Enzo.

"Okay, good. I need to get home."

"All right, I'll get Emily, and we'll ride north, straight up Fergusson Drive. Whoever is watching is bound to see us."

"Ride around for five-minutes just to make sure you pick up a tail. I'll see if Ben and I can borrow a car."

A knot tightened in my stomach. Crockett was going to hate having Enzo ride around with Emily.

"Done."

"I'll text when we are ready to leave."

And a sneaky idea emerged. I hung up and went to find Ben. Crawling trepidation tingled up my spine as I stepped into the backyard. I glanced skyward into the coming night. No visible drones.

Ben and Tom were still yabbering away about tools. No doubt they picked up where they left off before dinner.

"Sorry to interrupt, but I need to get home. Actually, we do." I waved my finger between me and Ben.

His eyes met mine and he nodded slowly. "How do you want to play this?"

"I'm sending Enzo and Emily back out to draw the brunt of the attention." I angled my body toward Tom. "I have an idea, but you are absolutely free to say no. We can jump on the bike." Could we? Yes, we could. Enzo

176

wouldn't mind if we rode his bike. Crockett would mind very much if it was his Harley.

"Spit it out," Tom said.

"You've got an SUV with lots of room. Could you and Ginny go visit someone near my street in Trentham, and let Ben and me be invisible passengers?"

Tom frowned as my words sunk in. "I'm sure Ginny would love that. I'm not overselling it; she's really enjoying all this. I need to ask one question: how dangerous is it?"

"Should be perfectly fine. No one knows your car, or that we know you, or that we are here."

Darkness slipped slowly over Pinehaven as we stood in the garage, making the lights inside seem all the brighter. I waited for Tom to decide if helping us was a good idea. It probably wasn't, but I had to try.

"We have some friends in Bartons Road. Is that close enough?"

"Yes." We could cross the park in the dark and get to my place pretty easily from Barton Road.

"Let me make a phone call. I'll see if they're up for visitors." He stopped talking and picked up a drill bit from the work bench. "Time I returned this."

"Thank you, Tom," I said, with a small smile.

"Don't thank me yet. They may not want visitors this evening."

Fair enough.

Tom went inside the house. I watched him until the back door closed behind him.

"What's going on?" Ben asked, his voice low, almost a whisper.

"Who's the puppet master? Because someone is pulling Alex's strings," I said. "Anything about this situation ring alarm bells?"

His light blue eyes stared into mine. "You want to check the recent reports," he said.

"Yes."

He didn't say anything else. It paid not to say too much when we couldn't guarantee security. The back door opened. Light from the kitchen spilled over the steps and onto the path. It disappeared when the door closed again.

Tom approached us, his expression neutral. I'd noticed that about him: he did neutral well and he gave little away.

"That went better than expected," Tom said. "Ginny and I will return a few tools to our good friend Mike. Ginny's getting ready. We'll drop in, say hi, give back the tools and leave. Quick visit."

"Thank you, Tom," I said. "Did you see Crockett and Alex?"

"Crockett is playing twenty-questions with her at the dining room table," he smiled. "She's not very good at the game."

Ben chuckled. "He'll keep at it for a while. I doubt anyone will notice our vanishing act."

I looked at Ben. "You don't want to tell Crockett we're leaving?" Interesting.

His head shook slowly. "I think we need to play this

close."

"Good call. But we can't leave him alone without warning. If something happens, he doesn't have us as backup."

Tom picked up a key fob and unlocked his car: a Mercedes SUV. Very nice.

"Should be more than enough room for the pair of you in the back seat. You won't even need to crouch or lie down. The back windows are dark tinted."

Perfect.

"I'm going to have a quick word with Crockett." Ben shot me a warning glance. "Just telling him we're going to recon the area and that Tom and Ginny are going to visit friends."

Ben's facial muscles relaxed enough for a small smile to form. "Okay."

I checked the night sky for anything unusual before hurrying into the house.

Crockett was still at the table with Alex. Ginny was nowhere to be seen.

"You good?" Crockett asked, as I walked toward them.

"Yes. We're going to do some recon before the move."

He narrowed his eyes at me. "We?"

"Me and Ben."

"You leaving the bike here?"

"Yes. Are you going to be all good with Alex?"

Alex looked up at me. "What about asking if I'll be *all good* with Crockett?"

"You'll be fine."

"He asks too many questions."

"If you answered them, it'd be over sooner, and maybe you and he could play cards or something."

Her eyes rolled toward the ceiling. "Do you have Cards Against Humanity?" Her voice sounded almost hopeful.

"I was thinking something more like Go Fish." I let that be my last remark and waved to Crockett. Ginny reached the back door at the same time as I did. I opened the door for her. I took the snip off the deadlock. We both waved before I closed the door and listened to it lock.

I hurried, head down, into the garage. Ginny took longer. By the time she reached the car, Ben and I were secluded in the back seat.

"There's a blanket on the floor," Tom said. "If you needed to scrunch yourselves down, you could pull it over you."

Ginny closed her car door and twisted a little in the front passenger seat. "This is exciting," she said.

"You can't talk to them," Tom said. "They're not here."

Ginny touched the side of her nose to indicate she understood. "It's still exciting though. It's like we're secret agents."

I liked her enthusiasm. Ben chuckled quietly.

"We all are tonight," he said.

I texted Enzo: Time to go.

Enzo: We're off. We're going to take Crockett's bike for a good run.

Me: I'd keep that to myself if I were you.

Enzo: LOL

Tom started the car and backed slowly out of the garage. The garage door slid down before he straightened up to drive out of their long driveway.

"We'll go the back way," he said. "Through Heretaunga and then across the train tracks."

"Sounds good." I knew that Sutherland Ave was directly across from Barton Avenue. So, it was simply a matter of crossing Fergusson Drive at the Sutherland Avenue traffic lights and driving straight down Barton Avenue. "Can you drop us off before you turn into Barton Road, please."

"That was my plan. It's nice and dark at the park end of Barton Avenue."

Perfect.

Chapter Nineteen:

[Donald: Secret Squirrel]

I hate it when Enzo's phone rings after dark because it seems so much scarier.

When he and Emily came back into the kitchen wearing their motorbike gear, complete with helmets, I knew it was Ronnie who rang.

"I don't suppose you can tell me anything?"

"Sorry, Lover. It's work."

Emily dropped her visor over her eyes and led the way downstairs. I followed Enzo. Nana and the *Cronies of Doom* were spying out the windows at the continuing drama across the street. And drama it was.

The garage door slid up with little more than a light groan. Enzo kicked the stand up and pushed the bike onto the driveway. He jumped on and started the engine. It rumbled loudly, echoing from the open garage. Emily hopped on the back and wrapped her arms around Enzo. They looked like Crockett and Ronnie. A sinking feeling twisted my stomach. They were going to put themselves in harm's way.

I waved once, as Enzo pulled out of the driveway and roared up the street. The Not-Neighbours paused their yelling to watch.

Back in the garage, I hit the manual door button and waited for it to close. The yelling across the road, recommenced.

It was going to be a long, scary night. I tossed my hair from my eyes and hurried up the stairs. It didn't do any good to think about it.

"Get on with what's in front of you, Donald," I said to myself once back in the kitchen.

Nana's practiced feeble voice called out, "Donald!"

I ducked my head around the dividing wall. "Yes, Nana?"

"Was that Enzo?"

"Yes, Nana. He's working."

"Well, dear, shall we have a sherry?"

I took a deep breath and exhaled slowly. "I'll get the glasses and the decanter, shall I, Nan?"

"You're such a good boy, Donald," Ester crooned.

They were up to something.

I carried a tray with the sherry decanter and glasses into the lounge. Frankie wasn't there.

I put the tray down and poured drinks, then passed a glass to Nana and to Ester.

"Where's Frankie?" I asked, taking a large sip from my glass, and settling into a chair.

"Powder room," Nana replied.

That was reasonable, I suppose. They're allowed to use the loo without an escort.

I downed the last of my sherry.

"Donald, you sip it, dear. Don't glug it," Nana said and took a tiny sip from her glass.

I stood and refilled my glass, while wishing I'd poured

myself a whiskey, and brought the bottle through.

A louder than usual commotion outside caught my attention. Nana bristled as I approached the ranch slider. "It's more nonsense," she said, flapping a hand at me.

"I know, but the racket has escalated," I replied, and peered out the net curtains. The reason became apparent immediately. Oh, Lordy.

Frankie was standing by our letterbox with her phone in her hand like she was filming.

"Will you three ever stop getting involved!" I rounded on Nana. "This is unacceptable."

The shouting intensified. I clutched at the front of my shirt and took a deep breath.

"You two stay put." I narrowed my eyes and glared at them. "I will get Frankie out of this situation." I sounded much surer than I felt. Wishing Enzo was still home didn't make it happen, so I straightened my shirt, adjusted my imaginary tiara, and hurried down the stairs before I could chicken out.

I ran out the front door to haul Frankie back inside, but she was gone. An angry voice rang out from the other side of the street.

"Do you own this old bat?" Bog-Mouth yelled.

Bloody hell.

I couldn't even fake a smile, so I grimaced and marched across the road. "Frankie, what did I say about staying inside?" I grabbed her by the elbow. She resisted and attempted to pull her arm from my grasp. I held firm and spun her back toward our house.

Bog-Mouth screeched, "She's been filming us, the old bat! I want her phone!"

"Not going to happen," I said, pushing Frankie in front of me to get her moving on the footpath. I checked for traffic. Frankie pulled her arm away and spun back to the Not-Neighbours. Phone in hand, still filming. Death wish, much?

I grabbed her again and saw Nana trotting out the front door with Romeo.

Bog-Mouth yelled and threw objects. I jumped as a lump of wood narrowly missed me. A door opened close by. Two women emerged from the house next door with a large muscly dog. I'd seen him before. A big mastador. Romeo turned toward him as he and Nana crossed the road to join us. I watched amazed as the dogs nodded at each other.

The women and the dog were in their side of the carport. Bog-Mouth and Whingy-Chick were yelling abuse and throwing things at me and Frankie. We were at the end of the driveway, next door, all of us: Ester, Nana, Frankie and me, and Romeo. The good neighbours weren't far behind us.

Their big dog growled and took a few steps closer to Bog-Mouth's side. One of the women with the dog called me over.

"Come with me," I said to Frankie, and the others. I still had a grip on Frankie's arm and encouraged her to move closer to the growling dog.

"This doesn't seem safe," Frankie said. Another deep

growl came from the big dog.

"You're a fine one to talk about safety," I rasped into her old ear. "This is not going well."

The older of the two women spoke, "I'm Samantha, this is Diesel, and this is my daughter Loralie. You're Donald?"

"Yes, I am." I paused for a minute taking in her hair cut and colouring. I was looking at my own handiwork. "I know you. You've been into the salon."

"Every three months for the last four years," she replied, running her hand through her short silver-streaked hair. That was definitely my work.

"You should've popped over and said hi," I said, tossing my fringe. "We love visitors. And what with this non-sense ..." I gestured to the Not-Neighbours. "... we need to stick together."

"Yes, we do," Samantha replied. "With luck we can run them out of the street, if not the town."

Bog-Mouth yelled louder, blanketing the area with her revolting language choices.

"What the fuck are you all doing out here? Mind your own business!" She squawked like a demented parrot. If it was my parrot, I'd put it down.

Diesel and Romeo growled. It must be sheer hell living right next door to the Not-Neighbours. It was bad enough being across the road.

"I'm sorry you have this next door to you," Frankie said trying to shake my grip. She was still filming with her free hand.

I sighed. Samantha inclined her head toward Bog-Mouth's screeching. "We share a wall. Half the time it sounds like they're murdering each other, and the other half is screaming, fake crying, and abuse hurling. She, in particular, can leave any time and make our lives better."

Nana shuffled her feet, managing to move herself closer to the trouble. The dogs noticed. Romeo and Diesel moved silently until they flanked the old troublemaker. She petted both dogs on the head with her gnarly thin hands. How she became the dog whisperer, I don't know.

The nonsense from Bog-Mouth stopped abruptly. Everyone froze as the snarling increased. Both dogs moved beyond Nana to the edge of the carport. Their eyes focused on the Not-Neighbours.

"I'm calling police!" Bog-Mouth screeched.

"Go ahead, dear," Nana replied. "Would you like me to dial?"

"No one dials anymore, you fucking, old bat!" She fumbled her phone. It slid from her hand and clattered onto the concrete. She picked it up and yelled, "You broke my phone!" Bog-Mouth spun the phone to show the crazy cracks on the screen. "You broke my phone! You need to get me a new one!"

Nana spoke, "No dear. You dropped your phone all by yourself." She took a breath and paused for a second Bog-Mouth wasn't getting any calmer. "It's time you started accepting responsibility for your actions."

Whingy-Chick hit Bog-Mouth on the back. "Ouch! Why'd you do that for, bitch?"

"Listen to the old woman."

Bog-Mouth spun on her screaming, "Shut up! You're supposed to be on my side."

"I keep telling you, lay off the meth, and stop being a massive bitch."

Frankie nudged Ester. "Are you getting all this?"

She nodded.

Bog-Mouth screamed and lashed out at Whingy-Chick, who stepped sideways. Unbalanced, Bog-Mouth fell into the car. She kicked it and picked up a hunk of wood, a fence paling. I guess there's more broken fence somewhere. I ducked as she swung the paling and let it go. The hunk of wood smashed into the driveway, narrowly missing Nana, and Ester. The dogs barked and growled.

Samantha called Diesel back as he was stalking toward Bog-Mouth. He listened and returned to her. Romeo followed. I wished Nana would listen.

Relief swamped me as sirens filled the air. Red and blue flashing lights rushed towards us from the right and left.

I said a silent prayer that none of the police officers knew Ronnie. Two call outs in one day, both involving the *Cronies* and Nana; this was a whole new level of bad.

Chapter Twenty:

[Ronnie: Now what?]

Ben and I chose our path across the dark park with care. We used the torches on our phones just enough to check there were no obstacles. Park benches aren't fun to fall over. We kept close to Domain bush and its deep tree shadows until we were opposite the playground. Ahead, I saw the yellow glow of streetlights on Brentwood Street. Every now and then an angry shout rang out: no words, just the noise.

"What do you think that is?" Ben asked, falling into step beside me as we crossed the grass toward the gates that led to Brentwood Street.

"I don't know, but I think we're going to find out."

It didn't take us long to reach the footpath to the gates. The gates were shut. I walked around the fence to the left until it was nothing more than a low chain. Using my phone torch, I stepped over the chain onto the driveway. Ben followed. Gravel crunched under our feet. We used our torches until we got to the road. There was a locked chain across the entrance. We avoided the chain by walking through a garden between the entrance and exit and emerged onto Brentwood Street. The yelling intensified.

As we turned the corner into Ruahine Street, we could see a lot of flashing blue and red lights.

"They look like they're at the intersection of Tararua,"

Ben said.

"Oh, that could be bad," I muttered, and broke into a run. Nana and *the Cronies of Doom* were foremost in my mind. "That's the Not-Neighbours."

Ben matched me shoulder to shoulder as we ran on the footpath on the other side of the road to the police. Our footfalls bounced off houses and echoed. I hoped police would hear us coming. It's never a good idea to appear from nowhere and risk surprising potentially armed cops. We slowed to a jog.

As we neared, I saw Romeo. White and black dogs stand out in the night. His eyes shone like small green torches. He looked possessed.

"This is bad," I muttered to Ben. We dropped our jog down to a walk. I scanned the sky for anything drone-like. I figured if they were serious about using drones then they'd have night-vision capability. I didn't see anything obvious.

The yelling, shouting, and swearing continued. It floated above low reasonable voices like an angry cloud. Glass smashed. A police officer stepped out of the shadows into the pool of yellowy light cast by the nearest streetlight. The officer turned; he must've heard our footsteps. He held up a hand to stop us.

Romeo saw me and wandered across the road to me. There was utter chaos in the street. More glass shattered. A woman screamed. Someone threw something heavy that smashed onto the driveway near a group of people. I couldn't make out who they were, until I recognised Donald's head toss.

Romeo leaned on me and whined. "Hey big guy," I said, rubbing his ears. "It's okay." I gave him a quick check-over. He seemed unharmed and wandered back to the group of people.

A low growl rumbled under the screeching. At first I assumed it was a police dog, then I saw yellow fur. The officer who stopped us approached.

"It's better to go back the way you came," he said.

"I live just here," I told him and pointed to my house. "And I have a horrible feeling that my cousin and Nana are involved in that ..." I waved a hand at the commotion.

My name rang out.

I searched the dark shapes and shadows for the person who called to me. A plain clothes officer crossed the road.

"Ronnie," he said as he joined us.

"Tony," I replied. "This is Ben. Ben, this is Detective Anthony Ryan."

"Pleased to meet you," Ben said taking his hand.

"Your Nana," Tony said, shaking his head. "Second call-out today here. Both involved June Tracey."

"Second." I let that sink in. "Twice in one day?"

"Yes. You didn't know? I thought that's why you were here."

"I'm on an assignment and not in communication as readily as usual, just came home to grab something. I'm not staying."

"That's a shame. I have a feeling this is going to go all night."

191

"Let's get over there and find out what the hell is going on," I said. "The sooner Nana and the *Cronies of Doom* are back in their rest home, the better."

"June said they were staying with Donald," Tony said. I heard the smile in his voice.

"I think they've stayed long enough, don't you?"

"You want them escorted home?"

Now that was a fantastic idea. "Yes!"

"Done."

Ben nudged me as we walked over to the gaggle of old ducks, with Tony. "Romeo is over there with another dog. He seems to have a friend."

And there he was, standing next to a large yellow dog in the carport. Both dogs had demon eyes. They were about the same height, but the other dog was younger and had a solid build. Neither liked the Not-Neighbours. They were good judges of character.

Broken glass littered the road and sparkled under the streetlights.

"Ronnie, thank goodness," Nana said, sounding extra feeble. "It's dreadful over there."

"So, I see. No doubt there is an explanation."

"Romeo has a friend. His name is Diesel," Nana said. If she thought that was going to stop me asking questions, she was wrong.

"Good, he needs a friend," I replied. "What have you been up to this time?"

"Nothing, why must you always think I'm up to something?" Extra feeble with a splash of cultivated innocence.

"Because Nana, I clearly told you to stay inside and not to get involved with anything."

Nana smirked. "We have video. You need that, don't you?"

Tony stepped closer to Nana. "I would like that, thank you."

"Who are you, young man?"

"Detective Ryan."

"Frankie," Nana said, reaching out to her. "This is Detective Ryan. He wants your video."

A filthy-mouthed woman with a dark stain across one eye and down the side of her face, shouted more obscenities. They seemed to be directed at Nana.

That's a great big nope fish in my book.

"Who is she?" I asked Tony.

"Monica," he replied. "Well known to us."

I left the weak yellow light and walked straight up to Monica.

"What the fuck do you want?" she yelled.

"To talk to you," I replied keeping my voice low and calm. "There seems to be a problem and I think we should talk about it."

"I'm not fucking talking to you, bitch."

I smiled. "Yes, you are."

Someone moved close to me. I glanced right and saw Ben.

"Fuck off. Get off my property."

I turned to Tony. "Who lives here?"

"Not them," he replied.

"Not your property. So, let's have a chat."

"It's my cousin's place. I'm living here. Fuck off and take those old bats with you."

"I live in this street," I said, and pointed to our house. "Right there. I have to listen to your bullshit day in and day out. And because you take your trash to the street, we all have an opinion."

She yelled something unintelligible.

"That's what I'm talking about." I stepped forward until I was within striking distance. "You need to have more respect for yourself, your family, and the rest of the community."

"You're on my property!"

"Not yours."

"Fuck off!"

I took another step closer, keeping my hands by my sides. She stepped back. She was one step from being up against the car.

"You owe my Nana an apology."

"I'm not apologising to the crazy old bitches. They should mind their business."

"Your business is all over the street. That makes it fair game."

She took another step back. Fear flashed across her face as she hit the car.

"Go away!"

"Interesting choice of words. Do you go away when people yell that at you?"

"Get off my property. This is assault! Police! Help me!"

She had a voice like a demented banshee.

Tony hurried over.

"What's the problem, Monica?" he asked.

"This bitch won't go away."

She put her hands up and shoved me. I rocked back on my right foot and regained my balance. I did nothing in retaliation but the smile on my face probably pissed her off.

Tony grabbed her by the wrist and spun her to face the car. "Hands behind you," he growled, as he snapped handcuffs on her wrists. "You're under arrest for assault."

"She assaulted me!" She screeched, trying to kick Tony.

"Whatever, Monica. Let's go." He passed her to another officer to put in a waiting police car.

I waved. "Bye now."

"Where's the other one?" Tony asked looking around the front yard. I saw someone looking out the front windows.

"Inside, I think."

"Good. She won't have much to yell about with Monica locked up for the night. Now, about your Nana."

My stomach dropped into my boots. "How bad?"

"Dangerous. She could've been badly hurt or killed."

"Let's get them home, and you the video footage. I'd like to speak to my cousin for a minute."

"Do I need to accompany you just in case?"

We grinned at each other. "No, but I might have to 'mum voice' him."

"I can probably handle that."

Chapter Twenty-one:

[Ronnie: Puppet master show yourself.]

Once we'd escorted the *Cronies of Doom,* and everyone who belonged to us, inside our house, the conflict between Nana and Donald heightened.

"I can't believe you'd be so reckless." Donald's voice hit higher notes than I ever thought possible. "You're impossible!"

Nana's tight smile didn't budge. "It's fine and dandy, Donald. No need for hysterics."

"The drama you conjure is beyond the pale. It could've been the end of you."

That was my cue to get on with things.

"Right, I have work to do. You three ..." I waved a hand at the *Cronies of Doom.* "... have a police escort back to your facility."

"You make it sound like a prison, Veronica," Nana said. "We are not inmates. We are free to come and go as we like."

"Maybe I should have you moved to a secure facility," I cautioned. "Don't test me, old woman."

Ben caught my attention. "We need to get this investigation underway."

I nodded.

"Donald, can I trust you to get these three troublemakers into the police car that should be waiting outside our driveway?" I checked my phone. There was a text from Tony saying he'd sent a car to retrieve them. "Don't let them escape or talk to anyone."

Donald took a deep breath. "All of this," he waved a hand around the room. "I tried my best."

As much as I wanted him to suffer and think I was going to haul him over hot coals, I couldn't do it. I knew what Nana and the Cronies were like. And now he did too. Welcome to my world.

"I know. And now you understand why I was worried." I punched him lightly in the arm. "I'll be in the bat cave."

"I am sorry," he said.

"I know. Just get them into that car."

I didn't say goodbye to the oldies. I filled a glass with water and went to find Ben. He was waiting in my bedroom for me. He'd opened the wardrobe and pushed clothes aside to reveal a doorway.

I handed him the cup. "Hold my cup."

I keyed a code into the lock on the door, a click followed, and I pushed the door open. The bat cave awaited. Lights flicked on, followed by a hum as a computer fired up. It was a smart bat cave. Every girl should have a hidden room slash bat cave.

Ben closed the door behind us.

Two office chairs were near a large wooden desk. On the desk I had two computers, one desktop computer and a laptop. A glow from the big monitor told me the desktop computer was ready to go. I wrestled my keys from my pocket and unlocked a drawer in the desk. From the back of the drawer, I retrieved a smallish metal box and unlocked it with another key. Inside the box were two flash drives and one larger external drive. Ben placed the glass of water out of the way, but near me.

I plugged the larger drive into the computer's USB-C port, then settled into a chair. Ben took the chair on my left. A few mouse clicks, and one fingerprint later, and I was inside the eternal drive accessing the *Genesis* files via a link. Before I got very far, a coded communication alert popped up on the screen.

"Every time I access this drive," I said quietly. "Every single time."

"What does it say?" Ben asked.

"You may call me Ishmael," I said.

Ben grinned. "I can see that. What does it mean?"

"It means, standby." I've seen that message a lot since MacKinnon passed me access to *Genesis*.

I carried on and opened the main *Genesis* folder. I wasn't sure what I was looking for, but I was looking, nonetheless. It seemed reasonable that there would be something about Alex somewhere. I couldn't even begin to guess what codename would be applied to her. I opened the most recent reports from our analysts.

"How far back could this go?" Ben asked, watching the screen as the last few months of reports opened like a deck of cards.

"She's twenty, so, probably not that far," I replied. It made sense that she would be a fairly new asset if that's what she was. I had doubts. Everything in my being told me she was working for someone, but it wasn't anyone good. Not that *Genesis* had good or bad. It was more preferred agents and officers, than not. Our officers, gatherers, analysts, and strike teams were made up of many nationalities. You could throw a dart at a world map and probably hit a country who had someone inside *Genesis*. Our criteria were not political. It was for the good of the world as a whole. The thing with Genesis was that no person was a representative of their country as much as they were the world. It was hand-picked individuals. I just couldn't imagine who would pick Alex the Influencer for espionage, apart from Crockett, and I doubted he'd be doing if his bosses didn't push him. I scanned screeds of reports, quickly looking for anything that would tell me about Alex. I shut every report as soon as I'd finished. Skim reading is a skill and a bloody handy one.

"You're faster than me," Ben said. "Slow down a bit."

"Catch up," I replied, trying really hard to do as he asked and give him extra time to read the file I'd just finished.

I'd read the fifth report before the incoming message arrived in the corner of my screen. I grabbed a pen and a single small square of cartridge paper from the unlocked drawer, and a small book covered in red and emblazoned with a gold shield. It was no bigger than a passport. I wrote the message on a piece of paper and watched it vanish from the screen.

How dreadfully *Mission Impossible*. Donald would love it if he only knew.

"Let's see what we've got," I said, opening the red codebook and looking for the first word in the message. It didn't take me long to have the solution. "Hunting pack operational in Upper Hutt. Bone fides not established. Consider unfriendly. Commandment Eleven."

"We knew about the surveillance. Shame they don't know who is doing it," Ben said. "Thou shalt not get caught."

"How'd someone know I'd come in here and do my sneaky login thing?" I asked, not expecting an answer, because the answer was more surveillance. This time it was friendly and probably electronic and somewhere in my house. Sometimes I hate espionage. It's the occupation that never quits.

"Let's check the rest of the reports," Ben encouraged. "We can decide what to do about the elephant in the room later."

I nodded and put the codebook back where it belonged. The piece of paper was scrunched and dropped into the glass of water on the desk. It would be a soggy unreadable mess by the time we finished reading, then I'd toss it down the waste disposal in the kitchen. Two more reports flashed past my eyes. Or that's what it felt like. Finally, I saw something: the abbreviation for hyperthymesia. H-SAM.

"Ding, ding, ding, we have a winner," I said, pointing at the last paragraph on the screen in front of us.

We read in silence. The person with H-SAM was identified as Nephilim. Nephilim was a witness to murder. No one was concerned about that, except us. What concerned *Genesis* was that she had, at different times, had access to the desk and documents of two different embassy officials. One was Russian and the other, Chinese. Neither wanted her working for us, or for the other party. She gained access as a social media influencer, doing her job. I could see how attractive she might be to two super-powers needing to push their agenda in a less obvious way, and garner favour in the world. The war was going badly for Russia. China wasn't happy with the world's outcry and finger pointing over COVID. Those two countries sure needed their images re-vamped.

I skimmed the rest of the information. She'd taken several contracts to promote goods created in China and Russia over the course of the last few years. They were publicity campaigns run by various companies to bring each country into a more favourable light, worldwide. And our lovely Alex wore a very expensive coat that contained a tracker from someone with a Russian name.

"Interesting," I said, leaning back in my chair. "Her influencer status got her a lot of places she wouldn't have otherwise gotten."

"She must've known that as soon as anyone figured out she had H-SAM, she'd be in demand and also danger," Ben said. "Nephilim. What is she, a giant, a fallen angel, or half-human, half-angel like the ones in *Supernatural*?"

I laughed. "Interesting codename, for sure."

"What do we do with all this information?" Ben asked, pointing at the screen.

"Act accordingly. Which one of them do you think got to her first and convinced her to work with them?"

"Ah, the old chicken and egg conundrum."

"Flip a coin?" I opened another file hoping for more but there was nothing. "Not only do we have unfriendly surveillance, but we have an unfriendly protectee."

"So, we know there are two layers of surveillance, or at least two. There's no way Crockett is going to flip her with two powers already working her. They could team up, or maybe they already have and work her together."

I smiled at Ben. "So, you worked out Crockett's task then?"

"Stands to reason," he said. "I was asked to give it a try, but I've met her, and I don't think she's got what it takes."

It was harsh but probably true.

"Our Department of Defence are interested."

"Of course, they are. They may change their minds if they get a face-to-face with her."

"Okay, let's keep Crockett in the friendly camp because he's working for the Aussies, and I prefer them to the hostiles we're up against. We still don't know who is pulling the strings. It can't be both hostiles, surely?" It very well could be. It could even be a four-way thing with someone from *Genesis* and/or New Zealand involved.

Another communication popped up on my screen. I got another piece of cartridge paper and wrote the message down before it disappeared. Then I took out the codebook and wrote the deciphered message under the code.

Nephilim puppet-master codename or call sign: Whiskey Tango Foxtrot. Vodka drinker.

"Can you reply?" Ben asked.

"Nope. One way comms from whoever the new boss is."

"Do you have any idea who it is?"

"No. I think this time it'll remain that way. Look at the shit that went down with the MacKinnons. It's better if no one knows anything beyond their own field." And whoever the new boss is, they're watching or listening to me. That I didn't like, at all. I pulled another piece of paper from the drawer and wrote a note to Ben. My money was on them listening, not watching.

The note said: When this silliness is finished, I want your help to isolate the devices in my home and office. I doubt they would've stopped with home.

It's probably in my bedroom. That would mean they'd know when I opened the hidden door and was preparing to access the link.

Ben nodded. "I'm curious though. Aren't you?"

"Yep."

"A vodka drinker," Ben said. "We're looking at a Russian team then. That's who got to her first."

"Looks that way. And she was wearing a leather coat given to her by someone working for a Russian. As far as we know, the public relations person was not a Russian. Josef Baranov is a Russian name." I put the book away, ripped up the papers, dropped the pieces of paper into the glass and watched them soak up water.

"We need to work out if the Russians are the first layer of surveillance, or the second."

I smiled at him. "Makes no difference to how we play this. We have two different sets of people trying to get to her, and one of them got a tracker on her. At least that faction is occupied thinking Alex is north of Upper Hutt. There's a chance there is still some kind of contract in the air. I can't imagine anyone wants her wandering around with what she potentially knows."

"Let's find out what that is," Ben suggested. He picked up the glass.

"Sure, why not."

I shut everything down, locked the box in the drawer, and locked the drawer. Ben led the way from the room and through my wardrobe. I closed and locked the door, then moved my clothes back so it didn't look super obvious that someone had been in my wardrobe. There were no sounds of life in the house. I figured Nana and the *Cronies of Doom* were safe at the retirement village. Donald was probably asleep.

We walked through the house, not speaking. In the lounge I spotted Donald on the couch. He was watching something on his phone.

"Hey, we're off," I said.

He looked up and smiled. "What've you done with my husband?"

"He's working, he'll be back in half an hour or so. Ask Emily to stay here tonight. Nana get off okay?"

"Yes. She really is impossible."

Oh, I know. "I'll see you once I've wrapped up this case," I said, throwing him a smile. "I'm not angry at you. Just so you know."

Romeo ambled over and leaned on me. "Be good old boy. You're in charge." I gave his ears a rub. He went back to his bed.

"I'm glad you're not mad at me," Donald said, and blew me a kiss. "Be careful and send my hubby and Emily home."

"Will do."

"See you. Bye Ben!"

We waved. On our way through the kitchen to the stairs, Ben paused to pour the now fully dissolved paper down the sink and give the glass a rinse.

The night was quiet. Amazing. We walked in silence back to the park.

Chapter Twenty-two:

[Crockett: She's a bloody delight.]

I sat with Ginny and Alex at the table. A large cat that felt like a feather folded itself onto my knee. Birman aren't heavy; they're all fur and fluff. Alex had a kitten in her lap. The presence of cats appeared to calm her. That wasn't a bad thing. She didn't have a lot to say about anything of significance. You'd think with a mind like hers she'd have something juicy to impart. I fiddled with a placemat on the table.

Ginny reached across the table and touched my hand. "What's the best part of your occupation?"

"I'm tempted to say, it's that we don't need evidence. No one's going to court and no one's calling their lawyer. And good luck calling the police."

Alex eyes flashed at me. "Is that like a threat?"

"Should it be?"

"What is that supposed to mean?" She clawed at the placemat in front of her. "It sounded like a threat."

"It's just the way it is. Think of it as a public service announcement." The horror on her face made me laugh.

"Oh. My. God. Who are you people?" Alex shuffled her chair back, distancing herself from me as much as possible, while still sitting at the table.

"I'm joking. Lighten up."

Ginny chuckled. "Time for some bubbles, I think." She

stood slowly and eased herself into movement. "How long do you think Ben and Ronnie will be?"

"I couldn't say," I said. "I don't know how far they went." She had a chilled bottle of bubbly in her hand and was removing the foil. "Do you want a hand?"

"No thanks," she replied, and with a pop the bottle opened.

She rejoined us at the table. "Chin, chin," Ginny said and took a sip from her champagne glass. I raised my coffee cup.

"Why can't I have my phone?" Alex asked.

This again?

"Don't be a galah. You know it's because it's not safe for you to post photos and talk to people right now," I replied. "Put a sock in the phone talk, will ya."

"How would anyone find me here?"

I took a breath. "Your phone can be tracked. Data from within your photos can give away your location. You could accidentally tell someone where you are or use a name that leads them here." Or you could talk to the person in your draft folder and straight up tell them where you are. Blimey.

We knew someone put the tracker in the leather coat they wanted her to wear, and that it was probably the Russians. What about her trainers? What's-his-name the shoe guy. I hauled his name in. Nigel Scott.

"Those trainers you were wearing, where'd you get them?"

"From that guy's company. They wanted me to use

them in some promo work."

"And Jo's wearing them now, right?"

She nodded.

I got up and walked to the back door. From there I could watch Ginny and Alex while I made a call. I rang Art.

"Yo, you good?"

"Yep. We're loving having big ol' targets on our backs."

"Might be another tracker. Check Jo's shoes."

"Will do. I'll hit you back."

He hung up, and I rejoined the women at the table.

Ginny sipped more wine. "I know it's frustrating for you," she said to Alex. "But Crockett, Ben, and Ronnie are trying to keep you alive."

"What if I don't want to testify?"

I waited. I could tell Ginny had some wisdom to impart. "That would be your decision, Alex. But if you don't, someone will get away with murder. Is that what you want?"

"No. But I want this to end. I want to get back to my life."

And there was the real problem. It sounded like she hadn't fully comprehended that her life wouldn't be the same. For all she was a pain in the bum, she was also a kid. She'd had her life ripped out from under her. I could see her point of view, but it didn't help her or us at all.

The back door opened. Ben stepped in with a smile on his face. "We're back!"

Ronnie and Tom followed him in. I'd wondered where

Tom went. I'd heard his car leave about ten minutes earlier.

"All okay here?" Ronnie asked.

"Never better," I said. "What's it like out there?"

"Quiet for the moment," she replied. "We have some intel and a story about Nana." She pulled out a chair and took a seat. Tom and Ben went into the lounge and sat on a couch each. Tom scooped a cat up and plopped it in his lap.

My attention returned to Ronnie.

"Have you heard from Enzo?" I asked. "My bike okay?"

"Yes, and yes. He and Emily rode around the whole time we were gone. It was all quiet on the eastern, western, and northern fronts."

"Does that mean they've moved south trying to find us?" Alex asked.

Ronnie shrugged. "Not necessarily. They can't keep drones up indefinitely. And driving around hoping to catch us in the open isn't feasible either. They don't know where we went. Upper Hutt has a big land area."

That's why I liked it so much. It's a city that feels like a small town and there are a lot of places to hide. I had a feeling Ronnie liked it for a similar reason. You could spread yourself out in the Wellington Region.

"Quick word with you," I said to Ronnie.

"Sure." She followed me to the back door.

I kept my voice low as I said, "Could be another tracker - this time in the shoes. I've asked Art to get back to me."

Just like that my phone rang. I showed Ronnie the

screen. She nodded. I answered, "Art, what've you got?"

"A tracker."

"Wonder which came first, the coat or the shoes?"

"Now we know why we're so interesting to other people right now."

"Yeah."

I nodded at Ronnie. She whispered, "Make sure they're okay to keep this situation going. I'll let Steph and Jenn know there are two trackers." She moved into the laundry room and used her phone. By the time she'd finished, I was already back at the table.

Ronnie adjusted her position and looked at Alex for a split second. Alex reacted by glaring at Ronnie.

That wouldn't get her far.

"Hey, Alex, don't be a dick for no reason," I said quietly. "Costs you nothing to be nicer."

She sneered. "My life is ruined, and you want me to be nice about it? Not happening."

Ronnie's head nodded in tiny increments. "I get it. I do. You just want to get on with your life." She leaned her elbows on the table and interlocked her fingers. "To be honest, I just want get on with my life as well."

"Then I won't testify, and you can let me go." Alex started to stand, but Ginny placed a hand on her arm and shook her head. "You can't make me stay, if I want to go."

"You're right, Alex. No one can make you stay if you really want to go. You should think very carefully about leaving and what will happen if you do," Ginny said with a small smile. "The reason you're here is what?"

I liked Ginny.

Alex plonked herself down with a sulky expression stuck to her face. "Someone tried to shoot me this morning."

"Yes, I heard about that," Ginny replied. "Who saved you?"

Alex rolled her eyes and pointed to Ronnie. "I guess they all did, but Ronnie got me out of it. We met an old man who knew her Nana. Mr Alan Christiansen. He was nice and helped us." She wriggled her nose. "Then we ran down an alleyway and across the train track and down another alleyway before we found a street and ended up somewhere else. A big building."

"Do you know where that was?" Ronnie asked.

Alex shook her head. "I didn't see any signs." She spoke to Ginny, "Ronnie had a friend there, a man called Aaron."

I mouthed 'Aaron' to Ronnie who nodded.

Ginny sipped her wine, then placed the glass carefully on a coaster.

"I know Alan Christiansen," she said to Ronnie. "How did he look?"

"He looked well," Ronnie replied. "I forgot to mention I'd seen him to Nana."

"That's great," Alex interrupted us. "You all know everyone. Look at you and your full lives. Why can't I just walk away now and go back to my life?" She glared at Ronnie and Ginny.

"Who will protect you next time someone tries to kill

you?" Ginny asked.

Frown lines appeared on Alex's forehead. "If I don't testify why would anyone try and kill me."

"What do you think will happen?" I asked.

"I'll go back to doing the work I love, and the murderer will go free." She shrugged. "I don't care anymore."

"No, not exactly. There's other evidence. You are the only eyewitness, and you gave a written statement."

"So, then, they don't need me."

"They do. You were called to testify. Remember. I know you haven't forgotten the subpoena you were given by the police prosecutor."

That was the reason we had the babysitting gig. The 'get her to court alive then send her off to her new life' orders. The whole thing was bogus. I just couldn't prove it. Yet.

"But I'm a special witness and no one knows about my testimony anyway, so if I disappeared now, who would care?"

"There'd be a warrant out for your arrest within minutes. Also, you'd best hope that we or the police find you before the bad guys do," I said. "You'd be all by yourself out there."

She smiled sweetly. "I'm never by myself. I have over five million followers across various platforms. They'd help me."

Ronnie stood up and walked away. I didn't blame her. Alex was getting on my nerves. Ginny was the only one at the table who didn't look like she wanted to escape. Ronnie poured herself a glass of water and stood in the kitchen drinking it while looking out the window. I could see her reflection from where I sat. Dark night and bright kitchen equals good reflection from the windows. She finished the glass and returned to her chair. The four of us remained silent. No one wanted to touch the five million internet strangers thing. Ginny sipped her drink. I finished my coffee. Alex pouted. Ronnie gave off a vibe like she wanted to kill someone.

"You know what I've always wanted to be?" Ginny eventually said to all of us.

"No clue," I replied.

"A Nephilim."

Ronnie blinked slowly and looked at her. "Nephilim?"

Alex froze. Her eyes cast downward to the cat in her lap.

"Yes, not the biblical kind, but the half-human, half-angel sort from Supernatural. Did you watch that show?"

"I did," Ronnie said. "Can't say I've ever wanted to be anything but human, though."

"Me neither," I said. "I did want to be a firie when I was a kid."

"Firie?" Ginny queried.

"Fireman," Ronnie said. "Aussies try and make everything sound cute."

Ginny laughed. "Whatever floats their boats I guess."

"I'll be back in a minute," Ronnie said. She stood and went into the lounge. I watched her beckon to Ben, and then the pair of them sidled into the hallway and closed the door.

"What's her problem?" Alex asked.

"You," I replied, truthfully. "You're a pain in the bum. We're not exactly living our lives the way we want this weekend, or hadn't you noticed?"

"What does that mean? You're getting paid, aren't you?" Alex sniped.

"Not enough to put up with bullets and your complaining."

"That's not very nice," Alex replied.

"Did I hurt your feelings?"

"No."

Chapter Twenty-three:
[Ronnie: WYSIWYG]

"What's wrong?" Ben asked me, as I leaned on the wall halfway down the hallway.

"Ginny said she's always wanted to be a Nephilim."

"Pardon?"

"She wanted to be a Nephilim," I repeated.

"When? What?" Confusion crowded his features.

"Just before. She randomly changed the subject with that."

"What were you talking about?"

"Nothing to do with Nephilim. We were trying to get Alex to understand what would happen if she walked away now."

"She's still being painful then?"

"Yep."

"And Ginny wants to be a Nephilim. Great." Ben leaned next to me. "It's gotta be a coincidence. That's all."

"Of course, I mean she's not likely to be bugging my bedroom or whatever," I said with a grin. "She's never been to my house." I let that sit for a second. How could someone who had never been to my home get a bug in my bedroom versus someone who had? Who had access to my bedroom that would have that kind of knowledge and equipment? It was a short list: Ben, Enzo, Crockett, Jenn, Steph, and Emily. I mentally crossed Emily off the list she had the knowledge but not the memory. Steph and Jenn were next off the list. We were partners. Partners don't spy on each other.

"You all right?" Ben asked, interrupting my thoughts.

"Yes. It's weird, though, right?"

"Yes. It's weird, but I've known Ginny a very long time and she picks up on things, so maybe not so weird because it's her."

"Okay. I just felt I needed to tell you what was said." I straightened my back in readiness to move. "I know she's your friend, but have you ever considered a background check?"

Ben's eyes widened, a flash of 'what the fuck' crossed his face.

"Unlike some people I don't background check everyone in my life."

"Maybe you should."

Subject closed.

"How come you still have access to *Genesis*?" Ben asked, brushing a strand of hair off my face.

"I don't know." That was true. No one had removed my access. Maybe no one knew I had access, but that idea didn't track, because somebody sent me messages every time I logged in.

"And you don't know who is at the helm?"

"Nope.

"And you don't know who sent those messages?"

"No. No clue."

"Any thoughts?"

"Probably not Ginny, and I'm sure it's not Chandler," I said with a laugh. It was either laugh or shudder at the mention of the current head of New Zealand Security Intelligence Service. Chandler was a horrible person who hit on anything and everything with a pulse in the most revolting way possible. We'd all been on the end of that nonsense, and no one wanted a repeat performance. "I better get back in there. Do you think there is any point in moving tonight?"

"While it's quiet, it wouldn't hurt to move," he replied, and leant in to plant a warm kiss on my lips.

"Can you find us a new location. I'm sure Crockett won't mind if you get on with that," I said. "I'll go back and see what I can get out of Little Miss Pain-in-the-Arse."

Ben laughed. "I'll get back to you when I've got us somewhere."

"Thank you."

"No problem."

I sauntered into the dining room and found Alex deep in conversation with Ginny. They were talking about beauty products. Alex got plenty for free to try, and was imparting knowledge, and suggesting which products would be good for Ginny's skin type.

I waited a few minutes for the conversation to finish. Glancing at my watch every twenty seconds didn't help the time to go any faster. Ginny saw me and wrapped up the conversation with Alex. I threw her a smile. "Thank you."

"Not a problem. I'll leave you alone," Ginny said.

Before I could stop myself, I'd suggested she should stay. She rose slowly from her chair and picked up her now empty glass. "I need a refill. I might be back."

Crockett stood up. "Have fun," he said, "I need to move my legs." He stretched, then went to join Tom in the lounge.

"Just you and me then, Alex," I said, sitting across from her. "I'm sorry this happened to you, but it's time for you to start talking. I know you're working for the Russians. Give me a name."

"I don't know what you're talking about. I'm a social media influencer. I don't know any Russians, that I know of anyway."

"A qualifier. That makes me think you're being truthful." I rolled my eyes. "One hundred percent truthful. Everyone who's innocent uses qualifiers. That I know of, anyway."

Alex slapped her palms on the tabletop. "I haven't done anything wrong."

"Of course, you haven't ..." I said. "I just asked for a name. Your Russian friend has a name. Everyone has a name. I want to know what his or her name is."

"Could be they, you know. Not everyone uses his or her pronouns." She rolled her eyes. "Your generation is so rigid."

"Right then, tell me their name?"

"I don't *think* I know any Russians in person," she sniped. "Why would I tell you if I did?"

"Because you ungrateful little shit, we are trying to keep you safe," I said slowly and quietly.

"I'm the one whose life is fucked!"

That was the first time I'd heard her swear. Maybe I'd hit a nerve, or perhaps she thought flashing a bit of temper was the same as righteous indignation.

"Problem?"

"Yes, you. I don't want to talk to you. I like Crockett more."

I saw his head turn at the sound of his name in my peripheral vision. With the sweetest smile I could muster I said, "Sweetheart, your problem is not me. Your problem is whoever you sold your soul to." With two trackers, I had a feeling she'd sold it more than once.

"I didn't sell my soul ..."

"Sweetie, you sold yours, and the souls of all your future bloodlines."

"You don't know fucking anything."

Again, with the language.

"Then enlighten me. I'm all ears. Give me a name."

"I was working. PR stuff."

"And that means what exactly?"

"That I was working. I had an assignment to do. Companies sponsor me to showcase their products."

"Okay, I get that. What I don't get is how that relates to your Russian friend."

"It was just work."

"So, you do know a Russian."

"So what?"

"That leather coat you like so much. The four-thousand dollar one." She nodded. "Do you know what we found sewn into the hem?"

She shook her head. "Is it ruined? Did you ruin it? Oh. My. God. If I don't do the PR biz they'll want it back and if it's ruined I'll have to pay for it. It's a really expensive coat." Wide-eyed fear gripped her, then she forced it away. "What was in it?"

She'll be paying a lot more than she realises to the people who gave her the coat.

"A tracking device. A tiny little tracker. That told whoever was monitoring it, where you were every single minute of the day or night."

I watched the information sink in. At first, she looked surprised, then shocked, then ripples of fear surfaced before she found something to cling to.

"They are tracking the coat, not me. Wouldn't you track something that expensive?"

I smiled. "Let's say they are tracking the coat and have no interest in you beyond all the social media things you're going to do for them. How much were those sneakers you were wearing?"

"Probably around the two-hundred-and-fifty-dollar mark."

"Not coat expensive then. Okay, so try this on for size ... there was a second tracker in the shoes."

She swallowed hard. "I didn't get the shoes from the *Alexandrite*."

"I know."

"Why would they have a tracker?"

"Gee, let me think. Why would a pair of sneakers have a tracker in them?" I tapped the side of my head with my finger as I pretended to think about her shoes. "Oh, I know! Because someone wanted to know where you were."

"Nigel Scott's company sells shoes. He's not a Russian. He's a Kiwi shoe salesman."

"Okay. He's a shoe salesman who had something on his desk, that was written in code."

"Maybe he likes codes," Alex suggested.

"Maybe. Sure. I'll buy that, who doesn't love codes? Where are his shoes made?"

She shrugged. "I don't know. Or care. I just had to wear them and take photos. It's a new brand they're trying to promote."

I pulled my phone from my pocket and did a search on the shoe guy. Turned out he didn't own the company. He was the CEO. The company was owned by Chinese interests. They set it up in New Zealand and other parts of the world, competing with all the other sneaker manufacturing companies. The shoes were designed and made in China.

"The company the shoe guy works for is Chinese," I said, while I put my phone back in my pocket.

"How does that make any difference to me?"

Chinese. Russians. Coats. Shoes. Trackers.

"Come be part of the winning team," I said, smiling. "You probably won't get killed."

"That's your pitch? Lamest pitch ever."

"Not as lame as what you've done. Jumping into bed with the Russians and or the Chinese. How's that working for you, Zoomer?"

She pursed her lips and wrinkled her nose, then said, "I don't know what you're talking about."

"Be careful who you choose as a friend, Alex. Not everyone is who they say they are."

"I've got friends everywhere in the world. So, what if some are Russian or Chinese or American or Canadian or whatever?"

"How many of them have you known since college?"

She looked confused for a second. "I left two years ago. I still know people. Lots of people. I was popular." Her lips twitched into half a smile.

"Were you really?"

"People like me. I'm pretty."

"That's all it takes on the internet, I suppose."

"They liked me at school too. I am a nice person."

"And you got excellence's on every test, didn't you. Without even trying?"

She shrugged. "Yes. Why?"

"Did anyone know about your special brain?"

She looked at her hands and picked at a manicured nail. "They thought I was weird." A tear trickled down her face. She brushed it away. "I told my best friend." Another tear ran down her face. "She was supposed to be my best friend. She told someone. Then everyone knew. They were always asking me what happened on certain dates,

223

trying to trip me up and prove I was lying."

"That must've been rough."

She wiped her eyes with her fingers. "I got through it."

"You don't tell people, do you?"

"No."

"Your fans?"

She laughed, but it was a sad laugh. "They like me. I'm not going to ruin that."

"And if your involvement with the trial makes it to the media?"

"You didn't notice the name on my social account you saw on my phone, did you?"

I shook my head. "No one seems to use their own name, and that's smart, or there are a lot of kids called XOXO-whatever or Blueberry Pop-Tart."

"Mine's a name, just not a real one."

"What name do you use?"

"Alexandra Fisher."

Alexandra Fowler. Alexandra Fisher," I said. "Nice work. Do any people from your school days follow you?"

"I don't know. No one has reached out asking if I'm that Alexandra."

"Okay."

"I don't know what will happen if they release my real name."

"Fingers crossed they get name suppression."

"Can I ask for it?"

"Yes. Can you help me?"

"Do what?" Alex asked, rubbing her face.

"Keep you safe."

"How?"

"By staying. By talking. By being just a little grateful that we are willing to take a bullet for you."

"I'll try."

"Okay. That'll do." It was more cooperation than we'd had so far. It was still going to be a long few days, but perhaps not impossible. "Let's start a new chapter without any scary plot twists."

"What happens now?"

"We're going to move again soon."

"I really like it here. Can't we stay?"

"It's nice, right?"

She nodded.

"I wish we could, but we need to move on. The longer we stay, the more danger Ginny and Tom could be in. And we don't want to endanger them."

"They're really nice people. I guess I won't see them again, will I?"

"Probably not." I sized her up. Everything had changed during our conversation. She wasn't prickly anymore. She was sad. I saw her in a slightly different light. She wasn't a brat; she was trapped behind the walls she'd put up to stop her secret escaping. And that made me wonder how the Russians and Chinese knew about her mind.

Someone must've seen something, or someone must've talked, and they went looking. It'd be worth the effort to recruit someone with H-SAM. How did it happen?

"Alex?"

"Yes." She made eye contact with me. "You came forward as a witness to the murder?"

She nodded. "I did. I rang 111."

"How'd the police know about your memory?"

"I described what'd I'd seen in the room, and they questioned me about the placement of things. When my account matched the photos they'd taken, they were suspicious. My recall was perfect." She shrugged. "It's always perfect. I can't forget anything. I can't forget seeing that man stabbing Ashley. I saw it in a mirror. I was in the bathroom getting a glass of water, and the door wasn't shut properly. I saw it. He stabbed her eight times."

Not being able to forget anything had the ability to be a nightmare. I didn't need to know about the murder, but curiosity is a real thing in my world. It can also lead to death.

"You knew Ashley?"

She nodded. "We were collaborating on a project. It was the second time I'd met with her."

Collaborating. Good choice of words.

"What was the project?"

"Oh, she is an artist." She shook her head. "Was an artist. Her family emigrated from Hong Kong when Ashley was very young. Her artwork depicted their lives as immigrants as they made a new life in New Zealand. The rich blend of cultures and how that looked from her point of view."

"What sort of artist?"

"Fibre. She used a lot of silk, beads, feathers, and embroidery. Some of her wall hangings were over two metres long. Most were about a metre and a half square."

"They sound amazing."

"They are. Nigel Scott the shoe salesman had one of her pieces on his office wall. Lots of people really liked her work. She had an exhibition that ran for a week, and I was there on the opening night, and on the third night. Doing the stuff you seem to have no patience for." She smiled. "I know all the selfie taking and live feeds aren't your thing."

"I think that's your generations thing, not so much mine," I replied. "So, it was getting the word out about the exhibition and exposure. That's what you did?"

"Yes. She was really happy with the work we did on that project. She sold everything. Wasn't a piece left at the end of the week."

"I imagine it paid well," I said, smiling. "It's not my thing, but you clearly have a passion for it. Good on you."

"And then we had a meeting about a new project later in the year. We were almost finished when I went to get more water, and the man came in."

"This is going to sound strange, but did police ask you about anything you might've seen on Ashley's desk?"

"No."

"Was the man known to Ashley?"

"Yes. She said his name. She said, Henry."

"What did he look like?"

"Asian. Dark straight hair. Brown eyes. He was thin and taller than Ashley but not tall. She was one-hundred

and sixty-five centimetres. He looked this much taller."
She held her thumb and index finger about three centimetres apart.

"Under one-seventy?"

"Yes."

"He didn't take anything?"

She shook her head. "He looked around her desk
though. I could see him before I hid behind the door."

"He left, she died. No one asked about her desk?"

She shook her head, her eyes met mine. "Do you have
a pen and paper?"

I pulled my notebook and pen from my pocket and
handed it to her. "There was a notepad on her desk with
three words written in messy writing."

Alex handed me the notebook once she'd written on it.
"It was written like that, messy, and rushed."

Sierra Papa Yankee.

I wondered if Henry wrote it, or Ashley wrote it.

"You ever seen Whiskey Tango Foxtrot written on anything in Ashley's office, or any other place?"

"Not there, but I was in a hotel meeting with two
clients, and one of them wrote Whiskey on some paper.
Like he was reminding himself to get some."

"Maybe he was," I said. "No mention of Tango or Foxtrot?"

"No. Why?"

"Just something I wanted to check. To clarify, Whiskey
Tango or Whiskey Tango Foxtrot mean nothing to you?"

"Nah, not a thing."

Interesting. If the puppet master's codename or handle was Whiskey Tango Foxtrot, she didn't know it. Things felt calmer with Alex being open and chatty.

Ginny touched my shoulder as she came back into the room.

"It's lovely seeing you two getting on," she said. "This is better, isn't it Alex?" She moved around and sat next to Alex again.

"Yes. It's better," Alex replied. "I didn't mean to be such a mega brat."

"I know that now." I wasn't having to force a smile. I probably didn't look like a serial killer trying to lure another victim at that moment. I hoped I didn't anyway.

"I think the men are making plans to move," Ginny said. "I've very much enjoyed your company. You are welcome anytime, Ronnie, anytime. And you, Alex."

"Thank you," Alex said. "When I've testified, I have to go live a different life somewhere else. But I won't forget your kindness."

That was true. She wouldn't forget.

Funny how many people say things like that, but we do forget because we're not Alex with a super-duper memory. Nana popped into my mind. That woman was going to be the death of me. Or maybe Donald. Yes. Donald. She'd be the death of him. They're almost the same person. How did that even happen? I could see it in Donald. What if he could see it in me? Oh. My. God. Am I becoming Nana?

I shovelled those thoughts aside. When my focus returned, I found Ginny and Alex watching me.

"Hello? Can I help?"

"You all right?" Ginny asked.

"Yeesss?"

"Is your Nana causing some problems?" she asked.

"Why?"

"Because you just asked if you were becoming Nana."

"Oh. That was supposed to be in my head. Sorry. Didn't mean to say actual words."

Ginny and Alex giggled.

"I'm going to start calling you Nana," Alex said between bouts of giggling.

"Please don't." Nope. No. No. No. How did that even come out of my mouth?

Crockett sauntered into view. "What's so funny over here?"

"Nothing," I said. "Absolutely nothing." I pointed at Ginny and Alex. "Clearly they've had too much giggle juice."

Crockett's eyebrows rose. "Okay then. Time to pack it up, ladies, we have a late-night check in."

"Great," I replied. "All ready. Let's go." I jumped to my feet.

"Careful, there, Nana, you might break a hip," Alex said with an almost straight face, then lost it with a peal of laughter.

I pointed two fingers at my eyes, then hers. "Always."

Renewed bouts of laughter sprang from her, fully loaded with tears. Ginny joined in and spluttered, "I'm going to wet myself!"

"You'll both need Depends at this rate," I said. "Who're the Nana's, now?"

Crockett let the laughter go on for a little bit then reminded us we were moving.

Sometimes all you need is a good laugh. That's it. It changes your perception of the world. Alex reeled in her borderline hysteria until it was little more than random hiccups and giggles. She avoided looking at Ginny. As did I. I knew we'd all be in hysterics if we didn't.

Chapter Twenty-four:
[Ronnie: On our own again]

We left Enzo's Harley in Tom's garage and our car in his carport. Instead of heading to my garage in Naenae and using one of the fleet cars, or two of the fleet cars, as Crockett and I had considered earlier, we were in Tom's Mercedes SUV.

Should anyone have spotted that during our uneventful trip home, they would've only seen Tom and Ginny, and then Tom by himself. There was no way to trace us to Tom. I was surprised he let Ben drive, and that they let us borrow their very fancy SUV.

I rang Enzo.

"Hey, you can call it a night," I said when he answered. I knew he was still riding around by the engine sound and traffic noise.

"Good. I'll drop Emily home, then head home myself."

"Keep Emily with you tonight. Thank you."

"Yeah, sure, of course. No problem. You all right?"

"Yes. Donald needs to debrief ... there was a situation with the *Cronies of Doom*."

I heard him sigh over his mic. "They're impossible, and I think they're getting worse."

"Yes, they are. Your bike is safe by the way. We've got it well taken care of. Can you keep using Crockett's and dress like him for the rest of the weekend?"

"You want Emily to continue to be you?"

"That'd be a good idea. Maybe go for a ride tomorrow."

"Will do. Take it easy. Tell Crockett hey."

I hung up. Crockett twisted around in the front passenger seat to see me. "My bike's okay, right?"

"I'd say so. Do you mind that I let him keep riding it?"

"No, I guess not. It's not the end of the world."

"You sure?"

"I fucking hate it," he grumbled. "It's not the end of the world, but."

I left that alone and peered through the tinted passenger window. No one had told me where we were going, just that we were leaving. I knew why. Tom, Ginny, and Alex didn't need to know. By the look of it we were going to Lower Hutt. There were plenty of motels there to choose from and they must've got one to agree to a very late check-in. Money talks, so I guess they pulled a decent amount from our budget to make that happen. It was just over an hour of doubling back and changing directions before Ben parked in front of a motel reception on Pharayzn Street. It looked quite nice with a gabled roof and brick work. He and Crockett went into the reception.

Moments later they were back with a key card and a very small bottle of milk. The lights inside the reception turned off, plunging the area into darkness. The 'No Vacancy' sign flickered, then shone red into the night.

Ben drove through an arch and into a courtyard, then pulled into a park outside a motel unit. We climbed out of the car and grabbed our bags.

The first thing I noticed was the lack of cars. There were no cars parked in front of any of the units.

"No vacancy but no cars," I said.

"This way," Ben said, leading us back four units. "This is us."

He opened the door.

I beckoned to Ben. "Let's make some hot chocolate." I had questions. He followed me to the tiny kitchenette. I filled the jug. "This place seems deserted."

"It is. We gave him enough cash to make it worth his while to give us a unit for the night. It's closed for renovations."

"Perfect."

Five minutes later we were sitting around in the two-bedroom motel unit drinking hot chocolate.

"This slaps," Alex said, taking another sip of her drink.

Ben and Crockett frowned at each other for a split second, then Ben spoke, "I'm sorry, I think I misheard. Slaps?"

"Oh my God, you are so old." Alex took another sip. "This slaps means, this is good."

"I must have misheard," Ben said. "Did you actually say the hot chocolate is all right?"

Alex smiled. "Yes."

I grinned. "We've turned over a fresh page. Welcome to Alex two point oh."

Crockett's deep laugh rumbled. "Nice to meet you new-Alex."

"Nice to meet you as well," Alex said, between sips of

her hot chocolate.

I let her drink her drink while it was hot. It gave me time to think.

Once she was settled in the bedroom she and I would share, I went back to the table in the main room to talk to Ben and Crockett.

A few things were bugging me.

"I've got concerns," I said as I took a seat. I reached for my cup and found it was empty.

"Spill," Ben said.

"First ... what do we know about Trisha Perkins the manager?"

Ben and Crockett looked at each other; they shook their heads. Ben started to speak, then stopped.

"That much. Right, I think we need to find out a bit more about her."

"Fair call," Crockett said.

"Let's dig deep into Perkins," I said. "Something is not adding up here."

"About the murder?" Crockett asked. "Because I have a gut rumble that says it isn't what we think it is, or what Alex thinks it is."

"Might just be gas," Ben replied.

Crockett grinned. "You'll be first to know. We're bunking in the same room."

"Think I'll take the couch," Ben said.

"Chicken?"

He nodded. "Hell yes, I am."

I knocked on the table. "Sorry to break up your fun

time, but where exactly did this job come from, Crockett?"

This time I wasn't contacted directly, Crockett was. That was not quite true, though. I did get a quiet heads-up. And Crockett brought us in as a team under my company name, *Wherefore Art Thou*. Steph, Jenn, and I are partners in the firm. Ben and Crockett have worked with me on various agency jobs in the past. We all work well together and are starting to develop a shorthand of sorts. We're the freaking Dream Team.

Crockett drained his cup and placed it on a coaster on the table. "It was a contact that came via my boss. I was told as much as you. In the notes, it said the police prosecutor reached out to the ASIO for help."

"Not police ..." Ben let that comment hit the table.

"No, and I get how strange it is, believe me."

"When does that even happen? It's a murder trial, police handle those. I didn't even know you could have an outside agency involved," I said.

"Then the police, or whoever it was, wanted us all involved, but went through my boss," Crockett said.

"Sounds fishy." I hadn't heard of it happening like that before, but then, I don't swim in the police pond so maybe that's what they do now. It didn't feel right, at all.

"My initial reaction involved putting on waders," Crockett said. "But I also thought, hey, they're paying well, and how hard can it be to keep a kid under wraps for a couple of days?"

"And yet, here we are in the middle of some shit," I

replied. "Okay, so the prosecutor went to the Aussies to keep Alex safe and deliver her to court. Clearly had no faith in police being able to keep her safe. That's weird. They're bloody good at what they do." That much I did know.

Crockett nodded.

"Is she really going into witness protection?" Ben asked.

"You read the brief as well as I did," Crockett said. "That's what we were told. What's the next thing causing that look on your face, Ronnie?"

I didn't know there was a look.

"The murder didn't happen like we were told. And we shouldn't have been told anything about it. But there it was in the brief. Vivian Street outside the offices of that shoe guy. A blitz killing, apparently."

"That's what they wrote," Crockett confirmed. "That, and they were worried about two gangs taking our special Alex out."

"Except, Crockett, that's not what happened. According to Alex, the murder happened inside the offices of artist Ashley Chu. Inside. Not on the street. Not on Vivian Street and nothing to do with her being at that building. It was some guy that Ashley called Henry. He stabbed her eight times. She bled out while Alex was hiding in the bathroom. She called police."

"Was he a gang associate?"

"Probably not the ones we were warned about if he was. He was Asian."

"Why lie?" Ben asked.

"Why did Ashley die?" I retaliated. "Alex dialled 111. Police had to be involved. There is a record of all 111 calls. How do you circumvent that?"

No one spoke for nearly a minute.

"Is Alex going into witness protection?" Ben asked. "Or is Alex expendable?"

I shook my head. "She's not going into witness protection. She's been recruited. I'm pretty sure that she's being wooed by two powers. She already working for whoever Nigel Scott is a frontman for, and by the way the shoe company isn't his, it's owned by the Chinese. He's just the New Zealand CEO. So, there's a little bit of gossip for you, and she's probably working for the Russians as well."

Silence fell.

"And, the kicker, I don't think she really grasps how bad this is or that these people aren't hiring her for her pretty face and her social media skills."

"What else?" Crockett asked.

"You'll love it," I said with a smile. "She was quizzing Ginny about me and Ben. She asked if Ginny had heard anyone mention *Genesis*."

"And?"

"And ... the puppet master is a Russian they're calling Whiskey Tango Foxtrot." I stood up with my cup in my hand. "I need another drink." That codename pretty much said it all.

"Jesus, Ronnie, how do you know that?" Crockett moved his cup and coaster.

"I just do. No questions about how I know shit."

"About how you know shit, Ronnie, can you use your woo-woo yet, or is this still the wrong kind of situation?" Crockett asked.

I filled the jug.

"I find people," I said, rejoining the boys at the table. "It's not much good for whatever the hell is going on here."

"Could you find the Perkins woman?" he asked.

"Yes. But we could also find her by asking Alex where her office is, couldn't we?"

Ben placed his phone on the table. I didn't notice he was using it until then. He raised his face until his eyes met mine. "I found her contact details on Alex's phone, but she's not responding."

"It's the middle of the night. She's probably smart enough to leave her phone in another room when she sleeps," I suggested.

"Or ...," Ben said.

Frown lines dug into Crockett's forehead. "This doesn't have anything to do with police, does it? Did you recognise the name of the prosecutor?"

"I don't think this is at all police related, and no, I didn't but I don't know everyone."

Ben picked up his phone again and twenty seconds later he showed us the court docket for Monday at the Supreme Court. "There's nothing here. No murder trial."

Now why would someone risk us checking the Monday docket and finding out there was no murder trial set down. Not a continuation. Not a trial in the early stages. Nothing.

"We've been set up," I said. "Why hire two spies and a former spy to keep Alex out of the way?"

Crockett's forehead lines dug in so deep I worried they were permanent. "Because if they used anyone else and it looked like Alex had vanished, then you'd be asked to find her."

Quite possibly.

"Where's the paperwork?" I asked, nudging Crockett's arm with my elbow. "I want a name and I want it now."

"What are you thinking?" Ben asked.

"Same as you," I replied.

Nothing to do with police or a trial.

"What is he thinking?" Crockett asked, as he rummaged in his bag. He looked up expectantly for a second, then carried on trying to find whatever he was looking for.

"That this is absolutely nothing to do with a trial or witness protection."

He stopped moving and straightened up.

"*Genesis?*"

Interesting that Crockett went there.

"Why do you say that?" Ben asked.

"Who else has the reach? Who else could re-route a 111 call and make all this happen?"

I smiled at him. "Really?"

Crockett grinned and shrugged. "Yeah, I know, any bad guy with tech smarts could do it."

"Why would *Genesis* want Ashley Chu killed?" I asked.

"I don't know. But someone fed us bs, and nothing makes much sense," he said.

"*Genesis* isn't behind this, but I don't think it's a million miles away from it either," I said.

He threw a manilla folder onto the table and zipped up his bag. "You know a lot about *Genesis*."

I thumbed through the contents of the folder, checking the information was what I remembered. It was. It definitely said she witnessed a murder on Vivian Street and that the accused was a gang associate. No mention of Alex having a manager. No mention of anything except the murder, the trial date and time, and that we were to deliver her to the courtroom, stay with her, and eventually put her on an airplane to her new life. On the page containing a headshot, and a brief overview of Alex, it said she was a social media influencer and had what is known as hyperthymesia. At no point was there mention of her working with anyone or being recruited by anyone.

Straightforward protection gig. I felt a smirk tweak the edges of my mouth. Nothing is ever straightforward when people are involved.

"So, this is a bunch of crap," I said, and closed the folder.

"We were supposed to wait with her at the courthouse, yes?" Ben said.

"Yep."

"Wait for what?"

"No idea, but we're not going to do that," I replied.

"Waiting for something that isn't on the docket smacks of a trap."

"Inside the courthouse, where no one is armed and there are cops everywhere," Crockett said, slowly. "That's one ballsy trap."

"Exactly," I said. "Who would see it coming?"

He nodded. "And the target is Alex?"

"Perhaps it's bigger than that. Think about it ... the three of us are there with Alex," I said.

"Convenient way to knock us off," Crockett said. "It could look like the target was Alex and we were collateral damage."

"So, what do you think?" Ben asked. "Want to try and find this manager, the Perkins woman?"

"I think we should. Won't hurt," I said. "Do we have a map? Because short of waking Alex, the only way to be sure where she is, might be using my skills."

"Tom told me there was a street map in the glovebox," Ben said. "I'll get it."

He grabbed the fob and hurried out the door into the night. Less than a minute later he was back with a folded map in his hand.

I unfastened the silver chain around my neck. It carried a pendulum; a quartz point set in silver. Fastening it in front of me so the quartz couldn't fall off, I took a breath and studied the map. It was a street map of Lower Hutt.

"What's on the other side?"

Ben flipped it over. Upper Hutt.

"There wasn't a regional map?"

He shook his head. "Just this one."

"Fingers crossed she's somewhere here then." I filled my mind with images of flowers and butterflies. It's my way of creating a calm space to work when I can't access my dedicated dowsing room. "Where does Alex live?"

Ben and Crockett looked blankly at each other.

"Does it matter?" Ben asked.

"Probably not," I replied. "Right, let's see what I can find."

In my mind I called the corners and asked for protection while I dowsed and to be shown the truth. Not a step worth skipping. Spirit is known to have a sense of humour, and sometimes, just be a right twit.

I held the pendulum over the map of Upper Hutt, letting it slip through my fingers until there was about fifteen centimetres of chain hanging, gripped by my thumb and forefinger.

It hung dead straight.

"Show me yes," I said, quietly.

The pendulum swung in fast clockwise circles.

"Stop."

It stopped moving and hung still.

"Show me no."

The pendulum tugged at my fingers as it swung in wide circles, anticlockwise. Okay. I was ready. I thought about Trisha Perkins. Concentrating on her name. That's all I had to use. Slowly, I moved my hand back and forth across the map, pausing regularly to allow the pendulum to pick up vibrations. Nothing. A lot of nothing. I reached the edge of the map.

"Can you turn it over?" I asked Ben.

He did as I asked. I started the process again, slowly moving across the Lower Hutt map until I felt the direction of the pendulum change to big wide clockwise circles.

"Show me where," I said.

The circles spun tighter and smaller until the pendulum stopped dead. I followed the point to a set of shops across the road from Countdown on High Street, around the 300 mark. "Thank you," I said and let the pendulum hang. I moved my hand and encouraged the pendulum to keep working. When the whole map was clear I took it back to the place it wanted to be. It was a firm yes to the question, is Trisha Perkins there? I let the chain slip through my fingers until the pendulum touched the map then let the chain go completely and watched. The quartz rolled until the point was across the road from the Countdown Supermarket.

Ben handed me a pen. I lifted the pendulum and drew a circle where it was.

"There," I said. "I think there is a multi-storey building about there. Maybe a COVID vaccination clinic." If I was remembering correctly.

"That's where we go, first thing tomorrow. See if we can't find this Trisha Perkins and have a talk," Crockett said. He patted my back lightly. "Good work. I don't get how that woo-woo of yours works, but it's interesting watching it all happen."

"Cheers. I think," I replied, then thanked spirit and put the necklace back on. Ben wrote the potential address in a notebook he always carried and then folded up the map.

We had a starting point. I was keen to check with Alex in the morning to see if that's where she met with Trisha Perkins. No doubt she'd require an office. Managers tended to have offices.

"Can anyone do that?" Crockett asked waving his finger in the air.

"I don't know," I said. "Maybe? They used to find underground water by dowsing with small branches from willow trees. This is just that, but not water, and not willow." I grinned at him. "It's completely different, but also not."

"When this is done, can you help me?"

"Sure," I said. "I'll help you find something that works for you as a pendulum and show you what you need to know."

"Thank you," Crockett said with a small smile. "What about you, Ben?"

Ben shook his head. "No. Can't say I've ever wanted to try."

"Scared?"

He chuckled.

Chapter Twenty-five:

[Ronnie: What happened?]

"Ronnie!" Crockett's voice rang out. "Ronnie!"

I could hear him calling as he moved through the room.

"Ronnie! Sound off!"

"Here," I yelled under a pile of whatever was on me. Maybe I didn't yell, and I imagined I did? The air felt thick and dusty. My mouth was dry. Was it an earthquake?

"Ronnie. Ben. Sound off!"

Crockett's voice sounded raw. There was an edge I hadn't heard before. I pushed my foot as far as I could. Something moved. I tried bending my leg to get more power. My right arm was trapped. I couldn't roll or lift my head. What on earth happened? Crockett's voice rang out louder now. I jammed my foot into whatever was trapping me. Movement followed.

I tried my voice again. "Crockett, I'm here."

Weight shifted. Dust-filtered light tumbled over my face. A shadow fell. Everything shifted. Hands reached in and lifted me from my dark, dirty prison.

"You in one piece?" Crockett asked as he set me on my feet. His eyes scanned me. His hands rested on my shoulders. Blue eyes looked questioningly into mine. A smear of blood across his face was the only sign of damage.

"I think so. You?"

He nodded. "Let's find Ben."

"Alex?"

He shook his head slightly. "I don't know."

I looked around the disaster zone that was formerly a motel unit. Dust, broken furniture, bricks, and general mess. Oddly the wall mounted television was undamaged and still on. No sign of the remote, or of Ben or Alex.

"You were where before this chaos?" Crockett asked.

"Sitting at the table." I looked around. "I'd just made coffee and was going to wake everyone up. Where is the table?"

He pointed to a piece of chrome. "That looks like part of a chair. I think the table was all around you, and also a dresser?"

"That sounds right. There was a dresser fairly close to the table."

"Where was Ben?"

"Bathroom. He was up."

We picked our way across the room to a broken door. "Ben!" I called, but it wasn't more than a rasp. My voice was failing me. I wiped dirt off my face with my sleeve. A moan from behind the smashed bathroom door, indicated Ben.

Crockett shoved his way through the wreckage of the door, and room. "Ben?"

"Yeah," he said.

Ben was sitting, leaning against the shower door. A

river of blood ran down the side of his head.

"You're hurt," I said, looking around for something to hold on the wound. "Thankfully you have your pants on."

I stepped over his legs and found a flannel in the basin. I handed it to him and stepped back. Crockett stopped me moving.

"There's blood on your back," he said.

I wriggled my back, side to side. "Feels fine. Might be coffee?"

"There's blood, Ronnie," Ben said, while pressing the flannel to the side of his head.

"I'll live. Where is Alex?" I shrugged off his concern. Surely, if there was a wound, I'd feel it, and I didn't. I was pretty sure it was coffee. I had a cup in front of me when whatever occurred. "And what happened?"

"I don't know where Alex is. I saw headlights and re-alised they were getting bigger and brighter. I dove to the ground right before the place imploded," Crockett said. We all stared at the gaping hole where a wall and door used to be. "Whatever crashed through that was big."

Not an earthquake then.

"Truck big," Ben added. "Did you see it?"

"No. I did see two sets of headlights. Next thing I knew, I was face down on the ground as far from what I thought the entry point was, as I could get," Crockett replied.

Fair enough.

"You yelled move. I think I remember that," I said.

Crockett nodded. "I think I did."

"Shouldn't there be fire engines and general mayhem outside by now?" I couldn't see flashing lights or hear sirens.

"Yeah. You'd think at five in the morning they wouldn't be busy," Ben replied. He was on his feet, still holding the flannel to his head. Blood spread from under his fingers as it soaked into the cloth.

"I hadn't woken Alex up yet. She was probably still in bed."

Alex was definitely in the bedroom when I got up. She was still asleep. I climbed over bits of furniture to the bedroom door. Ours was intact. The boys' door was matchsticks. The way the truck came through it, pushed crap which included a divan bed, couch, and chairs into the back of the main room. Some of it piled up against the remaining bedroom door and some of it smashed the other door to pieces. I pulled things out of the way and tossed them behind me.

A voice outside made its way to the massive hole. "Anyone hurt?"

I looked over my shoulder and saw Crockett shove debris aside toward the clear space in front of the massive hole. "Cuts and scrapes," he said. "Could do with a hand getting a path cleared."

I concentrated on the door in front of me. Ben's hand came into view. "You should sit somewhere," I said.

"Later," he replied. "Let's get this open."

I tried the handle. It moved but the door didn't.

"Push," Ben said. "Not pull."

Bloody hell. I tried again. The door opened. "Alex?" I peered into the dim room. The curtains were closed. I felt the wall by the door for a light switch. I pressed the switch down hoping we still had power. The light illuminated the room. "Alex!"

She wasn't in her bed, but the room was exactly how I'd left it to go make coffee at dawn. Wardrobe. I crossed the floor and opened the wardrobe. "Alex?"

Crouched at the bottom behind spare pillows, that were once on the top shelf, was Alex.

"You good down there?"

"Was it an earthquake? Everything shook."

I shook my head. "Not an earthquake."

"Someone drove a truck into the motel unit."

"An accident?"

"I don't think so. Come out of there. Get dressed, wear something with a hood, and pull it up before you come out of this room. Don't forget to grab your bag. We'll be moving as soon as."

"I heard someone calling out, so I hid."

"Good thinking, but it was probably Crockett trying to find us."

She nodded and stood up. "I'll get dressed. Will you wait for me?"

"I'll be right outside the door with Ben."

Ben was standing in the doorway. He heard, so he moved back into the disaster zone. I couldn't hear more voices out there but there were sirens in the distance. We needed to get Alex away from the motel before the three-ring circus arrived, and the questions started. Giving statements wasn't a great idea. Having her on display wasn't a great idea. The cold early morning air added an extra chill to my bones. We also needed to find anything that could be used to identify us. Somewhere under the mess was my jacket.

"You can't see my jacket, can you?" I asked Ben.

"Honestly, nothing looks like anything anymore," he replied. The flannel in his hand was red with his blood. There was so much blood that I could smell it.

"Stay here," I said and picked my way back to the bathroom. I knew there were more flannels on the vanity unit. I found two more and carefully made my way back to him. "Here." I folded a flannel into a smaller square and handed it to him. "Show me."

He lifted the sodden flannel. The wound was about twenty millimetres long and the middle gaped. He needed stitches. "Press the new flannel on that. We're going to have to get you medical care." I took the soaked flannel back to the bathroom and ran it under cold water. Nana would approve. But looking around at the chaos, there wasn't a lot of point. I guess rinsing the blood away was better than leaving a potential biohazard amongst the destruction.

"Ronnie, we're ready," Ben said. I joined him and Alex.

Crockett had cleared a path to the hole. The owner of the voice I'd heard was gone. There were no flashing lights. I could hear sirens winding through the air and coming closer.

"Time to get out of here," Crockett said.

Alex handed me my bag. "Thank you," I said and slung it over my shoulder. "Pull that hood over your face a bit more."

She tugged the front until it almost covered her eyes. I scanned Ben. There was blood all over his clothes. Not ideal. From where I stood, I tried to picture where everything used to be. My jacket was on the back of a chair. Ben's was lying over the arm of the couch. I tracked the path of the truck and hoping to see something that looked like our jackets. About a metre from where I stood I saw black.

"Wait a minute." I climbed over debris, maybe an armchair, and grabbed hold of the black. It was leather. It was my sleeve. I pulled until it came free. With a triumphant, "Ta da!" I shook the dust off, and dropped my bag so I could put the jacket on.

"Good work," Ben said.

"I'm not done." I hoisted my bag back onto my shoulder and decided that the position of my jacket meant that Ben's was maybe a metre further in. I moved carefully, kicking things out of my way that I couldn't pick up and move. "What colour jacket were you wearing?"

"My brown leather one," he replied. "Leave it. I probably needed a new one anyway."

Nope. I loved him in that jacket. Also, it would have his fingerprints and DNA on it.

Brown. Look for brown. I pushed a piece of broken couch with my foot. Bingo.

I bent down and yanked the jacket out from under the broken back of the couch. Watching my footing, I moved back to Ben and waved the jacket at him. Dust fell in clouds.

I held the flannel against his head while he struggled into the jacket. That looked better. At least no one could see the blood on his clothes.

The four of us walked out without looking back and made our way to Tom's car. Thankfully it was fine. Ben had parked it four spaces away from the unit. Had it been in front it would've ended up inside and at least one of us would be jammed underneath it now or splattered all over the main room.

We got in the car without speaking to anyone. Ben fished the fob from his jeans pocket. Crockett drove. "I need a direction."

"Hutt Hospital," I said. "Ben needs stitches."

He indicated left. Behind us, heading for the motel, I saw police cars with flashing red and blue lights. My dad called them party lights.

"Who did that?" Alex asked, inclining her head the way we'd come. "What smashed into the motel? Why would anyone do that?"

"That's three questions," I replied. "We don't know who. As for what, we think it was a truck of some sort. The why is a bit tricky." I scanned her face to try and get a read on how she was feeling before I proceeded. "Could be that the person hoped to kill us all, or just you, or force us to move, or it was a warning to let us know they can find us anywhere. Which isn't quite true because they did not find us at Tom and Ginny's."

And that told me no one was carrying a GPS tracker. By no one, I meant Alex the Influencer, and maybe Crockett.

Ben grumbled.

I thought about the destruction.

"Your motel owner will get his reno without having to shell out," I said keeping my voice even. "And he even made money tonight from a closed motel."

"Yeah," Crockett replied. "That would've been an opportunity to good to pass up."

Certainly looked that way.

Chapter Twenty-six:
[Crockett: Crazy town]

I don't know how we escaped the truck disaster, but we did. I headed for Hutt Hospital and dropped Ronnie and Ben at the door to the Emergency Department.

"We'll go park down the street," I said. "Ring when you're ready for a pick-up."

"Will do," Ronnie said, climbing out of the back seat and helping Ben.

I checked the car seat for blood before driving away. It didn't look too bad. We'd have to clean it before giving the car back to Tom.

"Where are we going?" Alex asked.

"For now, it's better if we're not all in the same place. So, we're going to park up somewhere."

One thing about five in the morning is, there is no shortage of on-street parking. I found a parking place without a streetlight. Sticking to the shadows of the early morning felt better than being illuminated. The street-lights were still on. Alex was in the back. I angled the rear vision mirror so I could see her and took off my seatbelt.

"Hey, Alex?"

"Yes?"

"Undo your seatbelt, it'll be more comfortable." And it wouldn't look like we're ready to leave in a hurry to any-one who saw into the car and noticed our seatbelts. I doubted they could, but you never know. She unclipped her belt. I heard it retract. "Where did you meet your manager?"

"Why?"

"Guess I'm interested in how your influencer thing works."

"She contacted me via one of my social media accounts."

"Wow, that's cool."

"Yeah, that's not what my parents said." She smiled at me in the mirror. "They were suspicious. Why would she want to manage me? What's her angle? That kind of thing."

"Reasonable. Parents worry. The internet is a bottomless pit of deprivation and abject terror."

"Yeah so they tell me, every chance they get. And it's forever. Don't forget that," she said. "The internet is forever ..."

"It's concerning. You've got a pretty daughter and she's all-over social media being sponsored by companies and making big money. Only natural that they would worry about you and who you meet."

"I never really thought of it that way. It felt like they were overreacting like usual."

"Give them some credit." I smiled. "She's got an office, your manager?"

Her head nodded. "In Lower Hutt. I've been there a few times, in the early days."

"How long has she been managing you?"

"Fifteen months, one week, and 3 days."

"Precise."

She laughed. "What happened at the motel?"

"We don't know. Well, no, we know someone drove a truck into the unit, but we don't know why or who or if it was intentional."

"They left, right? Drove through the wall then backed out and left. I thought it was an earthquake."

"Yep."

"Seems intentional."

"Yes, it does."

"How would someone find us there?"

I shook my head. "No idea, but we will find out." Good chance someone rang every motel and asked. When they got a hit or a suspected hit then money would be dangled like a carrot.

"What's stopping the same truck from finding us here?"

Nothing. That was probably not what she wanted to hear, though.

"Me," I said. "No one is going to hurt you."

"You can stop a truck, can you?" she said quietly.

"No, but I can get you out of the way of one."

"I suppose that's better than pushing me under one."

"Tell me what you know about the police prosecutor. Did you talk to him?"

"Yes. He rang me a few times to check my story and to remind me I was testifying."

"You didn't meet him?"

"No. He rang my parents' house."

"Refresh my memory because I'm not as good as you. What is his name?"

"John Douglas."

"What did he sound like on the phone?"

"A person," she replied with a frown.

"Did he have an accent?"

"No."

Kiwi then. "Cool. Were you friends with Ashley Chu?"

"Not friends, I did some work for her. She seemed cool."

I watched a car drive down the street and turn the corner. It was not exactly a high traffic time of day.

"Hopefully Ben and Ronnie won't be too long," I said, adjusting the mirror again into a driving position. "Are you warm enough?"

"Yeah," she said. "Why did you ask about the police guy?"

"We haven't come across him before. I just wondered what he was like." Keeping it casual.

"I have a question," Alex said.

"Shoot."

"What's going to happen on Monday?"

"What were you told would happen?"

"That's not an answer."

"I know, humour me. Tell me what you think is going to happen."

"You, Ben, and Ronnie are going to take me to the courthouse and wait with me in a room until it's time for me to testify."

"Are you giving evidence in the courtroom?"

"I think so. Why?"

"Sometimes they do a video link from another office in the courthouse for sensitive witnesses and kids."

"That wasn't mentioned."

"Okay, so we all wait in another room until you're called to the stand."

"You come with me, though, right? I don't have to go in there by myself?"

"If it's an open court then we can be in the public gallery. There will be court officers there to make sure you're okay."

"Oh."

Of course, we now know there is no trial set for tomorrow. I guess that's going to make things interesting in a 'why did I agree to this job' way.

"Did Mr Douglas say he'd meet with you beforehand?"

"No."

"Where are your parents?"

"They left for Europe two weeks ago. They were excited to finally be able to travel again after the COVID restrictions."

I swiveled in my seat and peered at her. The kid was staring at the back of the seat like she was trying to bore a hole through it.

"When did you find out about the trial?"

"On Tuesday."

She hadn't had time to do shit and then she's suddenly

uprooted and given to us, and her parents aren't even around to help.

"Tuesday this week?"

"Yes."

"Do your parents even know?"

She shook her head. "Maybe. I texted Dad's phone, but he hasn't replied. Maybe his phone doesn't work wherever they are at the moment."

"If he'd got the text, surely he would've rung to make sure you were okay with everything."

I cannot imagine a parent finding out their kid was testifying in a murder trial, and then going into witness protection, not picking up a phone and ringing. It doesn't feel right at all. It felt like something we needed to poke into. Nothing is said to the kid for almost a year, then it's all rush, rush, rush, while mum and dad are out of the country. Rush, rush, rush to what end? I had a feeling we already knew what the end game was: not just Alex's death, but a quick way to get rid of us.

Who would want us gone? As a unit? Or individually? Individually, we no doubt had a few takers. I chewed over our recent history. It wasn't a long association, but we'd wrestled with a few nasty people from several countries and prevented a couple of disasters. Doing that tends to piss the bad hombres off. But taking out a twenty-year-old, that was callous.

"What are you thinking about?" Alex asked. Sadness ringed her words. I felt bad for mentioning her parents.

"Not much. Just hoping my mates are okay and that

they'll be back soon."

"Can I tell you something?"

"Sure."

"Trisha asked me to tell her about things I saw and heard while I was working for various companies."

"Did she? That's not very ethical of her."

"She said I was helping her build stronger brands for them and getting the right influencer on board." Alex raked her fingers through her hair. "I think she was spying and using me."

Hello there, Alex, welcome to the real world.

"Did she ask for any specific information?"

She nodded. "She wanted information about *Genesis*."

"Isn't that a book in the Bible?" I really hoped I sounded like I had no idea. "Strange thing to ask."

"I've never read the Bible, I wouldn't know. I thought it was a power company." She shifted her position on the seat.

I chuckled because that's true, it is.

"Why is that funny?"

"Old person joke. One of those 'had to be there' things."

"Oh."

"Did Trisha give you questions to ask or tell you to look for things every time you met with a client?"

She shook her head, then smoothed her hair. "Not every single time but a lot. And she always asked me questions after I met with clients."

"How many clients did you mention *Genesis* to?" I

hoped I sounded interested and not like I was prying.

"Four."

"And they were looking for a new power company?"

She shrugged lightly. "I don't know, but I guess Trisha thought they might be. She said it was sort of a client survey."

That's one way of putting it.

"Who were the four you asked?"

"Nigel Scott, Ashley Chu, Andie Jones, Riley Hart. When we were at Ginny and Tom's house, I asked Ginny."

We knew about that. But it's less sinister now that I suspect she doesn't know what the question is about. Three names we'd come across before, but not that last one.

"What was it you were doing for Riley Hart?"

"My usual. He develops apps and creates video games."

That was not what I wanted to hear.

"How were you working for him?"

"The same as always."

"Not quite, Alex. How does the influencer thing work when it's video games and apps?"

"I see what you mean. Instead of photographing myself wearing clothes, or at events, I was filmed playing the games and using the apps."

"Sounds technical."

"It was. It wasn't just me out and about, I was playing online with other people and stuff like that."

"Fun?"

"Yes. The game he was pushing was a quest type game set in the real world, not a fantasy one."

"Was there a live chat feature?"

"Yes, most quest games have chats so you can keep in touch with your group and plan things."

"And you used it?"

"Yes. I played the game on an Xbox and also I had the game app on my phone so I could play wherever I was."

"It's on your phone?"

"Yes."

Her phone was in Ronnie's bag. That's not somewhere I wanted to be looking. We'd wait.

"Was it fun?"

She nodded. "I liked it."

Chapter Twenty-seven:
[Ronnie: Now what?]

The nice thing about New Zealand is the ability to run into people you know, even at the hospital. I took Ben up to the triage desk, a tired cranky looking woman greeted us, and handed me a clipboard.

"Fill this in and bring it back up," she said. "Go and sit down, someone will come for you. Might be a long wait."

"Okay, thanks."

Then a familiar voice called my name from somewhere behind the grumpy woman, "Ronnie?"

"Ange?"

"Everyone needs a neighbour who is an ED charge nurse. Wait there I'll come and get you."

I laughed. Ben looked confused.

"Ange lives in my street," I said to him. Next minute the side door opened; Ange smiled as she ushered us through to a treatment room.

"What happened?" she said, looking at Ben and his bloody mess.

"Car accident ..." I said, shaking my head. "But not like you'd think."

Her next few questions were for Ben. Full name, address, how the accident happened. All the fun stuff. Then, residency status.

"I'm a permanent resident," Ben replied.

That was the first I knew about that. He disappeared off and on for work - not just acting jobs, but his other work too. I don't suppose I'd really considered his residency status. He was here or not. We were dating or not. Life is only complicated when you put demands on it.

It was much warmer in there than outside. I took my jacket off and got comfy in a chair out of the way. Mostly I gazed at nothing while Ange cleaned Ben's cut and a doctor came in to view it. By the time I dragged myself out of the stupor I was in, due to lack of sleep and trucks through motel walls, Ben was stitched, and ready to go. I stood up, stretched, and took my jacket from where I'd hung it on the back of the chair. The wetness on my back had dried and was less uncomfortable.

"You've left a smear across the back of the chair," Ange said. "Thanks for that."

I smiled. "It's coffee."

She shook her head slowly at me. "That's not coffee. Turn around."

"I'm fine," I said, and didn't turn around.

"Just do what Ange asked," Ben said. "The sooner you reveal your coffee stain the sooner we can get back to work."

Because that's what I was in a hurry to do.

I huffed and turned.

"I'm lifting your shirt," Ange said. It stung a bit as she pulled it away from my skin. "This is not a coffee stain, Ronnie. You have a laceration, and it needs a couple of stitches."

"Is there a hole in my shirt?"

"No. It was in the wound."

"See, that's why I wear silk," I said to Ben. "Saves replacing shirts all the time."

Ange laughed. "How many times do you get stabbed during the day? And can you unbutton your shirt so I can clean this wound?"

I undid the buttons down the front of my long-sleeved deep red silk shirt with the coffee stain on the back. It was always going to be a coffee stain.

Ten minutes later, the wound was clean, I had three stitches and a waterproof dressing. I put my shirt back on and thanked Ange.

"Before you go," she said. "What was the carry-on with the Not-Neighbours yesterday?"

"You've been talking to Donald," I said. "No doubt he'll be waiting for you to get home from work so he can fill you in. Should be fairly quiet today, I might've got Bog-Mouth arrested. She'll be cooling off for the next twenty-four hours."

"Oh, my God. Bog-Mouth. That's perfect!"

"If it fits, it fits. I'll see you later," I said, waving. "Which way is out?"

"Right," she said. "Then left. It says exit."

"Thanks, Ange, for your help," Ben said.

"We don't get spunky actors in very often, so, my pleasure," she replied with a smile.

It took us a couple of minutes to get out the back of the Emergency Department and down to the road behind the hospital. I looked up and down the road and spotted Tom's car in a darkish area.

"There we go." I pointed to the car.

Hand in hand we walked across the road. The doors unlocked as we approached the vehicle. "Get in the front," Ben said, opening the passenger door for me.

"You two good?" Crockett asked as I settled into the seat.

"Yep."

Ben's door closed. Seat belts clicked.

"Where from here?" Crockett asked, starting the car.

The sky had lightened a couple of shades of grey since we left the hospital. I couldn't tell if the sun was going to rise, or the drab grey would stay.

"That address we looked at last night," I said. "It's not far. Go right at the end of this street, that'll bring us back to High Street. Turn left onto High Street and head into Lower Hutt."

"Where are we going?" Alex asked.

"To an office building in Lower Hutt," I replied. "You'll see soon."

"I'm hungry," she said.

"Me too," Ben added. "Coffee and food would be good."

I looked at Crockett. He smiled to himself.

"Detour," he said. "We've got time to eat."

"It'll have to be Maccas," I said, checking my watch. It was just after six. "The one on the corner of Raroa Road and High Street is a twenty-four hours."

"That'll do," Crockett said.

"You okay with that, Alex?" I turned my head to see her.

"Sounds okay," she replied. "Hotcakes and coffee, and they have clean toilets."

Good point.

Crockett parked in the parking area beside the Maccas, and we all wandered in, probably looking as rag-tag as we felt. Crockett ordered using an order terminal. For a change it worked. Today's little miracle. It could be a portend of joy to come. How often was a portend joy, I wondered. Never.

We waited in silence for a server to deliver our breakfasts. I quietly enjoyed that you could have table service at Maccas. There was no one else in the restaurant, but just in case people turned up we chose the furthest booth possible from the front of the restaurant. Crockett and I scoped escape routes on the pretext of using the loo. The nearest exit wasn't too far from our table. It was doubtful that people would use that door to come inside. It was a long way from the counter and ordering system. Just in case some rando did come in through that door we positioned Alex in the back corner of the booth. Ben was beside her to block anyone from spotting her through a large window and glass door.

By the time I was back at the table, our food had arrived. Everyone ordered hotcakes and coffee. The silence resumed as food was gobbled up like we hadn't eaten in days. I felt like *I* hadn't eaten in days. That's what not sleeping, and adrenaline did, made us crazy hungry for carbs.

I looked over at Alex as she finished her meal.

"Do you want more?"

She nodded and blushed slightly. "I'm really hungry."

"Me too. Crockett and Ben?"

They both nodded. Crockett peered into his coffee cup. "And more coffee, please."

"Another round of everything coming right up." I gathered all the rubbish and dumped it in the bin on my way to the machines in the front. A few minutes later I'd ordered and got another table tag with a new number and made my way back to the table. There was still no one else around. This was clearly the best time to hit Maccas. I stored that information away just in case.

"Welcome back," Ben said, smiling. "Everything okay?"

"Sure is. Why wouldn't it be?"

"I don't know, but you were frowning on your way to the table."

"Wasn't intentional. Maybe my face just does that now?"

He laughed. "Maybe. Hey, did you hear from Donald last night?"

"No. He was probably recovering from Nana and the *Cronies of Doom*. They're a lot to deal with and he was mostly on his own with them." I smiled. "They can sniff out weakness a kilometre away, so he stood no chance."

"You make your Nana sound hilarious and terrifying," Alex said. "Don't you get on?"

Crockett tipped his head back and laughed. "They get on like a house on fire, but I can see how you'd think they didn't. June is one hell of an old ..."

"If you call my Nana an old Boiler," I warned. "Or an old Trout."

"... Sheila," Crockett said, still chuckling. "She's fantastic. She invited me to her weekly poker night. They're sharks, the lot of them."

"She sounds fun," Alex said.

"She is," said Ben. "Unless you are dating her granddaughter and she would like you to marry said granddaughter."

"What about your family, Alex, what are your grandparents like?" I asked.

"I don't really know them. Mum's parents live in the UK and Dad's live in Poland."

"Is that why they're in Europe at the moment?" Crockett asked.

He seemed to know things we didn't about Alex.

"Yes. They've gone to visit the family."

I watched a deep sadness pull at her features until her mouth downturned and tears filled her eyes. She was a just a kid, and her world had vanished.

Our second round of breakfasts arrived.

Talking ceased while eating took over.

Chapter Twenty-eight:
[Crockett: Perkins]

It didn't take long to get from Maccas to the office building where Ronnie said Perkin's office was. She hadn't
picked up a residence, just the office. I can't pretend to be
an expert in Ronnie's special skill set, but I know from
experience she usually hits on a few locations. This time
just one. Maybe Perkins was a shut-in or a workaholic, or
maybe she was a few stubbies short of a six-pack.

I parked down the street from the building. Ronnie
and I were going to have a squiz, while Ben stayed with
Alex. That hour on a Sunday morning, High Street was
quiet and quiet is good. I still had no idea how the truck
incident happened and how anyone found us. But I had a
sneaky suspicion that the app on Alex's phone, the one
we hadn't investigated yet, was behind it. It wouldn't be
the first app to take control of a phone and transmit location data by turning the phone back on, intermittently.

"Why are we here?" Alex asked, looking around. "This
is near where my manager has her office."

"We know," Ronnie replied. "Crockett and I are going
to have a word with her if she's there. What floor is she
on?"

"Fourth."

We exited the car together and walked back to the
building. We stood in front of the entrance to the build-

ing staring at the glass doors in front of us.

"Let's see if it's open." I said, reaching for the door. It said push. I pushed. It opened and I held it for Ronnie. "Didn't expect that at this time of the morning."

"Nor did I," Ronnie replied, as she walked past me and into the foyer. "Okay, here we go. We have two lifts and a set of stairs."

I saw the building index on the wall before the lift doors. The fourth floor had a counselling service and a blank field. I tapped the blank part. "Maybe she hasn't been here long."

"Maybe," Ronnie replied. "Or maybe she doesn't want to advertise her presence."

"Publicity company that doesn't want to advertise. That doesn't seem like a red flag."

"Maybe business is so good that advertising is unnecessary."

"I'll take the stairs, you take the lift," I said with a smile. "Meet you at the top."

"All righty." Ronnie pressed the button and waved as I closed the stairwell door behind me.

Stairwells are always cold and mostly smell the same. I've never worked out exactly what it is, but I've narrowed it down to a probable mix of musty air and concrete. I took the stairs two at a time - not a difficult task as I have long legs. I was conscious to step lightly so as not to create echoing footfalls. At every second landing I checked the number on the exit door. Two came up fast but three was slower. When I swung the fourth door open Ronnie was waiting. The area was lit by soft lighting. There were no other signs of life.

"I think that must be her offices," Ronnie said as she pointed to a tinted glass door with gold lettering. It was opposite a frosted door that had a health department logo. "Cool name for a publicity company."

I read the company name on the door. *2:4-7 Impact.* "Interesting way to write twenty-four seven."

"Hmmm," she said and snapped a photo with her phone. "For later."

There were no lights on beyond the tinted door. The frosted door opposite gave off a soft glow; they probably had security lighting.

"Let's see if she's home." I bashed on the door with the side of my fist.

"You think she lives here in the office building?"

I banged again. "You only got one location from your ..."

"Don't say it."

"You only got one location. Last time I saw you use your *skills,* you hit several locations."

Ronnie nodded. "True. Usually, I pick up different energy strengths at various places but with her not so much."

I bashed again. A light turned on beyond the door.

"Someone is there," I whispered. I heard movement and stepped back. Ronnie followed. We stood next to the door, not in front of it. You never know.

A woman's voice called out, "Is there a problem?"

Ronnie smiled and replied, "Yes."

The lock clicked. A whoosh of air followed.

I stepped into view.

"Who are you?" said the short tubby woman in the doorway, as she clutched a suit jacket around her large shoulders. "The office isn't open until nine tomorrow."

"That's a shame. I have some questions," I said.

"Who are you?"

I thrust my hand out. "I'm no one you know."

She blinked, grabbed the coat with her left hand, and shook mine with her right. Must've been a reflex because she didn't look like she wanted to be friends. "I heard a female voice."

"That would be me," Ronnie said, stepping out of the shadows to stand next to me. "I'm his friend. And you are Trisha Perkins if I'm not mistaken."

"I am. Why are you here at this hour on a Sunday?"

"You might want to invite us in," I said, pushing past her. "Or not, but we're coming in."

"What is this about?"

"What could it be about, I wonder?" Ronnie said. "Why do you live in your office space?"

Perkins stuttered, "I ... I ... I'm between houses."

"Lucky you have this space then," Ronnie replied. "And where do you receive clients?"

Perkins grabbed Ronnie by the arm with her fat little fingers. "Get out! This is ... this is ... rude and intrusive."

I watched the exchange from about a metre inside the doorway, ready to help if required.

Ronnie threw the woman's pudgy hand off her arm. "Rude? Intrusive? Goodness, aren't you full of it this morning."

"What is going on here?"

"Let's sit, shall we?" Ronnie barged through another door. "I've found an office," she called out.

"Coming," I replied, and scooped Perkins up on my way by latching onto her right forearm and giving her a tug in the right direction. "Move your feet, or I will drag you across the floor."

She opted to put one foot in front of the other. Smart move.

Inside the office, I found Ronnie sitting behind a large wooden desk. She looked comfortable as she pulled out drawers and rifled through them.

"Stop it! That's my desk," Perkins squawked. "You have no right."

"I have every right, lady." She bent slightly and tugged another drawer open. "There's a safe in here. What's the combination?"

"I'm not telling you!"

That was my cue. I applied a little pressure to her arm. "Try again. Your attitude is not working for you."

"You can't just barge in here and give orders." I squeezed harder. "That hurts!" She tried to twist out of my grip. Not happening. Her fat arm was going nowhere. My fingers sunk into flesh and were swallowed by a generous blubber layer. "You're bruising me."

"My colleague asked you a question," I growled.

"I won't tell you."

I twisted her arm up behind her back. "You will."

"Ow, stop!"

I pressed it higher.

"Oww! Stop, stop." She took a ragged breath. I didn't let up the pressure until she gave Ronnie the combination. She rubbed her arm once I released it.

"Sit down," I ordered and dropped a spare chair in front of the desk.

She rubbed her arm and squashed herself onto the seat. I stepped back, giving her room, but close enough to do it all again. Nothing in me enjoyed causing a woman pain. I moved a step to the right so I could see Perkins and Ronnie at the same time.

Ronnie brought envelopes and papers out of the safe and placed them on the desk. "Let's see what we have," she said, smiling at the woman.

She started reading. After four pages she motioned to me with the papers she'd finished in her hand. I took them and skimmed over the contents. Seconds was all it took for me to know that Perkins wasn't simply a publicity manager who matched her clients to PR gigs. She was working for another company, one that looked to have an agenda.

"Can we track this back to the source?" I asked, glancing over the paperwork to Ronnie.

"Of course. Nothing is impossible when you have our resources." I didn't know if she was telling the truth or fudging the truth to cause more stress in Perkins. Her team of PIs can do a lot, so, there was a good chance it was the truth.

"I need to sit down," Perkins said.

"You are sitting down," I said. Perhaps she was more rattled than I realised.

"You're going to get me killed."

That's not usually the go to when things go pear-shaped unless of course she is up to no good with some bad, bad hombres.

"Shame," Ronnie said. "Maybe, be more careful who you work for and who you try and corrupt."

"I'm not corrupting anyone," she snipped. "I manage people and help clients run successful social media campaigns."

"If that's true, then how would us being here get you killed?" Ronnie gave her no time to reply. "You know who else manages people?" Ronnie said, looking her in the eyes. "Case officers. Handlers. Spy Masters."

"I ... I ... I don't know what you're talking about."

"Ah, if only that were true." Ronnie held up a piece of paper. "Didn't they ever tell you not to write anything down?"

Perkins eyes widened. "What are you talking about?"

That was the most unconvincing feigned innocence I'd heard since Ester tried to bluff over a hand while we were playing poker.

"I'm talking about a shopping list of things for Alex to find while in Nigel Scott's office."

"You're not making ... sense."

"Aren't I?" Ronnie held the paper up for Perkins to see. "Let me draw your attention to the top of your shopping list. It says Nigel Scott's office. The very first item: artwork." Ronnie touched the words at the top of the page with the index finger of her free hand. "What does that mean? What did little Alex tell you about his artwork?"

"Why would she tell me anything? Scott owns a shoe manufacturing business. She was hired to promote his sneakers."

"Let's look at number two." Ronnie arched an eyebrow at the woman. "What does that say?" She pointed again.

"It says desktop," Perkins muttered. "You can read."

"I can." Ronnie smiled and sniffed at the woman. "Something smells. Oh, I think I know what it is." She tapped the words 'gift for his desk'.

"What does 'gift for his desk' mean?" I asked.

"I was probably going to give him a gift and wanted to know what he'd like," Perkins said. "Is it illegal to give people gifts now?"

"That depends on the gift you gave him. For example, if you gave him something particular for his desk that say had ... a bug of some sort inside it."

"Why would I do that?"

"What did you give him," Ronnie countered.

"A bronze shoe."

"And where did you get it?"

Perkins clamped her mouth shut. We'd find out one way or another.

I read the last word on the short list: Visitors.

"Why would you need to know about any visitors to Scott's office?" I turned my head until I was eyeballing the woman. "Why does that impact on your ability to run his PR campaign?"

Her mouth stayed shut. I sighed.

Ronnie handed me everything she found in the safe. I flipped through it all, including some envelopes. They were interesting. The envelopes were all addressed to Perkins and had cancelled stamps on the upper right corner, but no return address anywhere. They'd been slit open across the top.

The woman squawked, "That's my mail! It's against the law to open someone else's mail!"

"Technically it's already open." I smiled at her and opened the envelope. I peered inside and extracted a piece of paper with a long series of numbers typed on it. That was interesting.

"What do the numbers mean?" I asked, showing her the paper.

"Nothing. It's private."

"Of course, then I won't ask again."

A small laugh came from Ronnie. "He's really good like that. Respectful of boundaries and privacy."

I took a photo of the numbers and sent it to Ben. It looked like it could be a bank account number, but instead of being written with breaks or dashes to separate the numbers, they were all run together to make one number. I opened another envelope and found another series of numbers. These were different numbers. Again,

I took a photo and sent it to Ben.

I got a reply fairly fast and glanced at the iMessage: Alex recognised the first series of numbers as the account that paid her for the work she did for Ashley Chu.

"This is interesting," I said to Ronnie, ignoring the whale of a woman jammed into the chair near me. "Alex was paid by the first series of numbers. It's a bank account."

I checked the remaining three envelopes. They all contained bank account numbers.

"Why does a company need so many bank account numbers?" Ronnie asked. I passed her the pieces of paper containing the numbers and she fanned them out on the desktop.

"If we break these down into the components," Ronnie said, "They're all different banks." She tapped the pieces of paper. "One is Kiwi Bank, then we have TSB, BNZ, The Co-operative Bank and finally ANZ."

That Ronnie knew the banks by their codes off the top of her head was pretty impressive. I couldn't think of a single good reason why anyone would have five bank accounts at five different banks. I was stuck on the envelopes. I had a feeling she sent them to herself. Why would a person post numbers to themselves in individual envelopes? If you wanted to deny you had anything to do with the accounts, perhaps. You could wave an envelope and say 'someone sent it to me' it wasn't my idea?

Perkins' chins wobbled as she shook her head. "It's so I can keep track of everyone."

Ronnie shook her head. Nothing wobbled.

"I have about ten employees and we manage to pay everyone from a single account. You know, the way most businesses operate."

"But the ..." Perkins stopped.

"The?" Ronnie asked. "The, what? The Russians do it this way? The Chinese like it done this way? The old man who lives under Ewen Bridge likes it done this way?"

I thought Ronnie was onto something.

"They're not business accounts, are they though?" Ronnie smiled a serial killer smile. There was no inkling of the smile anywhere but her mouth. "You set up five personal accounts and I just bet every deposit is just under the amount that would trigger the bank's money laundering alarms."

"This is a high value business," Perkins said with a bit of a gloat kicking about on her otherwise stodgy face. "We receive a lot more than that in one transaction."

"I'm sure you do, through your business accounts, but these aren't business accounts, are they?"

"This is none of your *business*," Perkins grumbled, her chins still free-wheeling from the violent shake.

"Oh, I think it is," Ronnie replied.

I enjoyed watching Ronnie work the woman.

"You should leave before I call police." It was the emptiest of threats. Perkins struggled to her feet. I reached over and applied pressure to her shoulder until she sank back into the chair.

"Stay," I growled. "We're not done."

Ronnie photographed everything she'd found, page by page.

"Who is it that puts the funds into these accounts?"

"That's none of your business," Perkins replied.

"Okay, great. It's none of my business but here we are, asking the questions." Ronnie levelled a cold glare at the woman. "Where's. Your. Laptop?"

Perkins jiggled in the chair like a jelly in an earthquake. "I don't have one."

Ronnie rolled her eyes. "I'll find it and you'll sit right there with my colleague while I turn this place upside down and inside out."

She stood and left the room. I stayed with Perkins. The woman turned toward me. The action caused a tsunami to roll through her body. It was hard not to cringe.

"Why is she doing this?" Perkins asked.

"She has her reasons."

"This persecution is ridiculous. I've done nothing wrong."

"I don't want to speculate on the stupidity of that statement. Let's hold off on the cries of innocence until my off-sider gets back with your laptop."

I leaned on the wall and watched her.

Did she seriously think we'd take her word for anything?

"Look, we can come to an arrangement. You seem reasonable." She tilted her head toward the door. Everything moved. "She isn't."

I shook my head at her. "That tactic won't fly. It might

work on the drongos you're dealing with on a daily basis. Trust me, lady, when I say, I am not one of them."

"I deal with CEOs and publicity people all day long. I can get you whatever you want."

"Good. All we want is the truth. Can you do that?"

"I haven't lied to you. I don't know what you are talking about."

Of course, she doesn't. Why would she?

"Let's try again. Where's your laptop?"

"I don't have one." Everything wobbled as she tried a sincere head shake.

Once that shit was moving it took a while to settle.

Ronnie marched through the door with a laptop under her arm. "Look what I found!"

"Can't be hers," I said. "She doesn't have one."

Ronnie laughed, then stopped abruptly as she slid behind the desk and into the chair. She placed the computer on the desktop and lifted the lid.

"Guess what?" Ronnie asked with a smile and raised eyebrows.

"Make my day," I replied.

"No password. No biometric scan. I'm in."

Fucking amateur hour. I was pretty sure the people who paid her expected a certain level of security, and it was two-step authentication and biometric data, above nothing.

"Bank accounts," I said.

Perkins squawked something that sounded like no. But I wasn't sure. Maybe duct tape would help shut her fat mouth.

"Guess what she's using?" Ronnie said, shaking her head in disbelief.

"Chrome?"

"Yes!"

Unbelievable.

It took Ronnie under forty seconds to open all the bank accounts and send transaction reports from the last six months to us. Then she downloaded everything from the date the accounts were created and copied it to a flash drive on her keyring.

"Would you like to tell us who you are working for? Because I'm seeing a few different company names here, and one of them is *Alexandrite*," Ronnie said. "And shouldn't contract work go through your work account and not a personal account?"

I swivelled back to Perkins. She gulped in air as if she couldn't breathe.

"I must've made a mistake and given them the wrong account."

"Looks like you made a lot of mistakes over the last six weeks. One would say that this many mistakes means it's on purpose. I count fourteen transactions from *Alexandrite*."

This was better than a ham sandwich.

"Anything else urgent?" I asked Ronnie.

"Yeah, the Chu woman. There's a single payment from *Alexandrite* with Chu as the reference."

"When you start to pick at threads ..."

Ronnie nodded. "I think I have everything we need to prove she's either money laundering, or on someone else's payroll."

"How much does money laundering get in New Zealand?"

"I think it's seven years, give or take. Probably depends if you're a spy or not, though." Ronnie never made eye contact with the woman who was gasping for breath; she kept her eyes on me. "Fourteen years for a spy, or is that still the one thing New Zealand has the death penalty for?" She did well to keep a straight face when she tossed out the death penalty part.

"I ... didn't ... do anything. I'm not ... a ... spy!"

"Beg to differ, but that's me, being difficult." Ronnie grinned at me and then stood and leaned over the desk toward Perkins. "When I started my career, I memorised part of the Crimes Act of 1961 and how it could pertain to anyone I dealt with, and myself. I have stayed up to date with all amendments."

I knew where this was going.

"In case no one told you when you dug yourself into a fucking hole, let me." Ronnie took a breath. "Section 78 of the crimes act deals with espionage." She smiled. "And it goes like this: 'Everyone is liable to imprisonment for a term not exceeding 14 years who, being a person who owes allegiance to the Sovereign in right of *New Zealand*, within or outside *New Zealand*, with intent to prejudice the security or defence of *New Zealand*, communicates information or delivers any *object* to a country or organisation outside *New Zealand* or to a person acting on behalf of any such country or organisation."

I interrupted Ronnie's lecture. "Did you get that part, Perkins? ANY. Object. Are bronze shoes objects?"

Perkins gulped and rallied. "That wasn't outside New Zealand."

Ronnie was back with her serial killer smile. "Let me continue, and yes, that bronze shoe, it does qualify because I have a feeling about that shoe. I bet it's collecting data."

Ronnie took a breath. "Where were we? Ah, yes ... delivering of any object to a person acting on behalf of any country or organisation — with intent to prejudice the security or defence of *New Zealand* and with the intention of communicating information or delivering any object to a country or organisation outside *New Zealand* or to a person acting on behalf of any such country or organisation." Ronnie pushed off the desk and glared at the now quivering sack of blubber. "Just in case you don't know what that means, it means, if you collect or record information." Ronnie sucked in air. "Or make copies of documents, or obtain any objects, or even draw a shitty sketch on a piece of torn paper, or take photographs with your bloody phone, or record sound or image, or deliver any object to any person ..." She took another deep breath. "If the communication or delivery, or even just the *intended* communication or *intended* delivery, is likely to prejudice the security or defence of *New Zealand*."

"I ... I ... didn't do those things."

"You did through an intermediary. You knowingly got Alex and who knows how many other of your clients to report back on what they heard or saw."

"I didn't!"

"You compromised at least one young woman," I said, stepping forward until I was towering over her. She stretched her fat neck to look up at me. Tears rolled back toward her hair line.

Her head shook, sending a tidal wave of motion down her body that was enough to make me step back.

"What are you going to do?" she asked between sobs.

"Already doing it," Ronnie replied with her phone in her hand. I could hear ringing. When it stopped ringing, Ronnie said, "We've got evidence that points to some form of espionage within New Zealand. Could be corporate espionage, or it could be a lot worse."

I couldn't hear the reply. Ronnie hung up. She winked at me and then said to Perkins, "And done."

"What? What did you do?"

"You'll see, in about twenty minutes when two people walk through that door," she inclined her head toward the office door. "And remove you."

Panic scrambled across Perkins' face. "What does that mean?"

Ronnie didn't answer. She smiled her serial killer smile and gathered everything she'd discovered into a pile. I knew she'd photographed it all and sent copies of everything to a secure email server from that laptop. I also know how Ronnie operates, and it would take anyone a while to discover we had the intel. We would leave the paperwork for someone. But who did she ring?

Chapter Twenty-nine:

[Ronnie: The more you know]

"Hey?" I waved a hand in Crockett's direction.

"Yeah?"

"Search this place before they get here," I said. "I'll stay with Ms Perkins."

Crockett nodded and left the room. It paid to have us both do a search just in case I missed something when I went searching for her laptop earlier.

I texted Ben: Everything okay?

Ben: Yep. Going to be much longer?

Me: Fifteen minutes maybe less. Text when you see a team arrive.

Ben: I'll recognise them?

Me: Men in grey.

My phone rang. Not Ben, but Steph. I glared at Perkins. "Stay put. I will be just outside the door, and I will be watching you." I moved my arm, so she saw the Glock in my holster.

I swiped my finger across the screen of the phone in my hand as I stepped outside the room. "Hey, what's up?"

"We have a clear image of a male entering the first safe house. He's Asian."

"Is the AOS guy still with you?"

"Yes."

"Get him, grab that Asian guy, and keep hold of him. Watch out for knives."

"Where do you want him?"

"Lock him up at the office. Keep a watch on him. Anything electronic that he's carrying needs to go in the faraday cage."

When we had the opportunity to revamp our offices, we decided to put in a secure interview room. This was the first time we'd used it.

"You still want surveillance on the house?"

"Just the electronic surveillance now. Can you keep an eye on it, please?" I couldn't commit to watching the video feed. Things were fluid and moving here.

"Of course. Everything okay at your end?"

"Yeah. I think we've found something, and someone, with connections to this mess." I thought for a second and decided to keep the rest of it to myself. "Be careful."

"We will. Stay safe," Steph said and hung up.

I walked back into the room. The woman had stopped crying and sat silently in the chair.

"When did this start?" I asked, quietly. "When did you make a decision to betray your country?"

"I'm not that person," she said, her voice laden with sadness.

"That'd be a lot more believable if we didn't find so much evidence to the contrary." I took a seat behind her desk.

"What's going to happen to me?"

"I don't know." That was honest. I didn't know. They could decide to use her, or they could lock her up, or she might disappear forever. I didn't think she was the best choice as a double agent or even an off-book informant, but that wasn't my decision to make.

"Who is coming?"

"Someone who will make some decisions on your behalf."

I was starting to understand why we were given the task of keeping Alex safe. We were the team that wouldn't leave well enough alone. We were the team that wanted answers. We were the team that defied orders and uncovered secrets. We were the team that gave absolutely no fucks about digging in even when we were told to back off. If I'd still been working for NZSIS I would've been fired so many times over the last couple of years. Good thing I'm not working for them on a permanent basis.

A silent alert on my phone screen caught my eye. I glanced at the screen and the message notification opened.

Unknown sender: Flash classified. Exfill now.

I jumped to my feet and left the room; over my shoulder I said, "Stay put."

I found Crockett heading into another office from the main reception area.

"We're leaving, now," I said.

Crockett nodded. "Stairs."

We left the offices and ran as quietly as we could down the stairs. At the bottom I heard the lift doors close and saw the number move from G to one.

Crockett held the front door open for me. Once out of the building, we ran to the car and jumped in.

"Go," I said to Ben, as I shut the front passenger door and saw him in the driver's seat.

"Where?"

"Don't care, but not here," I replied, pulling my seat-belt across my body, and clicking.

I saw Crockett's head move in the wing mirror. He checked behind us, then faced forward.

Ben did a U-turn as we passed the building we'd come from and headed north; I saw two black SUVs parked around the corner. How very clichéd. Ben didn't comment. Crockett tapped me on the shoulder.

"You see them?"

"Yes," I replied. "Perkins isn't our problem anymore."

"I doubt she's anyone's problem now," Crockett said in a half-whisper.

Ben drove north. He avoided the motorway by going the back way through Naenae and Taita, then passed the entrance to Stokes Valley. We were going against the early traffic. The morning shoppers and Sunday sports players were beginning to clog the southbound lanes on the motorway across the river. We turned into Silverstream, and instead of Ben taking a left and going toward Trentham, he drove through Silverstream and into Pinehaven.

We were going back to Tom and Ginny's.

I wasn't sure if that was smart or silly. I just wanted to be out of the way and have time to go over the info I had on my phone and check those emails. Perkins would be long gone and so would all the gathered intel. *Alexandrite* bothered me. This mess with Perkins didn't feel Russian. They usually make smarter choices when it comes to who they use. Perkins was not a good move. Although, they might've gotten away with it, if we weren't assigned as babysitters.

Alex spoke from the back seat. I'd almost forgotten she was there. "Are we going back to Ginny's?"

"Yes," Ben replied. "Do you have any objections?"

"No. I like it there."

Me too. It felt nice in their house, welcoming and calm. We could definitely use some calm.

Four minutes later, Ben pulled into the long driveway and parked in the carport. Nothing unusual about Tom's car coming home.

We piled out of the car, grabbed our bags, and walked around the edge of the house to the back door. Pierre sauntered up the path from the garden and rubbed around my legs. Even the cats were calm at this place.

Ben knocked. I kept an eye on the sky, just in case.

The door opened. Ginny stood there with a smile on her face. "You're back! Come in."

"Hope it's not too much of an intrusion," Ben said, kissing her cheek.

"Not at all. You know you're always welcome here.

What happened to you?" she asked, touching the side of his head.

"We had some trouble," Ben replied with a smile. "I'm fine."

Ginny nodded. "As long as you're fine." She greeted us one by one and ushered us inside. "Tom is at work. I'll let him know you're here."

"Keen to work Sundays," Crockett commented.

"He's always working. He was supposed to retire five years ago, and he can't keep out of the place."

Alex and I left our shoes just inside the back door. The men left theirs outside. Alex spotted Laila the kitten playing in a cardboard box in the lounge and went to play with her. I watched her for a moment. She seemed okay. But then, she didn't know what happened to her former manager yet. I wasn't keen on telling her. And I didn't one hundred percent know that Perkins was no longer breathing, but I strongly suspected that was the case. She'd somehow got herself out of her depth and she was shit at what they had her do. I don't know who came up with the bright idea to turn an amateur into a handler, but they were wrong unless the idea was to hang her out to dry if, or when, it all went sideways. Thoughts of Nana and Donald merged with the Perkins dilemma. I couldn't do anything about Perkins; she dug herself into a hole and she'd be in that permanently. Nana and Donald, though, I could do something about them.

I mulled that over as I lowered myself as gracefully as possible into a chair at the dining table.

"You all right, Ronnie?"

I blinked and followed the voice to the chair across the table from me.

"Yes," I replied.

"You look deep in thought," Ginny said. "Is there anything I can help with?"

"It's been a trying few days," I said with a smile. "I should probably check with my cousin and make sure Nana is staying out of trouble."

"How old is your Nana?"

"She says she's ninety-four, but she's been saying that most of my life."

Ginny laughed. "She sounds a hoot."

"She thinks she is," I said. I checked my phone. All quiet.

"Give your cousin a ring and check on your family. Everyone here is safe for now."

I picked up the phone and FaceTimed Donald.

He answered as I cursed him in my head for being so slack at answering and making me wait for eight rings. His face popped into view.

"Ronnie! Where are you. What can I see behind you?"

"Crystals or is it a salt lamp?"

Ginny nodded at my salt lamp comment.

"Fabbo! Oh, who is with you?"

"A friend," I said, watching his expression change from curious to dramatically curious. Trust me, it's a thing. "What?"

"I know all your friends and none of them like crystals

or salt lamps."

"She's a new friend." I dismissed his line of questioning, but I knew it'd creep back. "Have you heard from Nana?"

Donald nodded. His blond streak flopped over his left eye. He tossed it back. "Nana ... she's fine."

"Fine? I need more than that, cousin dear." I tried to see where he was by looking over his shoulder in the screen of my phone. I couldn't tell where he was. Odd. There didn't seem to be walls. "Where are you?"

I felt sure it was too early in the morning for them olds to be up to no good.

"Across the road."

"Donald!"

"Settle Ronnie. I'm not at the Not-Neighbours, and anyway, Bog-Mouth hasn't been released from custody yet."

"Where are you?"

"At the other neighbours. The nice ones."

"Donald, do not infect anymore people with your theories about the real neighbours and Bog-Mouth."

He tossed his head and chortled. "Too late. Anyway, I didn't infect them. They have to share a wall with the arseholes."

"And Nana?"

"Nothing to worry about, Ronnie. She's here with me."

"Oh. My. God. Will you stop!"

"Bog-Mouth is in jail and Nana is here at the other neighbours'. We're having a nice cuppa and then I'll take her back to ours."

"Why do you never listen to me?" I dropped my voice to a lower, more menacing level. "That old woman will find a way to cause chaos and it'll be on you. You thought I was angry last time ... well, my darling cousin, I will turn you inside out if there is another police call out because of Nana."

"Have a little faith, Ronnie. It'll all be fine. And by the way, where's my hubby?"

"He's working for me. He's doing what he does. He'll be back when he's done."

I waved at the screen. "Bye."

Donald disappeared. Ginny placed a cup of coffee in front of me and a plate of wine biscuits. "Excuse the baking," she said. "Had I known you were coming I would've whipped up something special."

We both grinned. She had the longest nails I'd seen on a person. I bet it was an effort to open a biscuit packet, let alone bake anything.

"Thank you, Ginny," I said, dipping a wine biscuit into my coffee.

"You're welcome. Don't worry so much about your Nana," she said, as she dipped a biscuit into her coffee. "She probably knows what she's doing. There's something to living into her nineties. She didn't get there by making poor decisions."

"I'm not so sure. I think she's been bloody lucky."

"I'd love to meet her one day."

Oh boy. I can see it now. Nana would like that way too

much. I didn't need Nana making friends with anyone else I knew.

It was bad enough she started inviting Crockett to her poker nights a while back. They were darn near besties. She didn't need another human to add to her collection.

"One day," I replied, dunking another biscuit. One day when we can ice-skate in hell.

"What sort of music do you like?" Ginny asked in a complete change of subject.

"I'm not super fussy but I don't like rap, though, as a genre."

"No one with taste does." Ginny sipped her coffee, then placed the cup on the coaster in front of her. "I quite like Phil Collins."

"So do I," I replied.

Of all the music in the world, Ginny likes someone who was in *Genesis*. My brain growled at me and warned me not to overlay my life on other people's. Some people think *Genesis* was a great band. Some people think *Genesis* is a power company. It's not suspicious to like or mention *Genesis*.

"What's your favourite song of his?" Ginny asked.

"Hands down, it's 'I Can't Dance'."

"That's a good one. I like 'Another Day in Paradise'," she said, then frowned. "Was that him or was that *Genesis*?"

"Aren't they interchangeable?"

"Probably." I could tell she was thinking. "That one was Phil Collins as a solo."

"Good to know."

I finished my coffee and felt a little more relaxed.

Crockett ambled over and showed me his phone and an open iMessage. I read the message and glanced at the top of the screen to see who'd sent it.

Enzo: Picked up a tail fifteen minutes ago. Took me ten to lose it.

I nodded. Crockett turned the phone and typed a response as he sat in the chair next to me. I could see his screen.

Crockett: Car or bike?
Enzo: Harley
Crockett: Stay safe and out of sight. Emily with you?
Enzo: She is. Lost the bike and made it home to yours. No drones in sight.
Crockett: Good.

I motioned to Crockett that I wanted his phone. He handed it to me.

Me: Enzo it's Ronnie. Steph, Jenn, and an AOS friend of theirs have a male locked up at *Wherefore Art Thou*
Enzo: What do you need?
Me: Your expertise and some answers.
Enzo: I'll leave Emily and the Harley at Crockett's and make my way to your offices.

Me: Thanks, Enzo.

I gave Crockett his phone back. There was a time when asking Enzo to get answers made me cringe. His methods are more akin to enhanced interrogation than a friendly chat. Enzo gets answers and he gets them fairly fast. This time it was a male he'd be interrogating, and I guess my squeamishness only shows when it's a female on the end of Enzo's special talent.

"Is everything going okay?" Ginny asked.

"Yes," Crockett replied. "Just checking in with everyone."

"That's good," Ginny said. She rose from the table and took her cup to the kitchen where she rinsed it and placed it upside down on the bench to drain.

Crockett bumped my elbow. "We can't move her again," he said.

"I know," I replied. "I don't know if staying here is smart or way too dangerous."

"We know there is no trial. Well, at least there is no trial scheduled in the public docket."

I turned my head and stared at him. "Public docket. Of course, if she witnessed a murder and the person who committed the murder is someone acting on behalf of a foreign power ... it's not going to be public. They want her in the room to positively identify him before he's either run out of the country or thrown in prison." Even as I said it, it didn't make sense. "They could've got the ID at any stage over the last year."

"This whole thing is a dog's breakfast," Crockett said.

"If he's on a diplomatic passport then whatever country is involved would've already sent him packing unless, he's a New Zealander or holds dual citizenship, and was working for his other country while here. Then maybe we could hold him and try not to let whoever that power is, have access."

"You're right about it not making sense. If the alleged killer was in custody, then why not ID him early on and get it over with? Why do it this way and take so long about it?"

"Okay, so, long shot ... He was caught, they locked everyone out except his lawyer." I was thinking out loud. "And the country who owned his soul would hire the lawyer so he didn't talk and so they were kept in the loop."

"Okay," Crockett said. "But ..."

"When Alex's name was given to the supposed court as a witness, the other power also got it via the lawyer. They can't have known Alex was there when Henry murdered Ashley Chu, until Friday when her name was released to the lawyer."

"Shit. That's a possibility."

"She's the only person who can one-hundred percent identify that Henry guy, isn't she?"

Crockett nodded. "I bet that's it. Didn't you have a photo from the surveillance cameras at our first safe house?"

"Yeah." I opened photos and pulled the image up on

my phone and showed him.

"Hey, Alex, come here," Crockett said beckoning the girl.

She did as he asked.

"Do you know the person?" I showed her my phone screen. "Is he familiar?"

"He looks like the man who stabbed Ashley Chu, but I'm sure that's not him. Maybe a relative, though."

"Thanks. You're sure that it's not him?" I held my phone so she could still see the image.

"Definitely. The person, Henry, who stabbed Ashley had a small, but clear, scar on his chin. That man has no scar."

"One other question." Something had just occurred to me. "Did you tell your manager that you witnessed a murder at Ashley Chu's office. or studio, or whatever it was?"

She shook her head. "No. I didn't say anything about it."

"Did she ask?"

Alex nodded her head. "Yes. She asked several times, and I told her I met with Ashley earlier that day and didn't see anyone there."

"Why?" I was pleased she said nothing, but curious. "Why did you lie?"

"She asked a lot of questions. I was tired of her prying." Alex fiddled with the back of a chair, running her fingers across the varnished wood.

"Is that the real reason?"

302

"Sort of. The police told me to say nothing to anyone."

Police or intelligence officers from the New Zealand Security Intelligence Service? I think we know it wasn't police. NZSIS had to know something was going to go down, but not exactly when, so they would've been monitoring all calls from that building, and I bet that's how the one-one-one call was intercepted. I wondered how much Chandler knew.

"Any other reason?"

Alex nodded. "Trisha would ask me to find out things. She said she was trying to help deliver the best service for the client, but she was really nosy, and it made me uncomfortable."

A warning pinged in my mind. Alex was bit by bit throwing her manager under the bus or telling the truth. Which was it?

"Good work, thanks. You can go back to playing with the kitten," I said.

I watched her cross the room and fold herself onto the floor near Laila to resume their game. It appeared to involve Laila hiding in a box and pouncing on a feather that Alex ran around the rim of the box.

"She's in danger, isn't she?" Ginny asked, getting up from the table and moving to watch Alex play with the kitten. Meg had joined the game.

"Yes." Maybe. "There's at least one foreign power interested in what she knows, and willing to commit murder if they can't get her to work for them."

Ginny turned and looked at me. "That sounds like

something I shouldn't know."

I smiled. "Perhaps, but I think you know a lot more than you're letting on."

Ben appeared in the kitchen. A frown moved his eyebrows downward and closer together. Almost monobrow territory.

"What's happening in here?" Ben asked walking into the dining room. Open plan living was the way to go. "There's a shift in the room energy."

I supposed there was. *Nephilim* and *Genesis* tangled with Ginny in my mind. Surely not? She couldn't be involved in this mess.

"Nothing to worry about, Ben," Ginny said, turning to face him with a beaming smile. "You know me, I get things screwed up sometimes."

"Sometimes," Ben replied. "Sometimes you do. But you don't seem to be struggling now. What's going on?"

Crockett nudged me. "What's happening here?"

I shook my head a fraction and pulled up the photo of Perkins' glass door, then stood. I moved to Ginny and showed her the picture. "What does 2:4-7 mean?"

"Twenty-four hours a day, seven days a week. Come on, Ronnie, you know that."

"Sure, if Perkins had written it twenty-four slash seven, but she didn't." It was something else. "What do you see?" I could hear my voice getting more intense with each word. "Ginny, what do you see?"

"*Genesis* 2:4-7," she whispered. "History of the heavens and earth when they were created."

When they were created. When *Genesis* was created. 2:4-7 Impact.

"The impact on the world when *Genesis* was created," I said, staring at Ginny.

"*Genesis* is about creation."

"Our version is about protection."

Crockett and Ben looked from me to Ginny and back, as though they were watching a tennis match.

"I didn't know there was another version," Ginny said.

Then it hit me. "Perkins didn't create the company; she just took credit for it."

"Why would someone do that?"

"Whoever was pulling her chain and getting her to use Alex and whoever else, created the company to hide their agenda."

Was *Alexandrite* also a cover? Were they funding Perkins enterprise? If so, it wasn't out of the kindness of some Russian's heart.

"Does that make sense?" Ginny asked.

"Yes."

"Sometimes the simplest solution is the correct one."

"Sometimes the answer is written in gold on someone's office door," I replied with a smile.

Ben held up his hand. "Excuse me, but what is going on here?"

Ginny looked at me, then Ben. "Nothing much. I just helped Ronnie see something." She smiled at us all. "It really is exciting having you all here."

"What do we need?" Ben asked.

"To get Steph to dig into the bank accounts of Trisha Perkins and find out who is behind all the deposits in those accounts," I said. "I can get to the office. She's already there with Jenn."

"No," Ben and Crockett said in unison.

For a second it looked like they were going to high-five each other.

Good grief.

"Okay, I can go to the bat cave, and she can meet me."

"NO!" They did it again. This time they high-fived.

"Okay, she can come here."

Ginny nodded. Ben and Crockett grimaced. "It's better than you leaving and getting yourself spotted," Crockett said. "She'll need her laptop."

I was already on the phone waiting for Steph to answer.

"Everything okay?" She didn't even say hello.

"Yes. I need you and your accounting skills."

"Okay. We've still got the electronic surveillance in place. Jenn and her mate are having coffee and gas bagging. There is no reason for all of us to be here babysitting the prisoner."

"Enzo is on his way to the office. He'll have a chat with our captive. I want you to run an SDR before making your way to me. Can you see my location?"

"Yes. I can. I will be there within the hour."

I hung up and smiled at everyone. "She's coming."

"You let Steph and Jenn track you and see your location all the time?" Ben asked.

"Yes, always. Why?"

"No reason." His blue eyes twinkled. "So, when we sneak off ..."

"They know or they would if they looked."

"No secrets."

"None."

"That's a good way to be, Ronnie," Ginny said. "Honesty. It's the best policy."

"Sure is," Crockett replied. "Along those lines ... do we tell Alex about Perkins?"

I shook my head. "No, we don't know for sure how that played out so there is no point saying anything unless she asks. If she asks, then we tell her what we know. That's it."

"Fair call."

"Have her parents checked in?" Ginny asked.

"They can't. We have her phones and they're off."

And that reminded me that we needed to check her personal phone for any apps that could switch location on while the phone was actually off. And she had a game app by the person we haven't come across yet: Riley Hart. I knew how I wanted to try to get into her phones, but I'd need a faraday cage. I would turn the phone on in the cage then turn airplane mode on and check for any apps.

"Strange question," I said to Ginny. "You wouldn't happen to have a faraday cage lurking around, would you?"

"They block cell signals, don't they?"

I nodded. "They shield devices so nothing can get a

signal to them or from them."

"I think Tom has something like that in the shed. He made it for something. I don't know what." She rolled her eyes. "You know what men are like. Half the time they make shit just because they can."

Or he's got a secret life.

My bag was by the chair. I fished both the cell phones out and stood. "Lead on," I said.

Ginny smiled and tottered toward the back door.

"Do you know what you're looking for?" Crockett asked before I reached the door.

"Something that doesn't belong, and anything created in China. I'll figure it out."

Crockett grinned. "That's three quarters of all bloody apps."

"Yeah. Needle in the haystack time."

Chapter Thirty:

[Donald: Oops I did it again, again]

I set Nana's hair and got her comfy under the dryer. Then I turned my attention to Ester. She wanted a pink streak in her platinum locks. Easy peasy. I tried talking her into a small rainbow on one side, but she wasn't having it. Frankie stood watch by the ranch slider overlooking the street. Every few minutes she'd pop into the bathroom with updates. I thought if I kept them busy all would be well. The most I could manage was two in the bathroom at a time. So, there was a floater bringing us all the news from the Not-Neighbours.

When Ronnie and I built our house, she insisted we had a huge main bathroom so I could fit a salon chair, and there was room for sitting, and washing hair, and all the business. Our mirrors give the impression the bathroom goes on forever. It's my favourite room in the whole house, well, apart from my bedroom.

"Donald!" Frankie's voice rang down the hallway and ended in a squeak.

I ducked my head out the door. "Still here," I said. She was hurrying toward me as fast as her arthritic hips could carry her.

"Oh, Donald, we need to do something. We must intervene," Frankie gasped while trying to catch her breath in the doorway. "It's awful!"

"What is?" I spun around and checked that Nana was still under the dryer. She was.

"They've shut the wee girl in the car. I didn't realise she was in there until just now. No one has been near that car in at least an hour and a half."

"Oh, no, thank goodness it's not summer." I finished wrapping a centimetre-wide piece of Ester's hair in foil.

"Donald. They're not outside, that child is screaming and crying. She has been for ten minutes. We need to call the authorities." Frankie finally had her breathing under control.

Nana pushed back the hood of the dryer. "What's happening?"

"The wee girl is locked in the car," Frankie said. I spotted her cell phone in her hand. "Who do I ring?"

"Lovely Liam?" I offered. It wouldn't hurt to have him check it out. It's not like the cronies were outside causing trouble. This was a welfare check. Oh, I liked that. Even Ronnie couldn't bitch about a welfare check. "Tell him they need to do a welfare check as the small person is locked in the car."

Ester reached up and patted my hand. "Well done, Donald. That's exactly what should happen," she said, beaming at me from the mirror. "Clever boy."

"Who has his phone number?" Frankie asked into the room.

Pick me! I do. Don't sound so eager, Donald. Deep breath.

"It's in my phone," I replied. "It's on the kitchen bench.

If you bring it here, I'll unlock it for you."

Frankie vanished, then returned holding my phone. She held it up, I looked at it, voila, unlocked. "Can I ring from your phone, or do I have to copy the number?"

"Just use mine, Lovey. He's in Contacts."

Her boney old fingers poked at the screen a few times. "I found it. Lovely Liam," she said with a smile. "He is lovely, isn't he?"

I nodded. Yes. No harm in looking.

What does Crockett say? Can't be good all the time. That man was really growing on me.

I carried on with the shades of pink effect for Ester, while Nana slid the hood down and continued the drying process. It was hard to believe she didn't abandon the dryer and rush out there on her broomstick.

Frankie spoke to Liam and from what we heard, he agreed to send a car over to check on the child.

Then, from nowhere, Frankie said, "They should check the adults as well. I've seen no sign of anyone in that entire time." A minute later she said goodbye and hung up.

"Over an hour?" Nana said, pushing the hood off her head again. "Have they gone out and left the child?"

Frankie shook her head. "I saw them go inside after they put the wee one in the car."

"And there's been no yelling?" Nana inquired.

Frankie bit her lip before replying, "None."

That was highly unusual. Those people couldn't be in the same vicinity for more than ten minutes without screaming, yelling, and fake crying. A chill weaselled its way inside my veins. What if something had happened to them? We wouldn't be that lucky, surely.

"Put that hood back, Nana," I said. "You'll be all ready to go in another ten minutes."

"What about me, Donald?" Ester asked. "I can't go outside like this." She frowned at her reflection. One side of her hair was covered in small foils.

"Ten minutes, police will take at least that long," I said. "I'll wash you out in five. A quick blow dry. You'll see. We won't miss anything."

Frankie scuttled away. She'd left my phone on the vanity. I wiped dye from my nitrile gloves with a paper towel and checked my messages.

Nothing from Ronnie or Enzo. I listened carefully over the sound of the hair dryer for sirens. Nothing.

Five minutes ticked by. I washed out Ester's hair and used the blow dryer to dry it off. Nana declared her hair was done.

"Wait, and I'll take the curlers out," I said, giving her a look. "Patience Nana, I've only got one pair of hands."

She huffed and puffed like an ancient dragon, but she waited. Another miracle. Maybe she didn't want to go to jail?

"What do you think, Ester?" I said, showing her the side of her hair and the little shaded pink section nestled in silver.

"Beautiful, Donald, thank you. They'll all be jealous at lawn bowls on Tuesday."

"Let them know who did it. They can book into the salon," I said, and blew her a kiss in the mirror. "Of course, no one will get those shades of pink, that's just for you!"

"Donald! The curlers," Nana piped up. "Hurry. Wait for me, Ester."

That was my cue. I removed her curlers, softened the curls with my fingers, and set her free.

"Nobody goes outside," I said. "Nobody. Am I clear?"

The pair of them smirked and hustled away. It's terrifying how sprightly they are when they need to be. I looked at the bathroom. It wasn't too messy. It'd have to wait. I couldn't leave them unsupervised for long. Just before I left the room, I put the curlers back into their box and tucked it into the cupboard.

Once in the lounge I discovered the ancient ones were gone.

I peered out the ranch slider. There they were.

Here we go again.

They'd doddered across the road and were gathered around the car. I raced through the house to the bathroom to grab my phone. I tried a cleansing breath, but it didn't work and I stormed down the stairs phone in hand, one-one-one on the screen, ready to push the call button.

"What are you doing?" I shouted from our letterbox. "Get back here immediately!"

Nana turned her head and smiled at me.

That old woman would be the death of us all.

I rushed over the street and grabbed her by the arm. "Come with me."

She tried to shake my hand off. "Look in the car, before

you overreact."

I bent down a fraction and looked into the car. The little girl was sobbing on the backseat, clutching a grotty, threadbare teddy.

No baby car seat to be seen.

Poor wee lamb.

Frankie was trying to talk to her through the glass. Ester tried all the door handles. "Locked," she said. "Where are the police?"

"Coming," I said. "Frankie rang, they said they would." I looked at Frankie for confirmation. She affirmed with a nod.

Nana marched up to the front door of the house with me in tow. I didn't know how to stop her, so I was along for the ride. It's been a good life. If it ends now, at least I married well.

"Hammer on the door, Donald," Nana said.

"Why can't you, old woman? You dragged me up here; I'm sure you can knock with the best of them," I muttered, mostly to myself, as I banged on the door. I banged a second time and called out, "Hello! Your wee girl needs help!"

Nana and I waited for yelling, screaming, and abuse, but nothing followed.

"There's something wrong," I said. Nana was a red flag for these people. If they heard us, they'd be yelling insults and stomping down the stairs to chase us off. "Are they dead?"

Nana's old eyes widened. "They do drugs," she said,

implying that they could be dead with her tone. "Your grandfather would break the door down."

My grandfather was a police officer. He would've had the law on his side. I tried the handle and it opened.

"I prefer doorhandles to brute force, Nan." I may have opened the door, but I did not want to enter. There was a smell. It was a rubbish smell, as if bags of rubbish were festering inside the house. It made sense. I'd seen them use a wheelie bin, but the thing was full again as soon as it was emptied. They could've done with putting out a bunch of council bags as well as the bin. I guess the excess rubbish inhabited the house and added to the ambience. No doubt rodents also lived there now. A shudder ran through me. I don't like rats and mice, or spiders for that matter.

"Go in," Nana said, pushing me.

"No. That's trespassing at the very least. And the police are on the way."

"Get out of the way then, Donald. I'll do it myself."

I planted my feet in front of the open door. "You'll have to go through me, old one."

"For goodness' sake, Donald, don't be so dramatic," Nana said, and pushed me sideways. Ester followed her in. I managed to get my leg in Frankie's way, before she attempted entry and went arse over kite.

"We don't all need to go to jail, Frankie." An attempted appeal to her goodness. "And what about the child? Someone has to keep an eye on her?"

Frankie and I turned back to the car. The wee girl

stared out the windscreen, her face covered in snot and crusty bits of food. I considered following Nana into the smelly house.

A loud sudden bark from next door startled me. I peered around the concrete privacy wall and saw Samantha and Diesel exit their front door.

"Over here, Samantha. Something awful has happened." I waved from the Not-Neighbours' porch.

Samantha waved back and walked Diesel through her carport and to the car in the Not-Neighbours' carport. Diesel shoved his nose on a back passenger window, leaving a slimy smudge. The little girl placed her hand on the glass. Maybe she liked the big dog.

"What's happened? It's been lovely and quiet for a couple of hours, apart from the kid crying on and off," Samantha said. "Diesel's been on edge. Too quiet probably."

"Well, still too quiet," I said. "Nana and Ester have gone inside to stir up some shit. Police are on the way. Frankie called them to do a welfare check on the kid who's been shut in the car for nearly two hours, apparently."

"She has," Frankie insisted. "Poor wee thing must've cried herself to sleep for a little while, but then she started up again."

"Where is that useless mother?" Samantha looked around and then looked past me into the house. "Not like her to be quiet, ever."

"Bog-Mouth is nowhere to be seen. She's been moderately less annoying since she spent the night in a police cell. Maybe she's still there." I could imagine how awful it was for the section on duty with her in there.

Samantha chuckled. "I love that you call her Bog-Mouth. I couldn't think of a better description if I tried."

Diesel investigated the car, then sat so the little girl could see him. She was babbling at him. At least the crying had stopped. I knew Romeo would be watching from the lounge window and wishing we'd brought him out.

In the distance I heard a faint siren. "About time!" I held my breath and put my head in the doorway. As I exhaled, I said, "Nana! Police are almost here. Get out of the house."

I turned my head and took a breath.

It was nasty in there. Very nasty.

A faint reply from Nana made it out the door, "I think they're dead."

Samantha and Frankie appeared confused for a moment. The three of us just stared at each other trying to get our heads around what Nana had said.

"Did she say dead?" I asked.

Frankie shook her head, then nodded. "Yes, I think so."

Samantha walked over to Diesel and clipped his lead onto his collar. "Police might have dogs with them," she said over her shoulder to us. "Did she really say dead?"

"Yeah, that's what I heard," I said.

I held my breath again and yelled into the doorway as I exhaled, "Get out of there, Nana!"

The sirens got louder with every passing second. Come on, Nana. Get out.

Finally, I heard Nana and Ester's voices nearing the door.

"Hurry up old woman, the cops are almost here." A car pulled up on the corner of the street; I could see the red and blue lights sending splashes of colour onto the grey road. "Nana, now!"

Nana appeared in the doorway. I grabbed her arm and helped her across the threshold and to safety near the car. Ester followed, her notebook in hand. She left the door wide open. Our fingerprints would be everywhere. I felt life draining from me. My fingerprints would be in the door handle.

"Donald, are you all right?" Nana asked, patting my arm. "You look pale and that's unusual."

She wasn't wrong. I'm usually no paler than a well-made dark roast coffee with milk and two.

"Nana, we're going to be in trouble," I whispered into her old ear. "So, keep your mouth shut and play nice."

Nana smiled. Her old thin lips stretched until they disappeared. "Donald dear, you are the biggest, most glorious drama queen. Everything will be fine. You'll see. I'm always right, you know that."

Always. I wondered if it was too late to adopt religion. God is supposed to be forgiving, so I gave it a shot. A little voice inside my head prayed. 'Dear God, I'm sorry for everything I've ever done and whomever I've done. Please, don't send us to jail. I'm pretty enough to be someone's toy-boy and I'm sure I could make a go of it, but what about my husband? And Nana is old. Thank you, yours sincerely Donald.'

"Are you with us, Donald?" Ester said, nudging me out of my prayer.

"Yes. Thank you. Or should I say no. I'm not with you. I had absolutely nothing to do with anything. You're on your own," I said as Lovely Liam walked up the street.

Ester slapped at my arm with her chubby little hand. "That, young man, is not very nice. I thought we were a team."

"No. Not when you decided to break and enter. No team here." I moved toward the car. "Romeo needs me." I flapped a hand at our house. "He's old, probably needs a wee." At that moment I caught sight of Samantha's face. She was desperately trying to hold it together and not laugh.

She probably shouldn't laugh, what with the dead in the house. If they were dead. Oh. My. God. The dead!

Liam stopped me from moving by putting his hand up in my path. "Donald, what's going on?"

"They're all dead. We didn't do it. The kid is trapped in the car. My dog needs a wee." I sidestepped Liam and took off across the street like my arse was on fire. I charged inside the front door and slammed it shut behind me.

I collapsed on the bottom stair.

Chapter Thirty-one:

[Ronnie: I hope you are joking]

I jammed my feet into my hiking boots, tucking my laces inside instead of doing them up, and followed Ginny into the shed. She turned a light on and walked to the far side of the large workspace.

"It's over here somewhere," she said. "Hold on, here we go." She lifted a drop cloth off the bench and revealed a metal box.

"Now I just need to figure out how to put a phone in it and still be able to turn it on without a signal escaping."

"That sounds tricky. If you turn the phone on out here it'll show up if someone is looking for it, that's right, isn't it?"

"Yes. How do you know things like that?"

"I watch a lot of true crime programmes on the telly and read a lot of crime novels."

That seemed reasonable.

I inspected the box. It wasn't as large as mine at work, but then mine was for storing a variety of tech gear. The box Tom made was maybe big enough for a laptop. It was front opening. I could see inside it.

"Microwaves make pretty good faraday cages," I said. That's what the box reminded me of: a microwave oven.

"Maybe this was one once," Ginny said. "I don't remember if it was or wasn't, but that's not unusual. You can use also heavyduty tin foil to block signals can't you?"

"Yes. You could line a wardrobe or cupboard with heavy duty tin foil and that would make an effective faraday cage."

Ginny chuckled. "Remember the protests, all those anti-everything people with their tin foil hats on because they thought the government was using some magic weapon on them?"

"No one will forget that part of recent New Zealand history. I loved how they started to get sick, and all the anti-vax lunatics declared it was the government turning electromagnetic weapons on them. Of course, it couldn't be COVID because they didn't believe in it." I put the first phone in the box and turned it on. Then I quickly turned airplane mode on and scrolled through all the apps while the phone was still in the cage. I figured it was shielded enough and if they picked up on the signal, we'd just have to deal with it.

I found four apps in the settings that I'd never seen before and hadn't heard about. All four were Chinese in origin. I scrolled through the home screen and app screens again in case I'd missed the apps, but there were no corresponding icons. I pulled a pen from my pocket and wrote the names of the apps on my palm. My next task was to look for anything created by Riley Hart. It'd be easier if I knew what his company was called. Maybe he just used his name? There was nothing that looked like a game at all. Then I turned the phone off and left it in the cage.

"Did you find anything?"

"Yes. Don't know if it's what we're looking for, but I think I'll leave that phone out here in the box."

"Good idea. Don't want to take undue risks."

I put the second phone in the box and turned it on, then enabled Airplane mode. I scrolled through all the apps in the settings of the phone and found the same four. Then I swiped through the phone's menu pages, but none of those apps had an icon present, just like the other phone. If Alex didn't open settings, she wouldn't even know she had extra apps lurking in the background. I checked them with the list on my palm. The same. I looked for anything designed by Riley Hart. Bingo. A game called 'Lives of Hart'. I looked at the phone to confirm for myself that it was her personal phone. That had to be it.

I turned the phone off and left it in the cage with the other phone. Then I closed the door on them both.

"Same?" Ginny asked.

"Yes. No icon, but definitely in the app list."

Ginny covered the box with the paint-splattered drop cloth, and we went back inside the house. I left my shoes inside the back door.

Crockett was rinsing a cup in the kitchen. "What'd you find?"

I showed him my palm. "These. And a game app called 'Lives of Hart.'"

Crockett typed the names into Notes on his phone. "Let's look them up in the app store."

We made our way back to the table.

Crockett and I both searched the app store on our own phones for each of the names I'd found on the suspect phones.

"I'm not finding anything," Crockett said. "For the four you found in settings."

"Nor am I."

"Let's see what Safari can find."

Still nothing.

I copied the names of the apps into an email and saved it in drafts. Then I rang Jenn's cell phone.

"Everything okay, Ronnie?"

"I think so. There's an email in our drafts folder. Can you run the names in it through all the databases we have access to?"

"All?"

"Yes."

"You want me to use your computer?"

"Yes."

"I've got company."

"I know. Do you trust him?"

"Yep."

"You know where the password is?"

"The lockbox in your drawer."

"That's all you need. Get back to me if you find something. And thank you."

"All good."

Jenn hung up. I smiled at Crockett. "If there is anything to find, Jenn will find it."

"Excellent work. That game app has a lot of reviews. That one was easy to find in the App store. Looks like people love playing it."

"Could be legit. Maybe it wasn't the way the other four supposed apps got on her phone."

Crockett's eyes moved up to meet mine. "There's one way to find out."

"Download the game and see what else we get." I could feel a frown forming and tried to smooth it with my fingertips. If I wasn't careful, by the time we handed Alex over I'd have deep permanent frown lines. "Bags not it."

"Real mature, Ronnie." He grinned at me. "Let's make Ben do it."

Ginny took a seat next to Crockett at the table. "You have an exciting career. Little bit more intense than breeding Birman cats."

A cat leapt onto Crockett's knees. "Who is this?" he asked, stroking the animal from head to tail.

"That is the old man of the family, Cricket. He's not usually that interested in knees." Ginny pointed to a leather covered footstool in the lounge. "That's his spot."

"Animals like Crockett," I said. "I think it's because they recognise him as kin."

Crockett ignored my comment and continued stroking the cat.

"What's next?" Ben asked, joining us with a large fluffy cat in his arms.

"You get to download a game app so we can see if it was the vehicle used to deliver some secret apps to Alex's phone." And potentially every other phone that had that game on it. What a great way to gather intelligence on everyone. Might even be better than TikTok at gathering information.

Ben put the cat down on a chair and pulled his phone from his jacket pocket. "What's it called?"

"Lives of Hart, spelt H-A-R-T."

He typed on his phone, then showed me the app store screen with the game on it. It matched the icon I saw on Alex's phone.

"Yeah, that's it."

"Here goes," Ben said as he authorised the download. It took no time at all to download the app. "Got it. Now where did it hide its extras?"

"Settings," I replied. "You're looking for these." I showed him my palm.

He scrolled down the list of apps in his settings. "They're here."

"Check to see if they're on your screen as icons."

He shook his head. "Nope."

"Okay, delete the app and see what happens." I stood and moved next to him so I could see his phone.

Ben held his finger on the app and chose 'remove app'. It disappeared. He went back into settings and the other 'apps' were still there.

"Now that's sneaky," he said. "Let's get rid of these too."

"Have you got something that will scrub all traces of them and the main app from everywhere it could hide on your phone?"

He nodded and cleaned his phone. Then he doubled checked everything was gone, powered down, and restarted the phone.

"Everyone who downloaded that game is carrying around something that is spying on them, and possibly turning their phones on, when they think they're off, while blocking any evidence of the phone being on. That'll be why there were four little hidden apps." Crockett said. "I bet people who spot them, scrub them, but if you don't know what's hiding then ..."

"Then those phones are listening devices and giving out GPS and storing keystrokes, maybe even taking video."

"How many game players are going to look for security breaches?" I muttered more to myself than the team.

"Judging by the number of TikTok users, and they were told publicly by the FBI and other agencies how dangerous that app is, I'd say none. Even when you tell them they still do it," Crockett said. "Here's a true nugget of info for you about TikTok. It actually beat Google as the most searched platform in twenty-twenty-two. What does that tell you about the intelligence of people in the world?"

"People searched for it, or people used the search bar on that app to find what they needed, rather than using Google?"

"Used the search bar. Astounding isn't it?"

"Yes and it tells me the world is absolutely fine with

unfriendly countries gathering their data," I replied. "What hope do we have against this kind of thing?"

Crockett shrugged.

"Who is Riley Hart, Ronnie?" Ginny asked. "That was the name you said?"

"A game developer, as far as we know," I replied.

"How would those extra things be included in his game download?"

"They are the two possible ways. Either he put them there, or someone else did," I said.

"Doesn't matter which because he isn't our problem," Crockett added. "That doesn't mean that no one will be told, they will. But we're not going after him."

"Now what?" Ben asked. He moved a chair so he could sit next to me.

"I'm waiting for Steph. Jenn is digging into databases looking for anything on the apps I found. Enzo is chatting to the person who arrived at the house we had staked out."

"Chatting, great description," Ben said with a laugh. "Heard from Art and Jo?"

"Not for a while," I said. "They had surveillants watching them."

"Should we be providing them with backup?"

"Just in case," I added. "Everyone is busy, I have no one to send. What about you Crockett?"

"My tradies, they'd make formidable foes."

"That they would, but can they handle counter-sur-veillance?" I didn't know much about them, except that

Art was considered one of his tradies. He was a carpenter by trade, and he could one-hundred percent hold his own in our mixed-up world.

Crockett nodded. "You know it."

"Can you get them in?"

"Sure can." He picked up his phone and made a call to Art and checked they were okay. Then he made another call.

"Hi Dink, it's Crockett here mate. Can you get hold of Plunger? Got a counter surveillance assignment for you both." I could only hear Crockett's side of the conversation. "Flick me a text when you two are ready to roll." He paused for a few seconds. "I'm sending you two to back up Art." There was more silence from Crockett and a low mumble from the phone in his hand. "Wouldn't hurt to be armed." Dead air. "I'll text the address. Take two cars. Usual check-in format." Crockett hung up.

"Good?"

"Yep."

"Does anyone need anything?" Ginny asked.

I shook my head. Ben and Crockett did the same. Alex was engrossed with her game with Laila and another similar looking, but bigger cat. Everyone was okay. I let that realisation rush through me. Everyone was okay. We just need to figure out a way to *keep* everyone okay and get Alex to the meeting. If people would just tell the truth, then it would save a lot of tail chasing.

"Crockett?"

"Yes, Ronnie." He turned his head and gave his full attention.

"You got tapped for this stint, and it was suggested you use me and Ben, yes?"

"Yes."

"We don't do babysitting gigs, so why us?" I couldn't help but feel Crockett knew more than we did and there was something underpinning the situation. It was more than Alex and her H-SAM and her witnessing a hit. And it was a hit because if another government was behind the murder of Ashley Chu, what else would you call it?

"I believe it has something to do with our inability to follow direct orders and your delightful location skills." He smiled at me. "We've been over this."

Inability to follow orders? Really? He wasn't wrong, though.

"Yeah, I know, but this is weird, isn't it?" I toyed with the edge of a placemat. "I'll sort of buy the inability to follow orders. The Dream Team does have a reputation for digging down and uncovering nonsense. But it's not unwarranted. We don't go looking for trouble. It just happens." I smoothed the mat edge with my fingers. "People don't give us all the information and then we discover things and on it goes."

"Like Nana tends to uncover things?" Ben asked with a cheeky grin.

I whacked his arm. "Don't start. You know bloody well that woman goes looking."

I glanced at my phone screen and saw a message pop up from Steph. I love doing that, nothing there and then I look, and magically there's a new message.

"Steph is two doors down the street and coming in on foot," I said.

"I will go and meet her," Ginny said. "That way if anyone is spying, they'll just see me greeting a friend."

"Thanks Ginny," Ben said. "Smart thinking."

Ginny teetered through the lounge into the hall. I heard the door open, then close. I forgot there was a front door.

Chapter Thirty-two:
[Crockett: Emily, Emily, Emily]

Steph and Ronnie set themselves up in Tom's office. Ginny was talking to Alex and Ben in the lounge. My phone rang. It was Emily. I swiped my index finger across the screen and rose from the table. I walked into the kitchen with the phone to my ear.

"Hi, Emily. Everything all right?"

"Hello, Crockett. No. It is not all right."

My heart dropped. "Are you okay?"

"Yes, I am okay."

"Good. Tell me what's going on?"

"Enzo dropped me off at Donald's house because I am pretending to be Ronnie." I wanted to hurry her to the point, but I knew not to. She would get there. "There are many police cars on the corner." She paused for breath. "Crockett, something is wrong with Donald."

"Police? Where are they?"

"The cars are on the corner, but the officers are at the ... the Not-Neighbours'."

"Okay. Where is Donald?"

"He is on the stairs. He will not move. I had to step around him to get up the stairs."

"Is he hurt?"

"There is no blood that I can see."

"Good. Where are you now?"

"I am at the top of the stairs. He is at the bottom. Nana and her friends, the *cronies*, are across the road."

"Do you need me to come?"

"Yes. I do not know what to do."

"Okay, give me ten minutes. I'll come to you," I said. Ben had joined me. "I'll be there soon." I hung up.

"Problem?" Ben asked.

"Police at the Not-Neighbours'. Donald sounds like he's freaked out. Emily doesn't know what to do. I'm going."

"Take the Harley. You don't have much choice. At least then you'll look like Enzo going home."

"Yeah, I was going to do just that. Let Ronnie know that Emily had a problem if she notices me gone. Don't mention the rest until I find out what's really going on."

"That's sensible."

"I'll see you soon." I opened the back door and sat on the cold top step to put my boots on. Then, I charged across the yard into the shed.

Back roads and taking it easy was my plan. Even with detours, double backs, and sticking to the speed limit, I was pulling up outside Ronnie and Donald's within ten minutes. I opted to come in from the north, so I'd avoid the police on the corner. I jumped off the bike in the driveway and watched the goings on across the road for a few seconds. I heard Frankie's voice. And I figured Nana and Ester would be in the thick of whatever was going on over there. I knocked on the front door. The door opened. Emily moved out of the way so I could cross the threshold. She shut the door behind me. I took off Enzo's helmet and set it on a table in the entrance way, next to a large vase of flowers.

"Emily, are you really all right?" I asked, taking her hand in mine. My massive paw swallowed her tiddler of a hand.

"Yes, Crockett. Thank you for coming."

"Donald, what's happening here?" I moved closer to him. "Hey, Donald." I touched his shoulder with my free hand.

Donald spoke but didn't look up, "They're all dead!"

Oh, shit.

"Who, Donald, who are dead?"

He pointed to the front door. "Not-Neighbours. Dead."

My eyes darted around my eye sockets as I tried to work out what could've happened. Nope, nothing.

"I'm going to need more information before I come up with a plan here, Donald."

"Wasn't me!"

"Never said it was. Just tell me what happened."

Emily twisted and looked out the window next to the door. "I know that policeman," she said. "He is Doug. He is coming across the road."

"Donald, tell me what happened," I said. "Make it snappy, bud."

"Nana, she happened. The little kid was crying in the car. Nana and those wretched women went over there, and I followed to bring them back." A loud knock at the door spurred Donald on. "I touched the door handle, that's all. Nana and Ester went inside. It wasn't me!"

"Okay. Settle down."

The knocker knocked again.

I spun Emily into my arms. "Shall we answer the door?"

She smiled up at me. "Yes."

With my arm around her shoulders, I turned the handle. Donald cowered on the bottom step. Light filled the entrance way, only to be partially blocked by a police officer.

"Hello, Doug," Emily said. "I remember you."

He smiled. "I remember you, too, Emily."

I moved a step closer and offered my hand, "Dave Crocker." Doug shook my hand. I checked the sky for any unwanted eyes. There was nothing obvious. "Come in."

"I wanted a word with Donald."

We could all see Donald hunched on the stair. "He's right here. Hope you don't mind if I stick around."

"Not at all." Doug stepped into the entranceway and quietly closed the door behind him. "Donald, the little girl is safe. I thought you might like to know," Doug's voice remained measured and calm, as if he was talking to a scared kid, not a grown-arsed man.

Donald nodded. "Thank you."

"Can you tell me what you know about the events across the road?" Doug held his notebook and pen, ready to write.

Donald took a breath. He wiped his eyes with his hands.

"It wasn't me. I didn't do anything!"

"No sense getting worked up, Donald. I need you to tell me in your own words what happened across the road," Doug said. He maintained a calm voice and manner.

"I'm a brown boy who was in the wrong place at the wrong time, and that feels like it would make me suspect number one." Donald thrust his hands out, wrists together. "Just arrest me and get it over with."

Doug looked from me to Donald, then ignored his outstretched hands, and patted him on the shoulder. "I'm not here to arrest you. I know you touched the door handle and opened the door."

"It wasn't locked," squawked Donald. "I didn't go in. I didn't do anything."

"Donald, listen to me." Doug crouched in front of Donald. "I need you to tell me your version of what happened. Can you do that, please?"

Donald wiped his watery eyes with his hands before telling Doug his version of events. I listened as Donald explained. When he finished, Doug thanked him.

"What happens now?" Donald's voice trembled.

"We are waiting on the coroner and forensics. The house is a crime scene and will stay that way for at least twenty-four hours. There will be guards posted." Doug stood.

"Do you know what happened?" I asked.

"It's too early to know, but it wasn't a drug overdose. The deaths were violent."

Donald grabbed at his own shirt front. "Oh my God!

Where's Nana?"

"She is talking to a detective outside the house." Doug checked his phone. "I'd better get back. I hope you are okay, Donald. We can get Victim Support to give you a ring or come over. Do you think that would help?"

Donald nodded. "I'm not going to be arrested?"

"No, you're not."

"What about Nana?"

"She won't be arrested either, although I'm sure Ronnie would appreciate it if she was taken into the station and given a severe talking to," Doug replied. "We are thankful that no one else was injured."

"We didn't see anyone go into the house," Donald said. "Frankie only saw the Not-Neighbours go inside. I was doing Nana and Ester's hair in the bathroom. It doesn't even face that way." His words came out in a panicked stream. "How could it be violent? Did they kill each other? How did it happen without us hearing anything? I don't understand what happened."

Doug nodded. "It's all right, Donald." Doug gave him a reassuring smile and patted him on the shoulder. "We think the perpetrators entered and exited the property through the back door. Someone on Tararua Street saw two males jump the fence."

"How do you know it was them who did it?" Donald asked. I guess he was making sure it wouldn't be pinned anywhere near him.

"As I said, two males were seen jumping the fence. The same people were seen to enter the back door. They left ten minutes later. One of them carried a child's backpack that he didn't have going in."

"The times work?" I asked.

"Yes," Doug replied. "I've got to get back. Your Nana will be home shortly. She's waiting for an Oranga Tamariki case worker to come and collect the little girl."

"At least they did something to protect the wee one," Donald said. "Poor little thing. Maybe she'll have a chance at a better life."

Doug smiled kindly at Donald and let himself out.

Emily sat down next to Donald on the step and put an arm around his shoulders. "You will be all right, Donald. Doug did not arrest you."

He hugged her back.

I gave Enzo a ring and left a voice mail that appraised him of the situation. It was the best option. He'd hear it when he had the chance.

"I think we should make a move up the stairs," I said to Donald and Emily. "Come on."

They followed me up. Romeo was waiting, wagging his long thin tail, and happy to greet me and follow me into the living room. I looked out the ranch slider without moving the net curtain. There were police cars every-where. I saw an ambulance. It was a bit late for that, but I suppose it was a formality. There was a white van parked near the house. People in white protective suits moved in and out of the house carrying cases - forensic techs, probably.

Crime scene tape fluttered in the breeze. A tent was

erected over the front yard, covering the area from the front door to the carport and providing some shelter and privacy for the techs as they worked. It'd also stop anyone taking photos when they were ready to bring out the body bags. The area was crawling with police and other people. A cordon was set up. It looked like half the neighbourhood was standing by it watching.

Lookie Loos. I could understand their interest. People were murdered in their street. Even though the people who were murdered in the street were the ones who also terrorised the neighbourhood, it's still disturbing to think of violent crime so close to home.

News crews joined the spectators. Terrific.

That was going to make it fun to leave.

I saw a reporter moving toward Nana. Disaster. That had to be stopped.

Donald gasped from behind me. "She can't talk to them. There'll be another death and I'm too young and pretty to die."

Emily moved up beside me. "No, Nana, no!" She turned around and fled.

She was gone from sight before I could stop her. I heard the front door open and shut, and watched Emily make a bee-line across the road to June Tracey.

"She's on a mission," Donald commented. "Pity the fool that tangles with our Emily."

I watched. To go out there I'd need to plonk the helmet on my head and that'd look suspicious unless I got on the bike and roared off. I wasn't planning on leaving yet.

Emily grabbed June by the hand, held her other hand up palm out to the camera, and said something. She towed June back across the street, Frankie and Ester hobbled along behind. The front door opened and a minute later closed. A commotion rose from the entrance way.

"I'll go see," I said to Donald. "You keep watching. I see why this has kept you entertained. It's hard to look away." I would've set up cameras and watched those idiots without them knowing and that would've provided an added bonus of footage to share with the police.

Donald nodded. "Now you see the dilemma I've had for weeks and weeks. It's like watching a very slow train wreck."

"You need cameras Donald. Talk to Ronnie about it when she gets back."

I greeted Emily at the top of the stairs. She still had June's hand in hers.

"I brought them home," Emily said, releasing June's hand.

"Yes, you did. Good work."

June scowled at me. "Was that your doing, Crockett?"

"No, ma'am, that was all Emily."

"I don't know that I believe you, young man. Emily doesn't behave like that," June said, and huffed her way into the living room.

Emily grinned at me. "I don't behave like that," she said with a shrug and a laugh.

The other ladies shambled up the last stairs and into

the kitchen before I could comment on Emily's use of a contraction. The Emily I knew didn't use contractions. The chattering from Frankie and Ester subsided as they moved through to the lounge. Emily was at the sink. She filled the jug and turned it on.

"Coffee?"

"Yes, please. Emily, you don't drink coffee."

"I feel like a coffee," she replied. "That's okay, isn't it?"

"Yes, it's okay. I just didn't think you liked it."

She placed mugs on the bench. "I could not remember if I liked coffee or not, but now I know I do. Or did. I want a coffee."

"How do you suppose you have your coffee?"

She grinned at me. "I suppose I have it NATO."

That wasn't a term I'd heard recently. NATO = White with two.

I watched as Emily made coffees. She didn't ask anyone if they wanted coffee or how they had their coffee. She handed me mine. "Hope I got it right."

"Black with one; yes, you did."

"I'll take these out. There is a tray somewhere?"

I put my mug down and located a tea tray in the pantry. I put the tray on the bench. "Do you want me to carry it?"

"No." She loaded the tray and left the room.

The second thing I noticed that day about Emily was her lack of limp. It was usually barely noticeable, but I could pick it, but not today. She came back with the empty tray and a smile.

"I got all the coffees correct."

She did better than I would've.

"Do you want to stay in here and have our coffee?" I asked, as I moved around the other side of the kitchen bench and perched on one of the four bar stools there.

"Yes. I would like that." She moved her mug across in front of an empty stool, then joined me.

"This is nice." I took another sip of my coffee.

Emily sipped hers. A smile danced on her lips. "I do like my coffee NATO."

"I'm glad." I turned so I could see her easier. "Would you like to go out with me when this operation is finished?"

"Where would we go?"

"Movies and dinner?"

"A date?"

"Yes."

"I would like that very much, Crockett."

"Do I have to stop calling you Milo now that you drink coffee?" I nudged her with my elbow.

She giggled.

"I still like Milo. And I still like you calling me Milo."

"Something has changed though, hasn't it?"

She nodded. "I can remember some things I couldn't before. It happens every now and then. Memories fight their way through the damaged parts of my brain and show me who I was."

"Who were you, Emily Jones?"

"I was a cop."

I let that sit for a moment. I did not know that. Is that how she remembered Doug? Ronnie told me Emily was a private investigator and they worked together.

She sipped her coffee. Emily looked happy. Her eyes smiled. There was no confusion in her expression at all. This is the Emily I had glimpsed a few times since I'd met her. I saw this Emily when we were working surveillance once, and I saw this Emily when Ronnie threw a Glock at her during an interesting mission. She'd always slid back into the Emily I'd first met. But I think little bits were starting to stick. She wasn't entirely the Emily she was when I first met her. That Emily had a note on her bathroom mirror that said, 'Good morning, Emily Jones.' Sometimes she forgot who she was. Last time I was at Emily's house the note was gone. Ronnie said once that she thought the real Emily was trapped inside this new version, and one day she might break through and come back to stay.

"Hey, Milo," I said and touched her hand.

She put her cup down and smiled at me. "Yes, Crockett?"

"I like spending time with you."

"I like that, too, Crockett."

That was all I needed to hear. Life was good. No matter what happened with Operation Hide and Seek, life was good.

Chapter Thirty-three:
[Ronnie: Lies, spies, and compromise]

Crockett was gone longer than I anticipated, and I hadn't heard back from Enzo. Maybe the captive was making things difficult. Steph made quick progress digging into the financials of Perkins and her business.

Her company was a legit public relations management company or whatever, but hadn't been around long, and definitely had some dodgy practices. Her business sprang into existence four years ago and opted to represent influencers. They didn't do anything but manage influencers. She had fifteen different influencers on the books; they were dotted all about the country, but the ones that got the most work were in the Wellington Region. It looked like she reached out to Alex without knowing how special she really was. That part was all good. It was the undercurrent and backers that weren't so good.

The personal accounts took longer. There were five accounts, all fed from different sources or what looked like different sources. Steph was still digging down into the layers-upon layers under the surface.

I left her to it and wandered through the house looking at crystals and semi-precious stones in the many large glass cabinets. Apart from amethyst and quartz, I didn't recognise much, but they were beautiful and somehow calming to look at.

Ginny came over to me as I stood near a cabinet in the dining room.

"How do you remember what they all are?"

"I don't," she said with a smile. "I know hundreds of them, but sometimes I need to look some of them up."

I sat down at the table with her across from me.

Ben came over and joined us, leaving Alex curled up on a couch with the kitten fast asleep in her lap. Alex was reading.

"Nothing from Crockett yet?" Ben asked.

"Nope, not from Enzo either."

"So, what was Crockett doing again?"

"Checking on Emily. She rang him about something."

"And he left this ..." I waved my hand toward Alex. "And risked being in the open because Emily rang him." I knew he liked her; we all knew he liked her, but it seemed a bit much.

Ben shrugged. "I wasn't the one who got the call, so I have no opinion."

Bullshit.

I narrowed my eyes at him. "Tell me again why he left?"

"Emily had a problem," Ben replied with a smile. "That's all I know."

"Where was this problem?"

"Wherever Emily is."

Steph hurried toward us through the kitchen with a grin on her face. "I've got something. Has anybody ever heard of a Russian named Novikoff?"

Ben and I looked at each other. Nope.

"Baranov, but not Novikoff," I said.

Ginny stood and went to join Alex. Steph slid into her vacated chair.

"Novikoff is who I found. The backer. The name behind the revenue funnels feeding those private accounts."

"Did you find anything else about him?"

"Oh, yeah," Steph said, grinning from ear to ear. "He made, and makes, his money from farming, oil, and his mining companies. He mines iron ore, copper, cobalt, diamonds, and gold as far as I can tell, with a quick look."

"Farms?"

"Sable farms. Mink farms. He owns four sable farms in China and exports sable and mink coats back to Russia. He also owns two in Russia. One of them is a hunting operation because wild sable is superior fur-wise."

"Sounds like you've had a crash course on fur trading," I said with a smile. "I can hear all the vegans shouting their displeasure from here."

"That's where he makes his money?" Ben asked.

"Yes, he has many legal revenue streams," Steph said. "Novikoff enjoys a lavish lifestyle. He is an oligarch. He's managed to continue his lifestyle despite the seizing of assets due the Russian Ukraine war. He lost a few ridiculously large yachts and a couple of islands, but the rest of his empire remains. Sanctions halted some of his fur trade, but not all."

"It's so hard to be filthy rich," I said with as much sympathy as I could. "I feel for him."

"Life is hard," Steph agreed with a smile. "His is going to get harder, I'd imagine."

"He wouldn't be able to just deposit overseas funds without triggering the bank's money laundering alarms, so how is he doing it?"

"He's funnelling money through legitimate businesses in the US, Australia, and the UK."

"He owns them?"

"He does."

"Okay, so we have an oligarch who owns actual companies and made his money legally, but then created a bunch of shell companies to fund Perkins privately. She wasn't running it through her business. He must've got her to open those accounts?"

"That's where it unravels," Steph said. "Perkins opened all the accounts. I cannot prove that it was at someone else's behest, just that she opened them."

"The big question is why he was going to such lengths to get information on companies here." I didn't mention the *Genesis* thing. That was not something Steph knew anything about. As much as I trust her and Jenn, there are some things they shouldn't know for their own safety. *Genesis* was very much one of those things. "Or was he? Maybe he was paying Perkins for something else?"

"I can track the money, but I can't give you any concrete reasons for it," Steph said. "No doubt you three can start plugging information into your secret squirrel databases and come up with a decent theory." She glanced around the room. "Where is Crockett?"

I shook my head. "Taking care of an issue, apparently."

"Fair enough. You heard from Jenn?"

"Nope. Nor Enzo."

We needed to drill all the way down on Novikoff.

"Hey Steph, you didn't come across the name Baranov anywhere?"

"Yes, I did. A leather goods manufacturer who deals with one of Novikoff's tanneries. The company is *Alexandrite*. It has five showrooms around the world."

"There is one in Wellington," I said.

She nodded. "Baranov's name came up as the business owner of all the stores."

"Transaction-wise, what did you see?"

"What I would class as legitimate transactions for goods. But I didn't dig far because that wasn't on my radar. I can get back into it and see how much more I can pull out."

"How do you even get into this stuff?" I asked.

Steph smiled, tapped the side of her nose, and said, "It might not be entirely legal so best we leave that alone."

Right. Enough said. Moving on.

"So, this oligarch guy is behind all the payments into the private accounts," I said. "How did he circumvent the triggers for overseas funds, because even I know, Australian money is overseas funds."

"They were spread about and made to look like payments for goods." Steph put her notebook on the table. "What was done here was payments for things sold on TradeMe and through eBay."

"Were there things sold?"

"I doubt it. I can't prove they weren't sold; there is a trail that indicates payment was made for various auctions of goods and services. And every transaction was under any triggering amount."

"Isn't it one thousand dollars for foreign money?"

She nodded. "I have taught you well, Grasshopper. So, they came in with many smaller amounts, but nothing that totalled a thousand dollars within a four-week period."

"That's all they needed to do?"

"Really someone should have noticed, but because there were reference numbers and auctions, it looked pretty damn above board."

"How did you know it wasn't?"

"I found the old auction pages for a few of the amounts by tracing the reference numbers. Looks like the same product was re-listed over and over again. That happens when people have more than one of the item, and it's common for stores using TradeMe and eBay, but I smelt a rat and kept digging."

"When you open an account, doesn't the bank ask a lot of questions, like how much do you think you'll be depositing in a set period and where the money will be coming from?"

Steph nodded. "I'm impressed with your memory, Grasshopper. But all the account owner has to do for a personal account is say, I'm using it when I sell things on TradeMe and maybe birthday/Christmas money from rellies. That could be any amount."

Ben leaned closer. "So, Perkins set up the accounts, told lies about where the money was coming from, this Russian dude put money in her account for goods he didn't receive, and she was paying her 'influencers' with that money. They thought they were on her payroll, but in fact they were being paid by a Russian."

"We can't say for certain he didn't receive any goods or services he paid for. It all could be above board. Maybe she has a side business and legitimately sells via TradeMe and eBay," Steph said to Ben. "Let's just say, you couldn't use what I found as evidence in court. I can trace the money no problem, but I can't give you motive."

"What were the auctions for?"

"Four of them were for marketing packages. I couldn't see details because they were closed. But because she was a public relations type person that could be above board and she may have sold actual PR packages." Steph reached for a glass of water in front of me and took a big sip. "I have no idea why Perkins would pay her 'influencers' from private accounts. That's not good business practise."

"But there is definitely a Russian oligarch feeding her accounts?" Ben asked.

"Hell, yes, there is," Steph said with a smile. "Now someone should make me a cocktail. I could murder a rum and coke."

"I heard cocktail," Ginny said from across the lounge. "A woman after my own heart. I'll be right there."

"You two enjoy your cocktails. Ben and I need to do some thinking," I said and motioned to Ben to follow me into the hallway.

Ginny laughed. "Is that what the kids are calling it these days?"

Ben waved over his shoulder and joined me in the hallway. We walked to the end by Tom's office.

"If the Russian part of this equation is above board, why did *Genesis* imply that the puppet master was Russian," I asked.

"Baranov and Novikoff know each other, or at least Baranov deals with some of Novikoff's companies. They're both legitimate businessmen."

I looked into Ben's pale blue eyes. "You're a legitimate actor. It's your profession. I'm sure almost everyone knows you from at least one series on the telly and has seen you in a few movies."

"Good point," Ben said, moving my long hair back over my shoulders with his hands. The warmth of his hands resting on the back of my neck felt good.

"Baranov could very well track all his coats. I would if I was letting some kid wear it for publicity purposes. She was worried about it, so it wasn't hers to keep."

"She was, or is, worried about it because she hasn't finished her publicity work with *Alexandrite*," Ben reminded me. "And they could ask for it back."

"Is Baranov behind the questions Perkins asked or was it someone else?"

"Let's call him and find out?"

As tempted as I was to yell out Baranov's name, I didn't. I knew that wasn't what Ben meant. It would've been funny, though.

I pulled my phone out of my pocket, chose Baranov from my contacts, and rang him.

I had nothing to lose. I wondered, as I put my phone on speaker, and we listened to it ringing, if he'd be at work on a Sunday. Did he have a life outside of the company? And if he owned stores in various countries, why did he live in New Zealand? My guess would be because it's a very nice place to live and a lot of people have landed on our shores looking for a better more stable life. It didn't have to be a sinister reason to want to live in New Zealand. I wouldn't want to live in Europe right now.

A voice message service kicked in. I smiled at Ben and left a message at the sound of the beep. "It's Ronnie Tracey. I'd like to talk to you about a full fur coat for my grandmother's birthday. I was thinking sable. Preferably wild sable. If that's something you can handle, would you call me back on this number, thank you." I added my phone number before hanging up.

Ben's hands moved from my neck to my shoulders. "That should get him interested."

"Nana might even get a coat. She'd love it. She still wears her fox stole every chance she gets. Pretty sure that was handed down to her from her mother."

"You're a generous and kind granddaughter, Ronnie." Ben dipped his head slightly, his lips brushed mine. "Nana is a lucky old woman."

Arm in arm we returned to the dining room. Steph and Ginny were deep in conversation about various precious stones. I noted Steph was halfway through her rum and cola, and Ginny had barely started her cocktail. I presumed it was vodka and lemonade as that's what I'd seen her drink before. My eyes landed on Alex. She was asleep on the couch; the book she'd been reading lay open and upside down on the floor. Two cats were curled up next to her.

"You two okay there?" Ginny asked when she noticed our presence.

"Yes," Ben replied. "I'll make us coffee. Any idea when Tom will be home?"

"Use his fancy espresso machine," Ginny said. "He trusts you. I thought he would've been home by now, so any time, I suppose."

"Thanks," Ben said.

"Do you need help?" I asked as I started to rise from the table.

"No. You sit there and supervise," he said with a chuckle.

As I listened to Steph and Ginny talking, thoughts started to weasel and wriggle in my mind. Two Russians. A dead artist. A tracker in a coat. A shoe salesman. A tracker in the shoes. Perkins' invasive questions. The statue she sent the shoe salesman. Lies about how and where a murder took place. The killer was Asian. *Genesis* said the puppet master was a Russian codenamed Whiskey Tango Foxtrot or maybe his/her call sign was

Whiskey Tango Foxtrot. *Genesis* analyst reports said they'd been aware of Alex for a while. She was code-named Nephilim. She was subpoenaed by the Crown to testify in a trial that we found no court docket for. Her parents were out of the country and hadn't reached out. A hunting pack in Upper Hutt looking for us and Alex. Surveillance and counter-surveillance. We were employed to keep Alex alive and deliver her to the court and then her new life.

The tangle of nonsense wound itself around and around, tighter and tighter.

A coffee cup arrived in front of me.

"Thank you," I said.

Ben took a seat next to me with his coffee.

"What were you thinking about?" he asked, his voice low enough that only I heard him.

I matched his volume, "Running over everything we know, I still can't make sense of the puppet master being Russian because it doesn't seem to be either of the Russians we know about. Unless we haven't come across that person yet?"

"You think Baranov is an actual fur trader and business owner?"

"No proof he isn't," I said.

"Likewise, no proof Novikoff is involved in anything more than purchases made from a myriad of shell companies via TradeMe and eBay."

"It sounds as dodgy as hell when it's put like that."

"Sure does."

I sipped my coffee and enjoyed the deliciousness.

"Has all your thinking come up with anything?" Ben asked. "And this is good coffee."

"Yes, it is, and no I haven't come up with anything. We still don't know if Alex is working for someone. We still don't know who the Russian is. We still don't know why Chu was killed, but I think that's the pivot point. We have no idea who rammed the motel."

"Alex said Perkins asked a lot of questions and she didn't always answer them. She said she thought Perkins was using her to spy on companies, didn't she?"

I sighed. Steph and Ginny looked at me, so I threw them a smile and sipped my coffee. Nothing to see here. "Great coffee," I said.

Ben placed his cup in front of him. "I have one question to ask you." He turned his head and whispered in my ear, "She was code named Nephilim by *Genesis*. Do you think we should be believing everything she says?"

Good point.

She's a kid though.

Isn't she?

I whispered back, "If she's playing us, she's really fucking good."

"To be fair, Ronnie, she doesn't have to be that good. We all discounted her the minute we found out she was a social media influencer who took selfies for a living. That's on us."

"I hate when you're right."

He slung an arm around my shoulders and pulled me

closer. "She makes me feel old."

Me too. "Reason enough to dislike her, right there," I replied.

"Wonder how much longer Crockett is going to be," Ben said, it was more a statement than a question, and no longer whispered.

"He could hurry up, that'd be great," I said.

Steph and Ginny were looking at semi-precious stones. Steph asked about a really pretty teal-coloured stone and Ginny launched into its history and metaphysical properties.

Ben and I drank our coffees.

Chapter Thirty-four:

[Ronnie: What if we're wrong?]

Crockett arrived back.

"Everything good at home?" I asked as he placed his helmet on the table.

"Umm, not exactly. We need to talk but I don't want you wigging out."

I cleared my throat. "I don't wig out."

"We'll see," he replied.

Crockett sat down. Steph and Ginny had moved out to the hallway. I could hear them discussing more stones and becoming besties.

"Spit it out."

"The Not-Neighbours are dead."

I stared at him for what felt like ages. Maybe it was.

"Dead?"

"Yes."

"And how does that concern us?" I tried for a measured calm tone. I knew how, I just knew. Donald and Nana. It had to be.

"Nana found the bodies in the house. Donald lost his shit thinking he'd be a suspect. Everyone is fine. Donald is not a suspect. Nana and the Cronies are fine."

"Uh, huh. Fine, you say."

"I do."

"And Donald is aware I'll kill him when I get home?

356

And Nana is aware she'll be put into a secure unit?"

Crockett smiled. "They are aware."

"That's good." I took a deep breath. "They'll be the death of me."

"Quite possibly," Crockett said. "Hey, subject change. Emily remembered she used to be a cop. Care to elaborate?"

I took another deep breath, counted to four, and let it out slowly.

"That's great news about Emily." I licked my lips. "She was a cop before she joined *Wherefore Art Thou*. Full-time. She served for ten years as a police officer, mostly here in Upper Hutt."

"Why'd she leave?"

"Because they didn't like her moonlighting for me."

"That's a bold move to make."

"Yeah. She liked working privately more than being part of the system." She liked being her own boss and running teams. All the slack created when I was away on missions, she picked up. I missed that Emily.

"She was different today. Confident. I couldn't even tell she has a half artificial leg."

"I'm glad she's remembering who she was, but I hope the memories of the accident are gone," I said. "They took her leg in the field. She was probably going to lose it later but that was bloody awful."

"Was she trapped?"

I nodded. Trapped by a mangled leg.

"Conscious?"

"I don't know." It was time to change the subject. My phone rang. I saw Enzo's face on the screen. "Incoming FaceTime," I said, and showed Crockett and Ben. Then I swiped my finger across the bottom of the screen. Enzo grinned at me.

"Hey, how's it going?"

"Got a little messy but I think we've got somewhere now."

"Great." I think.

"This guy's name is Steven Chu."

Oh shit.

"Any relation to Ashley Chu?" Ben asked.

"Yep. A cousin apparently. He doesn't seem to care much about his cousin. He was sent to kill her."

"Hang on. Some guy called Henry killed her."

Enzo nodded. "Yes, there were two of them. Their boss wasn't sure if Steven here would do the deed. I know he would've."

"Blood not mean much?" Ben asked.

"Not at all. Steven hated the New Zealand branch of the family because they left China and have spoken publicly about the conditions, hardship, and fear that caused them to pack up and flee."

"And what was he doing at our safe house?" I asked.

"The next part of the mission. Kill the person sharing Chu's stories and publicising her artwork, discredit Chu, destroy her art. The mission morphed because they found out she could formally identify Henry."

"Anything else?"

"Yes. Where is your protectee?"

I looked across the room. She still looked asleep. Just in case, I made a decision.

"Let's go out to the shed," I said to Crockett and Ben. Enzo nodded from my phone screen.

The three of us scanned the sky before running down the path, out the gate, and into the shed. Ben flicked the lights on after he'd shut the door.

"Okay, tell us," I said to Enzo. I held the phone in my hand stretched out in front of me, so both men could see Enzo over my shoulders.

"Steven Chu told me that Alexandra Fowler is a spy. Her parents are also in the espionage game. They're traveling in Eastern Europe. Their cover is that they're visiting family. Alex was groomed to be a spy from very young, as soon as her parents realised she had an incredible memory."

"Whiskey Tango Foxtrot," I said. "Did he mention that?"

Enzo nodded. "The name of the spy master."

"How old is Alex?"

"Older than we think," Enzo said. "She's not a kid, Ronnie. She's almost thirty."

I leaned against Tom's work bench. How the hell does that even work? Two years out of school ... lies.

"And the real reason Alex was using her influence status to further Ashley Chu's career?"

"Not sure about that. I only have the One China version." He was distracted by something and looked sideways. "Sorry, Jenn wanted to ask about Steph."

"Tell her she's good. Safe. Learning about crystals. I'm sure she'll be back at the office soon."

Ben spoke, "What's the One China reason for Alex helping Chu?"

"Because Russia doesn't want China to succeed, despite saying publicly they are a trade partner and ally."

"Just the usual, everyone hates China crap then," Crockett said. "Maybe if they weren't always trying to take over the world, people would like them better."

I smiled. "Really?"

Crockett shook his head. "Human rights violations, the way they attack when anyone speaks out, or up ... fucking COVID."

Enzo grinned at us from the phone screen. "Tell us how you really feel, Crockett."

"Enough," I said. "If you think you have everything he can give us then there's some cleaning up to do."

"I recorded the ... ah ... interview. I'll upload to your computer here before I steam clean my phone."

"Ask Jenn to handle the download from your device. She needs to use the secure computer. She knows where everything is."

"Roger that." Enzo threw a mock salute at me. "Once I'm done here, I'll head home. Hey, Crockett I heard the message. I'll take care of it. Thanks for the heads up."

I waved at my phone and hung up.

The three of us stood in silence for almost two minutes. Then, Ben said, "She's played us."

"Fucking everyone has," Crockett said. "This job of ours has nothing to do with Ashley Chu. Alex is valuable. The New Zealand government must want her and everything she knows. So does the Australian government. Her parents aren't visiting relatives, they've gone home. They got the fuck out of Dodge when they saw their cover crumbling under Alex's fingers."

"Why did we get her? Why didn't fucking Chandler take her as soon as he found out what she was?"

"He is a lazy arsehole," Crockett growled. "I wouldn't piss on him if he was on fire. We do all the leg work while keeping the lying little madam safe."

I agreed.

"And we just got rid of his China problem."

"They have Henry, though, right?" Ben asked.

"He won't be breathing," Crockett said. "He probably didn't talk either so the only way to get his partner was hope we did."

"His partner and evidence that China was behind the death of Ashley Chu," I corrected. "Our quiet little babysitting gig was the biggest pack of lies yet." We've been spun some castles made of sugar in the past, but this felt like an entire city of sugar. One decent shower of rain and it would melt into sticky puddles of goo that stuck to everyone in the vicinity. "Who were the bikers that shot at us?"

"Police have someone in custody. I think it might be time to give Chandler a phone call."

I made the call. Before he answered, I said to Ben, "Is

there hand sanitiser somewhere here? Because I'm going to need a bucketload after this call."

Chandler answered, "Ronnie, how lovely to hear from you. I hope everything is going well."

I was glad it wasn't a video call, and he couldn't see me almost vomit in my mouth.

"I'm very sorry, but I've rung to let you know that Alexandra Fowler was killed by some Chinese guy." A little bit of vomit rose into my mouth.

Crockett and Ben tried hard not to laugh.

"No, Ronnie! That was not the brief! You were supposed to deliver her tomorrow morning." Anger rose in waves through his voice. "This will be the last job you ever get from me. Mark my words. The very last!"

"From you? Interesting. Because this came from the Aussies, not you. You didn't give me shit."

"Who do you think gave it to them? Grow up. You owe me, Ronnie. You owe me for being completely inept."

"Nah. Don't think so."

There was a pause.

"Tell Crockett he can be my date tomorrow night," Chandler oozed. "That'll make up for some of your incompetence."

He switched gears fast from furious to horny. More vomit rose causing me to swallow hard.

"Don't think so, Chandler. He gave me a message for you. Crockett said he wouldn't piss on you if you were on fire. So, that date isn't happening. I think you should meet us at the courthouse in two hours."

"I'll be busy with my husband in two hours. So that won't work."

"It will work. You will meet us. If you don't, then I might have to tell people things."

"You think I'm scared of you? You don't even work for NZSIS anymore."

"Exactly, so, no one can silence me. But hey, if you don't think I know enough to sink your fucking ship, that's fine."

I hung up.

Crockett handed me hand sanitiser and Ben burst out laughing.

"He'll be there with bells on," I said. "Except it won't be the courthouse. We'll get set up and change the location."

"What do you have on him?" Crockett asked.

I squirted some sanitiser onto my left hand and handed the bottle back to him. He snapped the lid back on and put it on a shelf above the work bench.

"Let me get back to you on that. It's a laundry list of his cockups and coverups." I rubbed the sanitiser into my hands.

"Why did he want us to have her?" Crockett tipped his head to the living room.

"What has she been running all over the region asking?"

"About ..." his voice dropped. "*Genesis.*"

"What's the biggest threat to his position?"

"*Genesis.*"

363

"Who's the biggest arsehole in the country?"

"Chandler."

"Who's little Miss Prima Donna working for?"

"Faaaarrrck," Crockett said on a slow exhale. "He set us up."

"Not the first time he's done it, but it'll be the last." I needed to talk to Bill. If he wants little Miss Double-Agent-Lying-Witch he can have her. And if he'd like us to remove Chandler, he can help.

"How much do you think Chandler knows?" Ben asked.

"Not enough, or he wouldn't have sent us her," I replied. "I'm still trying to piece all the bits together. The Chinese part of this equation is probably real. Let's call it a side quest. The Russian influences." I shrugged. "We have a tangled sticky web."

"Do you think she is Russian and is here on a mission, a long one?"

I nodded. "Yep."

We hurried back into the main house. I strode across the lounge and woke Alex up.

"What's your father's name?"

She rubbed her eyes. Amazingly her ridiculous eyelashes didn't fall off.

"What?"

"Your father's name, what is it?"

"Why do you sound so angry. Why do you need to know my dad's name?" She was awake now, but I doubt she'd really been asleep.

"The man you called your father, what is his name?"

A flicker of something crossed her face before she could stop it.

"Dad's name is Warner. Warner Fowler."

"What's his middle name?"

She shook her head slightly before answering. "Truman."

"Whiskey Tango Foxtrot."

A cold smile graced her lips. "I suppose we aren't buddies anymore. I almost liked you, Ronnie."

"And I guess his real name and yours aren't so English sounding."

Crockett appeared next to me and showed me a text on his phone. "There you go."

Chandler: Two hours.

I took his phone and replied: Change of plans. Location to be advised.

Chandler: Unacceptable.

Me: No worries I'll call a press conference instead.

Three dots appeared as he typed. Then disappeared. Then reappeared.

Chandler: Fine.

"Well, that's good. I need to talk to a friend and then we can get set up." I handed Crockett back his phone and looked down at Alex sitting on the couch. She was stroking a cat. It wasn't all lies, then, she did like cats. "How long have you been working for Chandler?"

Alex smiled. "I don't know any Chandler."

"Sure, you don't."

"I think you're getting confused, Ronnie. Twisting everything up, looking for a conspiracy."

"That's what it would look like if we didn't have proof."

She appeared more interested. "Proof. I don't see how you could have proof of something that isn't true."

"I suppose you're innocent and haven't done anything wrong. Just a kid doing her job as an influencer, but definitely not passing information to various countries."

"Why would I do that? And how would I do that?"

"I'm not debating this with you, Alex. You did it. End of story. You're not twenty. You're not innocent. You're here under false pretenses."

We were 21 Jump Streeted by Chandler. Alex is a fucking spy. She lied and lied to get close to the team in the hopes that she'd find something out about *Genesis*. And not just for Chandler; for the Russians, and probably for the Chinese, or maybe the murder of Ashley Chu was all them.

"It's over, Alex. We're dropping you as a client."

I left her where she was and joined Ben, Crockett, Steph, and Ginny, who were all in the kitchen. The room was full.

"Steph, thank you for all your work on this. And Ginny, thank you for your hospitality. We have some answers. While I'm thinking about it, can someone find out if Ashley Chu really was murdered?"

"Ashley Chu?" Ginny asked. "The artist?"

"Yes."

"No, sweetheart she's not dead. She has an exhibition opening in Auckland in a few days, all new work."

"She does?"

"Yeah, I saw it in the newspaper."

"Do you have it?"

Ginny went into the laundry and found the newspaper. She returned and handed it to me with the story about Ashley Chu. I read. She had an exhibition opening, just like Ginny said. I pulled my phone out and did a search on her name. Her website came up. There were stories about her artwork, a story about her family, and a small picture of her. I searched for more pictures and could only find images of her art. Digging deeper, there was a story buried under many, many pages of links. Ashley Chu stabbed. I read the story. She was stabbed in her office and left for dead by an unknown subject. Why was that story buried so deeply?

"Ronnie?" Ben touched my hand.

That's when I realised I had a death grip on my phone. I relaxed my fingers a little. "Yeah?"

"What are you looking for?"

"The truth."

Chu was left for dead. There was no follow-up story. No mention of her recovery or funeral. The picture in the newspaper of Chu was similar to the image I found online, but not similar enough for it to be the same woman. All the artwork on her webpage was pro-China. It depicted the farm her grandparents owned before emigrating.

There was no mention of why they came to New Zealand and none of the wall hangings were of places here.

"What?" Ben asked when I lifted my eyes from the screen.

"I think they replaced Chu with a lookalike," I said, fully aware of how insane and impossible that sounded.

Ben slid an arm around my shoulders. "I think we all need some sleep." He kissed the side of my head. "It's been a roller coaster of a few days."

A warning pinged in my mind.

Chapter Thirty-five.

[Crockett: Tell your story walking]

"Ronnie, you ready?"

She nodded. "You know what to do?"

"Of course. I'll ride home. Drop the bike, change my clothes, get my rifle bag, and set up before you tell him where we are meeting." I'd be lying in the wet dirt ready to do my part for however long it took for Chandler to arrive at our meeting place.

"Text Enzo. Tell him and Emily to go for a ride."

"What about Art and Jo?"

"They're fine at the office."

"Okay. You coming with me, or going with Ben and the thing in there?"

"Ben and the thing," she replied. "And to think we believed her."

"If you have a brain like hers, I guess when you're fed backstory and intertwined backstories at that, it's no problem keeping it all straight and being believable. Don't think we can beat ourselves up over this, Ronnie." She didn't look convinced. "She conned us all. She played a good game. But at least we figured it out."

"I suppose we did. Why do I feel so stupid then?"

"Because we aren't used to being played like that when we have home advantage. And you're not alone feeling stupid." I hung my bag over my head, then pulled my helmet on. "See you at the location. Hopefully you won't see me."

I waved to Ben and Ginny. Steph was already gone. Alex was locked in a bedroom until Ben and Ronnie were ready to move her.

It didn't take me long to get home and it wasn't much fun. That fucking Sheila ruined our day, and it was raining again. There isn't much fun in riding around in the rain. I was conscious of the other issue: the gang issue. Not the pretend one but The Alpha Brotherhood situation. It felt like someone told them where I was and how to get to me. I'd put money on that someone being Chandler. If that was the case then it wasn't over yet, or it could crop up at any point. They might lie low for now, but they'd be back.

I showered and changed into another set of all black clothes. I took the clothing out of my bag and tossed it into the washing machine. There was no point putting the washing machine on; I wouldn't be there to hang it out. That was tomorrow's job. Might even stop raining by then. There ya go, there's your positivity, I thought to myself. I chose a rifle from the floor safe. I added a scope and a longer magazine. From my wardrobe, I took a soft gun case - the type hunters use. I could carry it over my shoulder. It was still a gun case, though, and not exactly subtle. I put the case back in the wardrobe and went with a different plan. I had a soft guitar case. That would work better. I could carry that, if I made it look like a guitar was in it and not a rifle. I hurried out to the shed and took some polystyrene packaging from a box. I laid it on the garage floor and moved the piece around, trimmed some, and created a guitar like shape. That'd do. Then I hollowed out enough so I could put the rifle in it.

That wasn't too shabby an effort. Back in the house, I assembled the polystyrene around the rifle and slid it into the soft guitar case. After a little bit of buggering about, it was all good. I checked the time. There was plenty of time to meander over to Bartons Bush. A lot still bothered me about Operation Hide and Seek. I made a phone call to my boss.

"It's Crockett. Who are Chalmers and Clark because I doubt they're cops."

"Wait a minute, I'll see what I have."

I heard paper moving over the line then typing. Eventually Craig's voice came back, "Andrew Chalmers?"

"Yes."

"He's not a cop. He's intelligence with New Zealand. Supposedly posted overseas."

"Great."

"The other name Cassandra Clark?"

"Yes."

"Also, intelligence with New Zealand. Also, currently overseas."

"Thanks."

"Do we have a problem?"

"You could say that. It's being handled."

I hung up. Another piece in the puzzle that made it look like we were being set up. I made one more phone call. I rang Dink and pulled him and Plunger away from the surveillance gig, but while I was doing that I had another idea.

"I want you two to set up surveillance as best you can near the cricket pitch at Trentham Memorial Park. The one that is right before the stop bank."

"West of the clubrooms?"

"Yes."

"Is Art free, he'd be handy."

"Should be now. Give him a bell and text me if you see anything."

"Looking for anything in particular?"

"Anyone connected to Chandler."

"Jeesssuuus."

"Yeah, this could go off like a frog in a sock."

"How long do you want us out there?"

"I'll let you know. When I do, pull back to Bartons Bush, or get the fuck over that stop bank."

"Gotcha."

"There'll be some clean up work to do, so don't go far."

I hung up and made my last call. Ronnie picked up on the first ring.

"I'm moving out to get set."

"Good. I'll put a call in to Chandler and tell him where to meet us," Ronnie said. "Exact location?"

"The cricket pitch before the stop bank at Trentham Memorial Park," I said.

"Nice and open," Ronnie said. "Don't let that prick get away."

"Where are you now?"

"I just got home. I need to do something in case this goes tits up."

"Alex the liar?"

"She's with Ben for now."

"Stay frosty."

"You, too."

The last thing on my list was a quick wee and something to eat. There's nothing worse than lying on the cold wet ground hungry and needing a wee.

It didn't take me long to get to the park. I walked and didn't see a bikie anywhere on the way. Mind you, I could get to Trentham Memorial Park without going near Fergusson Drive or Ronnie's place. That would've helped make sure drones didn't spot me. We didn't know who controlled the drones yet. It could be the bikies, it could be the Chinese, maybe some Russians were still around. Who the fuck knows? I went in the gate off Holdsworth Avenue and walked down the bush track until I was near where I needed to be. There was no one around. It was drizzly, cold, and not the sort of day people wanted to walk dogs or play at the park. I climbed over the wire fence and moved through the bush and trees to the far edge. In a gap through the trees, and the bush, I could see the cricket pitch, and past that I could see the trees that lined the golf course. I found the best place to hunker down and wait. Water dripped off leaves above me. The ground was muddy in places, but mostly leaf litter.

Carefully I removed my rifle from its hiding place and

got comfortable. I used the sight to look for Art, Dink, and Plunger. Either they weren't there, or they were well concealed.

I knew where I would go if I were them. I'd be at the very edge of the clubrooms, on the golf course side. I moved the rifle to the left, then up about man height. There was someone there. Where else would I go? Into the trees on the golf course. I moved the rifle barrel slowly all the way to the right. Nothing. I moved it back to the centre and caught a glimpse of a hand. Then the last place I'd go would be over by the stopbank; there was a bench near the golf course trees. I went up from there to the top of the stopbank and along it. I couldn't see the third person. They were either really good or not there.

Chapter Thirty-six.
[Ronnie: 60 seconds to midnight]

I side-stepped Donald with my hands up. "Can we do this later, please?"

"No, Ronnie, you don't understand, I nearly went to prison for murder."

"I'm sure that's melodrama on your part, Donald. I have to do something." Life as we know it depends on it. I turned sideways and squeezed past him as he stood in the hallway trying to block my path. "I need two hours and then I'm all yours."

"I'm putting a timer on!" He said, huffing and puffing like a pissed off steam engine.

"You do that."

I escaped into my bedroom and locked the door behind me. Very quietly I said, "If you are listening, then you're not going to be surprised when I reach out in a few minutes."

I shoved my clothes in the wardrobe aside and punched the code into the door lock. The lock clicked, I opened the door, and stood there for a moment as everything sprang to life. With care I closed the door, walked to my desk, and slipped into the chair in front of the computer.

I went through the procedure of getting the flash drive from the drawer safe and all the security measures, then accessed *Genesis* via my link.

There was a flash drive in my pocket that Steph had given me. It contained everything she uncovered. It also contained everything we found at Perkins place, including the interesting contents of her laptop and emails. I uploaded everything to the secure server, under a date heading. Before I'd finished, a message flashed onto the screen. I wrote it down, got out the code book and translated it.

'Designation changed from gatherer to temporary strike team.'

I carried on uploading the files. A chat box appeared. I'd never seen one of those before inside *Genesis*.

Three blue dots moved inside the chat box.

Word appeared.

Genesis: Lethal force authorised.
Me: Clarify target
Genesis: Chandler

I didn't know how to respond, so I watched for a few seconds until the three blue dots started moving again.

Genesis: Confirm target
Me: Affirmative, target Chandler
Me: He's not coming out without telling his husband and staff where he's going.
Genesis: Not your concern.
Me: I'm not alone

Genesis: We are aware that you have Ben Reynolds and Dave Crocker with you.

Me: Roger that

Genesis: Fowler goes to Defence. She is their problem now.

The chat box disappeared as the uploads finished. Before I left my bat cave, I texted Chandler the meeting place. Then I double checked everything was locked and secure.

Donald was waiting in the kitchen.

"Not now, Donald."

"I know," he said. "You're busy, busy, busy." He pointed to his phone. "I've got a timer on."

"See you soon then."

I patted Romeo and ran down the stairs. I had no idea what would happen in the next little while. Crockett was in place. I rang Bill while I walked. Walking seemed like a good idea to clear my head. And it really wasn't that far to Tom and Ginny's. Four kilometres in the rain had the potential to feel a lot more than four kilometres though.

"Where are you?" Bill asked.

"Walking," I replied. "You want the package?"

"Yes."

"Brilliant." I looked around. "I'm coming to you. Then you can drop me off and pick up the package."

"Sounds like a plan."

"Did you find out where the photo came from? Drone or CCTV?"

"Potentially. A body dropped early this morning. I got a note stuck to my door that looked like a suicide note and moments later MP's found a body in a car. Pretty sure it was CCTV; the body was that of a corporal who had access required."

"Nice. Was it suicide?"

"Don't know yet, but it could be that he was trying to warn me about a double agent in the organisation. Thing is, Ronnie, he was the double agent. And now he's dead."

"Could still be suicide." The level of guilt at betraying your country could easily lead someone to suicide. "I'll be there in twenty minutes."

I stuffed my phone in my pocket and scanned the skies for any sign of drone activity. Not knowing if whoever was still after Alex, or us, or Crockett, was still in play, caused some unease. I didn't allow myself to think about the next step. I knew it was going down that way. I'd even asked Crockett to grab his rifle. I decided as I walked to meet Bill that thinking too much wasn't going to end well. There was no sense thinking about what I'd decided was the next step before I got the go ahead for that next and final step.

Drizzle turned to rain before I reached the Messine Centre. I was glad for the black cap on my head keeping the rain off my face, but also wary. It wouldn't be the first black cap to leak dye. Puffer jackets aren't the most waterproof, but I was warm, so I didn't really care. I pressed the buzzer at the door. It didn't take more than a few seconds for Bill to appear and open the door. He jangled car keys from his hand.

"Ready to go?" He surveyed me. "You're going to drip all over my upholstery."

"Sucks to suck."

"I have an escort ready."

"Might need it."

I followed him to his car.

"Wait," he said when I opened the passenger door. He grabbed a towel from the back seat and threw it over the roof to me. "Sit on this."

"Seriously?"

"My car, my rules."

"Fine." I spread the towel on the leather seat before I climbed into the car. "Happy now?"

"Yes."

"And we are waiting for?"

"That," he replied. Another car pulled into the car parking area.

Bill started the engine and led the way, with me giving directions.

"Park down the driveway," I said. "The house behind just sold and there is no one living there at the moment."

He parked in front of Tom's garage, his escort parked behind him. I led the way through the gate and to the back door.

Ginny was already there with the door open. "Hellaire," she said to Bill. "I'm Ginny, you must be Ben and Ronnie's friend."

"Hi, I'm Aaron," Bill said with ease. He shook her

hand. "Shoes by the door, I take it?"

"Yes, please." She looked past him to the escort. "And you must be more friends."

"They're with me," Bill said. "We won't be in your way long. Just picking up a package." He motioned to the men behind him to stay where they were. They stood in the rain.

Bill and I went inside with Ginny.

"The package is in the spare bedroom, Aaron," Ginny said with smile. "Through that door there and first on your right."

I went with him. Ben was outside the bedroom door. "You good?" I asked.

"Yep. She's finally shut up," he replied. His greeting to Bill was quiet, "Hi, Bill." They shook hands.

Ben opened the door.

Alex was sitting on the bed. "I've seen you before. You're Aaron," she said.

"That's right. And you're Alex," he replied. "Come on, time to go for a drive." Bill extended his arm toward her.

"Why would I go with you?"

"Because I asked nicely," Bill said. "That can change in a heartbeat."

Alex shuffled to the edge of the bed, planted her feet on the carpet and stood. "Anything is better than being here with these losers."

I smiled and inserted pure joy into my words, "Have a great rest of your life, Alex."

She glared at me as Bill led her to the back door.

"Her shoes are beside the door," Ginny said.

"She won't need them," Bill replied.

I shoved my feet back in my hiking boots.

One of the waiting soldiers stepped forward and slapped handcuffs on Alex. Surprise registered on her face. The other soldier stepped forward. I followed as they escorted her to the waiting car. Another soldier stood in the rain by the back door of their car. He placed his hand on Alex's head, forcing her to duck as she climbed into the back seat. As soon as they were all in the car, the driver backed out of the driveway. Bill jumped in his car, waved, and followed.

I walked back inside, pulled my shoes off, and left my wet jacket in the laundry.

"You ready Ben?"

"Yes," he called. "Just saying goodbye."

I followed the sound of his voice and found him in the lounge with Ginny and four of the cats.

Ginny gave him a hug.

"Thanks for everything, Ginny," I said.

"You're welcome. It was fabulous to finally meet you."

Ben and I waved as we left.

"How's the time?" Ben asked at the Sutherland Avenue traffic lights.

"He'll be here in about ten minutes," I said. "Go right and in from Brentwood Street."

We entered the Brentwood Street carpark for the park and drove to the furthest parking area.

"Why did the moron agree to meet us?" Ben asked. He

opened the boot and took out a black and white golf umbrella.

"Because he honestly thinks he can weasel his way out of what he did." Or he's planning on trying to remove us from the equation.

We walked around the sealed path that took us under the trees and curved around the park to the stop bank. The path followed the bush. I didn't want to be out in the open, stomping across puddle filled rugby fields. Rain pelted from the sky, bouncing off the umbrella shielding us, and splashing up from the sodden ground.

"Where are we meeting him?"

"Over on the cricket pitch."

"In this rain, he'll melt long before he gets to us."

That would be a fitting end to a massive bitch.

Ben linked his arm with mine and held the umbrella over our heads. We strolled down the path, just a couple out for a stroll in the pissing rain. Nothing to see here.

Over the fields near the water fountain, I saw a familiar car. I smiled at Ben. "He's so damn cocky that he drove up in his own car."

"Let's go pop his balloon."

"With pleasure."

We waited on the path by the cricket pitch. There was no one around. My phone buzzed. I checked it. Crockett.

Crockett: I need you two to move two metres to the right.

Me: Okay.

"Ben we're moving right about two metres, but let's make it look good."

I probably shouldn't have said that. Ben grinned, unlinked our arms, then he swept me to him and danced me two metres further along the path, while holding the umbrella over our heads.

Across the field I saw Chandler scurrying like the rat he was with his plain black umbrella. Water splashed as he moved. I didn't see anyone else with him.

That wasn't like him at all.

Mr Cautious came alone.

We waited until he was halfway, then walked out from the path to the centre of the wet cricket pitch, making sure we stayed in the same position.

When he was close enough to be heard he said, "Ronnie, what have you done?"

"Wasn't me. You did this." My phone buzzed once in my pocket. "It's all on you, Chandler. All on you."

He squinted at me in the pouring rain, confusion settled, a small hole appeared in the middle of his forehead, and he slumped to the ground. His open umbrella rolled across the pitch as blood mingled with rain and vanished into the grass.

"Come on," Ben said. We walked to the end of the park almost to the stop bank, then found the sealed path, and followed it around into the bush. At the junction of three paths, I saw Crockett climbing over the wire fence with a guitar case.

"We should do something about the body," I said when Crockett joined us. We couldn't leave it there for random strangers to find, or kids. That would not be a fun time. And really, police involvement would just get messy.

"It's taken care of. The tradies are dealing with it."

Ben moved the umbrella to his other hand. Crockett walked with us to the entrance on Holdsworth Avenue.

"Want a lift?" I asked. "The car is over there."

He smiled. "Think I'll walk. Is Emily at yours?"

"I don't know."

Ben tried to hand him the umbrella, but Crockett refused, "You take it, mate. Rain doesn't hurt me."

"Hey," I said. "What's the clock on?"

"Sixty seconds to midnight," Crockett replied. "Sixty seconds until Doomsday."

"Do you think we just made a difference?"

He nodded. "Course we did."

The End.
[Whiskey Tango Foxtrot]

Acknowledgments:

Nicky Hurle - for being a wonderful editor and long time friend.
(Thank you Nicky, from the bottom of my tartan covered heart.)

Big thanks to *Robyn and Duigald* for saying yes and letting me turn them into great characters. (Recurring characters at that. They'll be back!)

Margot Kinberg - for making sure Ben is still American and being a golden grammar hammer.
https://margot-kin-berg.com/

Pete Turner - for being an awesome go-to espionage guy and for his unwavering encouragement. Everyone need a friend like Pete.
https://www.breakitdownshow.com/

Geoff Inwood - for answering questions and listening when a sounding board was needed especially when it came to Crockett. And for being my Knight from the Order of Chrome.

My children and father - for being amazing humans and for always being super supportive.

And *Chrissy* - for keeping me sane!

Last but not least by any means:
Readers - without readers a story cannot breathe - so thanks for the oxygen!

About the author:

Cat Connor is a prolific crime thriller author hailing from New Zealand. Her expertise in the genre is reflected in her engaging and suspenseful narratives, which have garnered a loyal following. Her work is known for its intricate plots, dynamic characters, and relentless pace, keeping readers on the edge of their seats until the very end. She has authored multiple books, including the popular "Byte" series, which follows the exploits of an FBI unit that investigates serial crime.

Cat's passion for crime and espionage is evident in her writing, as she strives to create a world that is both authentic and thrilling. Her meticulous attention to detail and extensive research have won her critical acclaim and accolades from readers and peers alike. In addition to writing, Cat enjoys speaking on topics related to writing and publishing. Her talks are known for their candidness, humour, and practical advice. With her unique blend of talent, expertise, and passion, Cat Connor has established herself as one of the most exciting and accomplished authors in the crime thriller genre.

Her other passions include music, reading, tequila, red wine, coffee, and chocolate. When she's not writing she can be found binge watching TV shows and spending time with her much adored animals; Diesel the mastador, Patrick the tuxedo cat, Dallas the tortoiseshell Birman, and Jimmy the Thug.

You can follow and contact Cat at the following places:

Website: **www.catconnor.com**
Twitter: @catconnor
Facebook: @cat.connor
Instagram: @catconnorauthor

Also by Cat Connor:

Array - short stories from within the series
If I Was A Carpenter - SSA Kurt Henderson's story
Dead Flowers - SSA Sam Jackson's story